TWO SCANDALS AND A SCOT

#5 The Duchess Society Series

BY

TRACY SUMNER

WOLF PUBLISHING

Two Scandals and a Scot by Tracy Sumner

Published by WOLF Publishing UG

Copyright © 2023 Tracy Sumner
Text by Tracy Sumner
Edited by Chris Hall
Cover Art by Victoria Cooper
Paperback ISBN: 978-3-98536-163-2
Hard Cover ISBN: 978-3-98536-164-9
Ebook ISBN: 978-3-98536-162-5

WOLF Publishing - This is us:

Two sisters, two personalities.. But only one big love!

Diving into a world of dreams..
   ...Romance, heartfelt emotions, lovable and witty characters, some humor, and some mystery! Because we want it all! Historical Romance at its best!

Visit our website to learn all about us, our authors and books!

Sign up to our mailing list to receive first hand information on new releases, freebies and promotions as well as exclusive giveaways and sneak-peeks!

WWW.WOLF-PUBLISHING.COM

Also by Tracy Sumner

The Duchess Society Series

The DUCHESS SOCIETY is a steamy new Regency-era series. Come along for a scandalous ride with the incorrigible ladies of the Duchess Society as they tame the wicked rogues of London! Second chance, marriage of convenience, enemies to lovers, forbidden love, passion, scandal, ROMANCE.

If you enjoy depraved dukes, erstwhile earls and sexy scoundrels, untamed bluestockings and rebellious society misses, the DUCHESS SOCIETY is the series for you!

#1 The Brazen Bluestocking

#2 The Scandalous Vixen

#3 The Wicked Wallflower

#4 One Wedding and an Earl

#5 Two Scandals and a Scot

#6 Three Sins and a Scoundrel (Coming 2024)

Prequel to the series: The Ice Duchess

Christmas novella: The Governess Gamble

Fill your paper with the breathings of your heart.
—*William Wordsworth*

TWO SCANDALS AND A SCOT

FIRST IMPRESSIONS
(KINDLY FILCHED FROM THE WICKED WALLFLOWER)

A fateful Mayfair evening 1826

"Always got a book in yer hand, don't you, lass? Even when it's too dark to see the page."

Startled from her musing, Theodosia Astley glanced up from her perch atop the stone wall bordering her brother's lush garden to find Dashiell Campbell leaning carelessly against the veranda's balustrade, a crimson-tipped cheroot dangling from his lips.

"Am I intruding?" he asked when he knew he was. "I have a spot of time before the guv picks me up round the corner. On Albemarle, so we're not seen fleeing a duke's terrace in the wee of the night."

Theo sighed and shut her book. The 'guv' being Xander Macauley —and Dash, his latest pet project.

"Not what I'd planned for this evening's theater, escorting you bonnie ladies home. Mostly to save your unruly sister from further disaster. The chit has a certain penchant, nae the first of her fixes I've been involved with if the truth be crawling from my throat and into the night. The guv has taken a sharp shine to her, he has."

Theo started to argue, but he was right about Pippa *and* Macauley's fixation, so why bother? She was, however, unwilling to tell this uncouth scamp that this was her favorite spot on the entire estate. Her *private* spot. Lest he expect to find her here again.

She also didn't tell the Scottish lout that he should call her Miss Theodosia. Or that being alone with him was a risk to her reputation. Which was laughable because no man would be tempted to take advantage of Theodosia Astley. Besides, she couldn't rudely dismiss him when he'd helped her. Helped Pippa. He'd spirited her sister away from that inane ball without anyone in the *ton* or, heaven forbid, the Duchess Society, knowing she'd been kissed to within an inch of her life by the most infamous blackguard in England.

If Theo was correct in her assessment.

Her love hypothesis was still in the testing stages.

Dash strolled over when she failed to object. More of a swagger. Ridiculous when he hadn't done enough in his brief life to earn the right to swagger. He gestured to her book with his cheroot, resting his hip on the banister two paces to her left. "I reckon it's a bonnie read the way you're hugging it so."

She dropped the novel to her lap, title down, reluctant to reveal that tonight's selection was rather lurid. Nothing academic by any measure. Theo enjoyed a rousing romance as much as she did a stimulating text on chemical processes. Mostly because she suspected she'd never have a love story of her own. Therefore, it was fitting to read someone else's.

Shrugging, she ran her thumb along a crease in the leather spine. "It's passable."

Dash hummed a vague reply and threw a calculating glance around the space. "This is quite the posh plot. I dinnae think I've ever seen a garden as grand. Nae outside Glasgow, anyways. The botanical garden there is a handsome sight to behold. I visited as a lad, crawled in through a busted gate. Slumbered beneath the stars, if me memory serves, before they pitched me out."

She understood his wonder.

Some days, she could hardly believe she'd landed in this luxurious world. Her half-sister Helena's marriage to the Duke of Leighton had catapulted Theo from the rookery to Mayfair in a short day. Then she was introduced to darling Pippa, the sister of her heart, who she'd do anything for. Even lie through her teeth about perilous adventures with men likely to break Pippa's heart. "Capability Brown is rumored to have designed this in 1790," Theo finally murmured when it appeared the young Scot expected her to say something.

He turned to her, his smile close to irresistible, a fact he was well aware of. His eyes were a pale, moonlit blue, gleaming with humor at something she hadn't meant to be funny. This often happened as the things she found humorous no one else seemed to. His hair was a heavy fall over his brow, black as tar, not a hint of any other color. He tilted his head, his amusement growing at her inspection. He had a crooked scar on his chin that she wondered how he'd gotten and a light dusting of freckles across his nose.

Theo glanced shyly at her book when she couldn't see the words in the wash of hazy light unless the text was pressed practically to her face. She wasn't taken in by the aristocratic charms dangled before her so often of late, so why be entranced by this?

Her life was littered with arrogant nobs who couldn't wait to share their titles and the number of estates attached to each, their stories repeating themselves in dismal glory. How many times they'd met King George and been invited to Carlton House. Grievances about attending class at Cambridge or Oxford, discussions that infuriated her because she would never be allowed to study at either. She chewed on her lip in vexation. Men were only circling because her massive dowry was enough to raise shipwrecks from the sea.

Plus, her brother-in-law was a peer of the realm, holding one of the oldest titles in Christendom. This circumstance did alter societal perceptions.

To put it bluntly, Theo had a status she'd never wanted nor knew what to do with.

She was plain and bookish, and a hundred sumptuous gowns made by the costliest modiste in the city weren't going to change that. Or a duke for a brother. Or a pocketful of blunt. She often thought to remind her family of this fact, but she didn't want to disappoint them.

"What is swirling around in that keen mind of yers, lass? I see sparks shooting from yer eyes with the rapid pace."

She glanced at Dash again, intrigued despite herself.

Of course, he wasn't attracted to her. Or cultured enough should he have been. Roan had strict standards regarding the gents who would someday court her. This scoundrel, a pair of dice in his hand every time she saw him, would never make the list. But he *was* interesting. She'd heard Roan and Helena whispering about him being the shrewdest cardsharp in England. Maybe even a master pickpocket before being plucked from the stews. One thing was certain. If he kept his bridle clipped to Xander Macauley's, he'd be wealthy as Croesus in a few years.

According to Dash—a comment she'd overheard, not been told directly—he was going to own his own gaming hell and planned to burn through the *ton* like a flash fire.

She had no doubt he'd someday rule the city. Charm every person he stumbled upon. Hop in and out of every bed.

Because if his lilting accent wasn't enough to entice, there *was* the matter of his face.

Not that Theo cared about such things—if she ever fell in love, the man would be a noteworthy academic with a predictably unappealing countenance—but Dash Campbell was blindingly good-looking. The kind of splendor that halted people, men *and* women, on the street. Full, stumbling stops. She'd seen it happen. A hazard rather than a boon to her way of thinking, bringing attention to oneself no matter the situation.

She would have hated being that beautiful.

He knocked his hair out of his eyes and took a lengthy pull on his cheroot, his patience for companionable silence over. His signet ring, housing an emerald that she questioned how he'd managed to find the money to purchase, glittered on his pinkie. "Maybe a brilliant lass such as yerself could help me. A wee project I'm undertaking."

She scooted to the wall's edge, hooking her slippered heel on a jutting stone. "Me?"

"*Aye.* In the writing of me book."

Theo blinked, as stunned by those seven words as any she'd ever heard. "Your book?"

Dash skimmed his gaze her way, the trace of vulnerability mixed with devilry tugging curiously at her heartstrings. "Marked cards, reflectors, holdouts, manipulations. I ken them all. Collusion. Conspiracy. I have a chapter name for each already thought out. Breakdowns of the major games. Hazard, poker, roulette. Faro, even. Ways to spot tells. Or put the doings to yer own use should that be yer gambit. Nae a topic I've missed."

Theo brought her book to her mouth and laughed into pages that smelled faintly of mildew. "You want to write a book teaching people how to *cheat?*"

He rounded on her, his bum coming off the balustrade. "I'd sell more copies in one month than that Austen chit does in a year. Do ye ken how many lads in this loathsome city are losing what piddling blunt they have nightly? Desperate to find a way to stop the bleeding? I used to hold lessons in the back of my flat in Glasgow, then in Shoreditch. More demand than I could keep up with. Every grandee in town sailed through my battered doorway, yearning to ken what I ken. How do ye think I met Macauley? He was there, as was every gambling proprietor in England. My book would be solid information from a professional."

"Solid information from a professional," she repeated, charmed to her toes.

He blew out a furious breath, tossed his cheroot to the ground, and promptly stomped on it. A tantrum from a man she'd never seen the least flustered. "Forget I asked, Lady Theodosia."

"I'm a miss, not a lady." When he went to stalk from the garden, Theo scrambled up, grabbing his sleeve to halt him.

He gazed down at her, his white teeth a flash as his lips parted on a fractious sigh. A man in defense of his dreams. He was tall and lean, on the side of gangly. His jaw covered in a faint dusting of jet stubble, patchy in spots. His clothing was informal but high quality, likely thanks to his patron. He smelled of a spicy, masculine fragrance that was subtly enticing. Theo didn't have enough experience with such things to guess what it was.

The most intriguing piece? He fairly vibrated with emotion. Sentiment flying across his face like rubbish in a gust while they stared, making her wonder, *what is he about* for the only time in her eighteen years. People mostly ignored her, and she them. She saved her wonder for science, math, history, art.

She documented this unusual development like she would a lab experiment, stunned by the split-second camaraderie.

No one understood grand plans—or being underestimated—better than Theodosia Astley.

She released his sleeve when it occurred to her that neither of them was wearing gloves, and his skin was scalding hers. A strange feeling seeped into her belly, weakening her knees. She swallowed hard against the temptation to tuck a stray lock of hair behind his ear. "Can you read?"

His shoulders went back, a fighting stance. "Nae very good."

Theo held back a smile at the mystery of life, knowing he wouldn't appreciate her delight.

Dash Campbell, rookery pickpocket and renowned cardsharp, a young man with perhaps the most exquisite face in England, had presented a challenge Theo couldn't have turned down for the world. "I'll help you. Reading first. Writing after. One requires the other."

He glowered, tiny plackets settling beside his lush mouth, his eyes clear enough to dive into. He really was unjustly attractive. "Canna I nae dictate it to ye? Less time involved. I'm a busy man, what with the gaming hell and keeping blokes from swindling the Devil's Lair and all."

"Do you think to work for Macauley forever?"

He rocked from one boot to the other, his gaze narrowing. Trying to figure out her game. What he'd never understand was how she didn't *have* a game.

What she presented was what she was.

"If you plan to open your own business at some point, Mr. Campbell, even manage the accounts for your publishing venture, you'll need to read well. And write well. Maths would be a useful subject to add to the list."

A wild grin broke through his skepticism. "I'm brilliant with numbers, lass. I can count cards like no one you've ever seen in your wee life. Then add them in my noggin like a whirlwind."

"You can do this arithmetic on paper as well?"

He glared and wiped his fist beneath his nose, looking more boy than man. "I can pay ye. My reserves are growing like a weed shooting right through the cobbles. Regular monies from Macauley, every Friday without delay. I dinnae think he's a bloke to miss a payment."

Theo laughed, utterly, unexpectedly enchanted. "Oh, no, *no*. You misunderstand. I wish to be your teacher. Life is a very thorny predicament and working at any position is not easily attainable considering where I've landed. It might be the best I can hope for." She shrugged, her hand going out as if to shoo a fly when it was her dream she was flicking away. "You'll be my first, and maybe only, student. I have texts. Loads of them. Materials. We can use the blue parlor—"

The kiss was soft. Tender. Barely there before it was over.

He didn't touch her anywhere else, only his lips grazing hers. His sweet scent filled her nose, her heart thumping hard, then gone.

All gone.

Theo blinked to find Dash pulling away, his lids sweeping up to reveal eyes gone blue as ice. "Why did you do that?"

He nodded to the book she clutched, forgotten. "Ye looked so lost for a wee second there, I wanted to snap ye out of it. Someday, yer fine fella will come, lass. Flesh and blood. Blue blood, I expect yer clan is planning for. With only you in his sights. He willna be tucked up inside some dusty pages, in yer mind his only existence. Dinnae worry about that." Dash strolled three paces away, then threw the full force of his charm over his shoulder. "But I thank ye for the lessons. I accept. Then I'll owe ye. And someday, lass, that owing will be worth something."

Astonished, Theo watched him stroll from the garden.

Worth something.

She bet it would.

Scandal #1

Chapter One

When managing a crooked gamble, best not leave your secret bits
on display.

Dashiell M. Campbell, *Proper Etiquette for Deception*

A celebratory occasion gone wrong
London, 1830

Theodosia Astley never planned on becoming a runaway bride.
Never planned on becoming a bride at all.

At one time, her dreams had been scrawled across her
mind like the majestic illustrations in the fairy tales she'd been gifted
as a child. *After* her sister's celebrated marriage and Theo's incredible
shift in circumstance with her arrival in a duke's household. The first

books she'd ever owned came during this time, to this day tucked on her Mayfair bookshelf between Longfellow and Wordsworth.

Impractical whimsy, those dreams. Although her cat, Mr. Darcy, found them reasonable. Found the most bookish chit in London captivating when no one else did.

Not even the man she'd agreed to spend her life with found her captivating. A man she'd thought to enter into a doctrine that would have granted him fiscal control.

Personal, intimate *control*.

Well, she would, from this second forward, stick with cats.

Mr. Darcy understood her *joie de vivre*. He purred every time she mentioned attending Oxford or becoming the first Vice-Chancellor of Clare College. Ridiculous, when women weren't even allowed to attend university. Become professors of mathematics or philosophy. Theo would have settled for Shakespearean literature when she'd have chosen Austen over the Bard of Avon any day of the week. Though he was deliciously quotable. *A thousand kisses buy my heart* was beautiful.

It's why Theo repeated it at least once a week. Although Shakespeare wrote largely about deception and revenge, more where her heart was lodged at the moment.

Lowering the carriage window, Theo pitched her tiara, a cheap imitation Edward Biggerstaff had given her for her birthday, into the shimmering twilight. Her brother, the Duke of Leighton, had once been fond of offering tiaras to women he no longer wished to associate with, or so rumor went. He'd not been impressed when she showed him hers, even as she'd stressed that gentlemen on academic salaries couldn't afford trinkets from high-priced jewelers on Sackville.

But fake was fake, wasn't it? Her lousy fiancé and his blasted baubles.

Theo watched the circlet shatter against the cobbles with little regret, paste diamonds and rubies glittering in the muck. Rage was the emotion flowing through her, not sadness. When studious women rarely got angry because everyone knew the brain ruled the heart. Which matched what society had taught her: Women weren't supposed to show any emotion outside simpering contentment with their situation. Tedium often eradicated with potent doses of laudanum and brandy.

Theo had gotten herself in this mess, and she would get herself out of it.

She should have paid attention to the warnings pinging like a ball around her gut, an area of the body a rogue scientist by the name of Lucifer Henry considered a "second brain." In a furtive corner of her mind, she'd even disliked Edward—a horrible precursor to marriage, true—because he, a professor of economics, held the dream she desired with her entire being as easily as he would a blossom in his hand.

If the world weren't so tilted, favoring every male on the planet, her ambitions might have been possible. Cambridge. Walks along the river Cam, texts tucked under her arm as she rushed to class, crossing the Clare Bridge, the scent of lavender and honeysuckle stinging her nose. Or Oxford, her second choice. She would have liked to be an Oxonian. Now, a withered spinster surrounded by felines and books was the probable scenario. Her reputation ending up where it had started. In the gutter.

One didn't survive stolen carriages and broken engagements and pregnant mistresses showing up at pre-wedding balls even if they were sisters of dukes.

Roan, her brother-in-law, the Duke of Leighton, was not going to be happy that she'd absconded without telling him. Run right out of the gala that he and his duchess, her sister, Helena, had been planning for weeks. He had a fierce temper, legendary with proper justification. One he'd been in the middle of unleashing on her fiancé when she'd crept from the ballroom, the group of friends the *ton* called the Leighton Cluster closing around him like a bloom at sunset.

Theo dropped her head to her hands and blew a noisy breath through her gloved fingers. She hated to cause her family and friends angst. Spawn a scandal which London loved better than they loved dukes.

Dear heaven, she'd unwittingly given society a rip-roaring one. Perhaps the finest this year, and with her brother and his friend's antics, that was saying something.

3

Theo's answer to the arrival of her betrothed's *very* expectant mistress had been to commandeer the first carriage in the line flanking Leighton House's drive, invite a stray dog inside to stink up the interior (though adding comfort since it would be days before she was reunited with Mr. Darcy), then utter a directive that sounded as if it were taken from a lurid novel: *I must leave this instant*.

The coachman, his hair as vivid as the wash of ginger across the horizon, had winked as if he heard this request every day and wrenched the carriage into motion, heading she knew not where. Away, as she'd requested.

Now, here she was. Alone. In a lavish coupe with a possibly deranged driver. Her family, her books, her cat, her reprehensible fiancé, and his ungainly lover sliding farther away with every click of the carriage's wheels.

This felt, in turn, marvelous and dreadful.

Taking deep breaths, she sought her bearings. *Calm, Theo.*

It was a posh carriage she'd chosen. Luxurious. Modern. Seats upholstered in a striped plaid satin, the doors and windows framed in gold leaf. Four candlelit lanterns polished to a high sheen flickering brightly. A spirited team of four as splendid as the Windsor Greys leading them through a street clogged with hackneys and carts, yipping dogs and shouting children. Theo knew exceptional horseflesh when she saw it.

Someone would soon be missing this vehicle when they left her brother's party.

Theo turned as the pyrotechnics began to pop over the misty evening sky, fluttering ribbons of silver and gold piercing holes in the city's eternal haze. The Duchess Society had suggested fireworks as an appropriate commemoration for a pre-wedding fete. Theo watched until the carriage turned a corner, a fast bank no driver of her brother's would have taken, and the sight was lost to her. Leaving behind a throng celebrating a marriage that the bride had had a tremor in her belly for months when thinking about.

The first proper life she'd tried to fashion behind.

Whatever path lay before Theo was uncharted. And tainted. Why that felt *right,* in some odd sense, eluded her. She'd think on that later, when the pulse behind her eyes had slowed to a dull flicker.

Theo sighed in whispered shades of relief and fury. One of which wasn't a suitable emotion when a woman was tossing aside her intended. She'd suspected Edward desired her immense dowry and connections to a duke, his entry into society, more than he desired her. But he'd seemed perfect. An academic, if she could not be one herself, what she wanted.

And once she gave her word...

Theo thumped her fist on the windowpane, her wrath hotter than the congratulatory rockets exploding over her brother's gardens. She didn't renege on promises—not usually—but it seemed her fiancé did. She might live in Mayfair, bow as elegantly as a queen, pour tea like a countess, make idle conversation as if she'd been born to the role, but her principles had been molded by a childhood spent in the stews. Filthy streets, the sounds of breaking glass and drunken laughter, an empty hearth, a vacant cupboard. An upbringing no one mentioned, of course.

An upbringing that had shaped her.

She was as constant as a draught horse, an excellent judge of character not swayed by society flash, the Queen's English, or empty promises. Although a fat lot of good this steadfastness had gotten her. Like every woman in history, when given a choice of men, she'd chosen *poorly.* Her own particular trap to be fooled not by a set of Hoby boots but by a set of scarlet don's robes. A sizable vocabulary, she'd come to find, did not make for an honorable man. Or it didn't guarantee one in any case.

A lesson learned and not forgotten.

Another reminder to stick with cats.

Sinking deeper into the velvet squabs, Theo's gaze caught on a length of silk in a twist at her feet. She lifted the cravat to her nose, inhaling her first full breath of the day even as her belly tumbled to her toes.

The scent was elusive but familiar. All too familiar.

Expensive. Refined, but with a spicy edge. Belonging to a newly formed man, one she didn't particularly *like*. Or trust. Winding the strip around her trembling fingers, she glanced about, seeking confirmation that she'd made a worse mistake than imagined.

Oh, bloody hell.

Dashiell Campbell was sprinkled about his carriage in bits and pieces, invading her space as she'd unwittingly invaded his. Closeness they'd not shared in over a year.

A little pillow nestled on the opposite seat covered in a distinctive plaid. A ridiculous knickknack a woman purchased for a man that he couldn't toss aside until he'd tossed *her* aside. The Campbell tartan, she knew, because she'd looked it up at Hatchards in the *History of Clans and Colors*. Boredom, not interest, being the reason for her inquiry. If it was true interest, she would have purchased the tome. It was not the fact, certainly *not*, that a tidbit about a distinguished Scottish author, a countess, and an aggrieved husband had hit the scandal rags the morning of her trip to Piccadilly. She'd read the story over tea and toast with that burning in her chest she got when she envisioned Dash's exploits.

With a shuddering breath, Theo searched every corner of the conveyance, knowing it would be there. The man didn't travel without his blessed book. The manuscript she'd helped him write. Three hundred pages that had changed him from a man she enjoyed a little too much to one she didn't recognize. Recognize in bearing, not appearance. His beauty was still dazzling enough to light a thousand chambers.

She'd often wondered, did someone with such Greek god splendor stun themselves when they caught a passing glance in the mirror? Although Dash had never seemed more than mildly engrossed by his good looks, merely opportunistic. Like people had from the dawn of time, he used his attractiveness to his advantage. She'd watched the demonstration multiple times, those first seconds when a person stumbled upon him. Parted lips, ragged sighs, dropped parasols, flushed cheeks. Even once, at an insipid winter ball at the Duke of Markham's, Lady Bonham had taken one look at Dash in formal attire, tripped over her slippers, and landed *on* the dessert table. Theo grimaced to recall the melee that had followed.

Grinning like a fool, Dash Campbell sold every copy of *Proper Etiquette for Deception* in his possession that day.

In the end, this was the element that had shattered their friendship. He had a *gift*. He could write. His subject may well have been common—gambling and how to cheat accordingly—but his prose, *ah*, exquisite. Lyrical. As gorgeous as his silly face.

A gift he was *wasting*. Crashed carriages and widowed countesses, drunken brawls and races down Bond at midnight, minor transgressions, perhaps, but ones she couldn't easily forgive. Because they were part of the bigger calamity.

He was throwing away what she would have killed for. A *career*, a talent all her own. When he was coming to not need the money, his fortune from investing with Tobias Streeter and Xander Macauley, part ownership in a gaming hell and other ventures, growing along with his fame.

Of course, *Proper Etiquette for Deception* was on the floorboard. Two copies, in fact. Endorsed, she'd wager, with his wispy signature and a pithy sentiment meant to captivate. "Joyful reading" or some such blather. Dash's tome was the most popular narrative to arrive in London since the Bible. Theo pried his literary masterpiece from the stray pup's mouth, groaning over the gnawed corner. Knowing exactly where she was going in the book, if not her journey, she flipped pages until she located the chapter explaining how to mark cards.

A vision of Dash bent over her brother's desk rolled through her like mist. The only place he and Theo, and her chaperone, Mrs. Danbury, had been allowed to work without risk to her reputation. An oil lamp sparking blue in his jet-black hair, the scent of him, that slightly ribald fragrance he'd worn before being directed down more polished paths, circling the room. She'd loved that aroma, a bit of the rookery right there in Mayfair.

Now he smelled like everyone else.

Sounded like everyone else after the Duchess Society had smoothed away his vowel's hard edges.

"*What's that fetching word, lass? The one for cheating.*"

Theo smiled, taking a sip of chamomile tea, wishing for the sun to sit in the sky a little longer. At sunset, her time working with her student was over. Dash had his gaming hell to run, and she had a ball or some other pointless event to attend. Therefore, these moments were the best of her days. "Duplicitous."

He'd looked up then, and she would never forget. His lips, the lower plumper than the top, a crime that, silently shaping the phrase. His eyes had gone the palest indigo, icy and mysterious, nothing ordinary, a watery blue like hers. Wonder and, buried deep, an emotion he reined in for most, humiliation because he had to ask. "Spell it. Dinnae rush. You ken to go slowly."

She'd gone slowly that afternoon, done everything he asked of her. Spelled and edited. Suggested chapters to expound upon and those to remove. Reworking his sentences, offering sharper phrasing. Gently, taking care to protect his self-esteem when a man's could be crushed effortlessly beneath a satin slipper.

Together, they'd fashioned an entire book from a loose idea and a few notes scratched on foolscap wadded in a scamp's trouser pocket. A truly gifted writer, he'd only needed help filling in where his lack of education left him deficit. Come to find the rough-edged Scot, once the most infamous cutpurse in London, was brilliant in his own way. Why, he could compute rows of figures without quill and paper, count cards so well he'd been booted from every gaming hell in town until Xander Macauley, one of her brother's best friends and de facto leader of the Leighton Cluster, asked him to manage his establishment four years ago.

Keeping enemies close was Macauley's initial plan.

Theo had been surprised to find they shared a hunger for knowledge. Except she'd had to hide her cleverness behind dainty teacups and stitched samplers. Dreary watercolors of landscapes and pianoforte drivel.

While he'd hidden his quite contentedly behind his beauty.

And their unfortunate childhoods, they'd shared this as well. Although Dash had never wanted to discuss his. What had happened to put that sorrowful look in his eyes when anyone mentioned Scotland? When he started anxiously twisting that signet ring round his knuckle. His manner became alarmingly chilly when she asked—even if for a short time, she'd been his best friend.

Or so he'd said.

She glanced at the book in her hand, to the window where twilight was creeping around her like a cloak. Lifting Dash's cravat to her nose, she drew a man she no longer knew into her soul. A man who'd once told her he owed her—because listing her as a contributor in his book couldn't be done. Not unless she wanted ruination of the kind her brother and the Duchess Society would have had an apoplexy over.

Although she'd abandoned any good intent now.

Theo brushed the silk strip across her cheek, debating. She needed a means of escape. *Temporary* means. Out of London means. Somewhere to hide until she determined what to do. She'd get in touch with Leighton's sister, Pippa, the one person in this world who might understand why she'd done what she'd done. In the way that she'd done it.

Pippa had once been a girl without dreams, too.

It wouldn't be long before Dash realized his carriage was missing. He'd track her down. For all she knew, his driver could be taking her to his front door this very minute. If that were the case, how could he refuse to help her? After she'd helped him become the biggest sensation to hit London since George IV ascended the throne.

He would protect her. This she knew. The Leighton Cluster was loyal, and Dash was a solid member in standing.

Although...

With a sigh, Theo flipped the book back to the puppy for his entertainment.

There was the matter of his vow. Following their tender, innocent kiss.

Barely there before it was over. Dash hadn't touched her anywhere else, only his lips grazing hers. *"I thank you for the lessons. Then, I'll owe you. And someday, lass, that owing will be worth something."*

A young man, impressionable and impulsive, asking a duke's daughter to help him had shocked her to her core. She could still see his face in the moonlight, his pure blue eyes so sure, the crooked scar on his chin gone pale with his wide smile. "Solid information from a professional," he'd said, full of what she'd considered naivete about his topic's potential to attract.

Well, he'd shown them all. Even her. She hadn't thought his

manuscript would sell, not one copy outside the Leighton Cluster's pity purchases.

She scrubbed her fingertip over a smudge on the windowpane. A man in defense of his dreams was a highly admirable thing. Attractive, even. Fascinating. If he'd continued on the path of steadily composing and not gone down the different-chit-each-night one.

She had a verbal voucher, and he owed her.

The only problem with her plan was the flutter that attacked her heart when she was around him. And the heat. Low, similar to an oil wick burning its last, but present. If she could only turn it down as she did her bedside lamp each evening. Although a shade of attraction was normal regarding the man considered the most handsome in England, wasn't it?

She slumped back, verdict made. Desperation bred decision.

Theodosia Astley was calling in her marker.

Dash had a damned good idea who'd stolen his carriage.

An engagement party with a missing fiancée and one conveyance less than should be lining the drive. Wasn't too confounding a puzzle to solve now, was it? He released an aggrieved breath and sought to calm himself. Though a fine mount, the sleek filly he was currently directing down West End back alleys, an asinine effort to draw less attention to the debacle he was involving himself in, wasn't his. He'd hit Leighton's stables at a run after finding his barouche, the Wourch he'd had shipped directly from Germany, thank you very much, missing. Taken the first saddled beast the groom could present and left the estate at a gallop. He could ride like no man in London if put to the test.

Somehow, he'd *known*. Immediately and without a whiff of uncertainty that she'd stepped into a mess she'd think she could save herself from. Like dog shite on one's boot, it wasn't that easy to remove.

Dash had searched the ballroom seconds after her engagement gala detonated like an explosive and thought: *foolish, reckless lass*. Though he might have run himself had he been in the same bind. Scottish good sense hitting him square in the chest as he elbowed his way through the high-class throng, not even letting up long enough to tell her brother, His Grace, about his intention to find the missing bride. Leighton had been too busy thrashing Theo's husband-to-be to a veritable pulp, which was expected from the duke with the fiercest temper in England.

Dash had merely acknowledged that he had to find her.

Because no one understood Theodosia Astley like he did.

He hadn't spent a year in her brother's study only writing a blessed book. He'd analyzed his partner in literary crime as intently as she'd analyzed him, sly glances across the duke's massive mahogany desk telling him much of what he needed to know. *Wanted* to know. Bugs under a microscope and all that mince. The *minutiae* of life. A new word he liked to repeat as often as he could, cementing it in his mind for future use. Minutiae the brainy lass loved. The little things. Surprising and thrilling to find this was a curiosity they shared.

Learning, words and writing, pieces he'd not known he had a knack for until a studious wallflower with hair the color of raw sunlight showed him.

For this, since he'd been unable to repay Theo in any other way, he would intervene in the muddle she'd embroiled herself in. He cursed beneath his breath, his fingers clenching around the reins. Stealing carriages and fleeing celebrations, what was she thinking? He'd return her to her brother under cover of darkness with none the wiser. They could lie and say she'd fled the ballroom to go have a crying jag in her bedchamber. Although Theo was the least likely woman he knew to weep over a lump like Edward Biggerstaff.

Or so he hoped.

He also goddamn hoped she'd ducked from view as his carriage careened through the city streets, his groom acting as his driver because his coachman had come down with a fever of some sort. There were only five Wourches in England to Dash's knowing, so the vehicle was sure to attract attention. He didn't think Theo wanted to heap scandal on her family's shoulders, of course not, though he could tell them that she didn't much care about heaping it on her own.

That was her con, her scam, her *gift*.

He could have written an entire chapter detailing Theodosia Astley's poker face. When he'd caroused with some of the shrewdest gamblers in the bloody world. Dash dodged a stalled vegetable cart, his hand tensing around the ribbons and sending his mount into a scattered stride. She was no society miss. No rule-follower.

Complacent, he decided, the perfect word for what she *wasn't*.

She only pretended to be. Following the decrees laid before her because it's what one did to survive. Same as him. Neither of them had to like it.

Theo presented a bonnie picture. *Aye*, bleeding hell, did she. The picture the Duchess Society and her brother, the duke, her sister, the duchess, wanted her to present. She'd done a fair job of safeguarding the ruse. Guarding the edges—perimeter, he believed that was the word—of any ballroom she stepped into. Fresh as a flower, concealing her bold inquisitiveness beneath a winsome, purely false smile.

Beautiful, but in a way you had to discover, like buried treasure.

He tilted his head, thinking hard, digging his heel into the horse's flank. Ostentatious. *Aye*, nothing ostentatious like his looks. All flash and no substance.

There was devilry in her eyes. So light a blue they seemed bottomless, like the loch down the way from the Glasgow workhouse where he'd resided for a time. He'd bathed in that pond every evening in the spring and summer, teeth chattering but body clean. Washing away grime, blood, anguish. Theo's gaze cut through him like that ice-cold water, reaching deep. Areas he'd blocked off, shut down, hidden.

No lass, to his mind, should be the most intelligent person in any parlor. Speak more than one language and like *maths*. But she was—and a damned danger because of it. *Poor Leighton* was all Dash could think as he kicked his mount into a gallop upon passing Wapping and the West India Docks. She and his stolen carriage were just ahead if he had it right.

The tricky part of this rescue mission would be ignoring the itchy sensation he got under his collar when he stood too close to her. Heat flowing down his neck and along his limbs like a caress every time he caught a glimpse of her charmingly crooked front tooth. Blood humming a tad much for mere friendship when he realized how she'd matured in the years he'd known her. Curves and smiles and a decided hint of knowing. The scent of lavender that seemed to linger, drift around his mind long after she'd left. A problem, indeed.

He didnae know why Theo Astley, of all lasses, got to him. She wasn't his usual kind. He preferred the gaudy chits with guffawing laughs and shallow minds. Sequin and glitter types.

Women who never asked questions he didnae care to answer.

He'd worried a bit about concealing that spark, or had, until Theo cut off their friendship like a chicken's head with an ax for no reason he could fathom. Perversely, he wanted her more for the fiery, angry looks she tossed his way of late. Vivid-bright lust, he imagined, if he let it loose. Licentious. *Aye*, a lovely word for what he could feel if he let himself. Which he wasn't going to do. But he repeated it anyway —*licentious*—a whisper lost to the ripping wind because he loved the sound and didn't want to forget it.

He wasn't captivated by everything in a skirt. He was choosy—but was often chosen.

What was a man to do but say *aye*?

Dash caught sight of his carriage as he directed his filly onto Narrow Street, heading toward his gaming hell as he'd expected. The least suitable place to deliver a duke's sister on the run, but his groom, Meekins, a lad who'd arrived last week from the Shoreditch workhouse by way of Pippa Macauley's charitable organization, wouldn't know a respectable woman from a lightskirt. Pippa was the wife of his partner, Xander Macauley, the man who'd taken Dash under his wing, saved his life truth be told, and he'd do anything for him. Including hiring castoff orphans. He'd fill his house with gap-toothed scamps if it would pay Macauley back.

Dash's cheeks stung as he imagined what Meekins thought. Assumed the chit who'd climbed into his employer's conveyance was one of the sequin and glitters was what. A pre-arranged situation, something Dash had arranged multiple times, he'd admit. Chit enters carriage, then bed. Wink, wink, nudge, nudge.

This didn't go along with anything Dash wished Theo to think about him.

He'd tried around her, he really had. Always using the correct fork

13

and keeping his serviette in his lap, not dinging the sides of his teacup with his spoon, that sort of class. She made him want to be good, better, honorable—a *gentleman*—when everyone else made him want to be very, very bad.

Let's face it. Bad was easier.

Consequently, he'd avoided Theo the past year. *After* she started avoiding him. A move he couldn't completely blame her for as he was getting sick of his bloody book parade, too. It wasn't her fault she reminded him of his past, being impoverished and uneducated, having to ask that even simple words be spelled for him. Vowels tripping over each other, proclaiming the unpleasant side of his Scottish heritage. He was embarrassed by that lad and more embarrassed to feel attraction to that part of her.

The rookery lass he could see shining through occasionally.

When she seemed proud of her former privation. He admired her loyalty to herself.

Angling his mount alongside his carriage, Dash shouted to Meekins, jerking his chin to signal that they keep moving. The groom grinned and winked—*winked,* dammit—gesturing with a wiry shoulder to the interior of the carriage. *I have her.*

Dash grimaced, nodded, accepting the reputation he'd earned for himself. He simply didn't want that reputation to spill over and stain her.

A persistent drizzle that promised to become a downpour had started, the streets muddy, the cloudburst soaking through his formal coat as his overcoat was hanging on a random hook at the duke's. A dreich day. His splendor in wait for a wedding that was not happening. Expelling a sigh, Dash maneuvered his horse to the side, then followed the carriage down the lane bordering the gaming hell as his mount took two dancing steps backward in confusion.

He couldn't confront the obstinate lass on a city street.

But the back alley of the city's most infamous gambling establishment would do.

Dash patted his waistcoat, and the dice pocketed there. His heart was racing when this was a game, like any other. One requiring solid strategy. He was, if nothing else in this bonnie life, a man quick on his feet, a man willing to gamble.

Except, Theo didn't play games.

And he wasn't a man known to chance anything, especially his heart.

Chapter Two

Even if you're counting cards, expect the unforeseen ace to hit the table.

Dashiell M. Campbell, *Proper Etiquette for Deception*

Dash Campbell was even more handsome than memory served—when it had only been an hour since she'd seen him lounging against a ballroom pillar, the Countess of Geden-Mills coercing him into something wicked. Mere minutes before Edward's pregnant dilemma had showed up and ruined everything.

Theo peeked out the window in time to see her savior make a slithering dismount from his horse, tiny furrows of displeasure radiating alongside his mouth. Exasperation should not make a man more attractive. It was *unjust*. He had on another of his bold plaid waistcoats, a signature style young men in the *ton* had started to emulate. A formal set of clothing for an event that had splintered like a ship's hull against the rocks.

She thought the conveyance stopped too suddenly behind the Devil's Lair, that she'd heard hoofbeats blending with the steady rhythm of the carriage's grays.

Lands, he'd caught them quickly.

Caught her quickly.

He stomped through a puddle, his thighs flexing in trousers flawlessly cut for his form. Scooting forward on the seat, Theo squinted. He was limping. *Ah*, yes, she'd read about the accident. Another mad race through London at dawn ending in chaos. Reckless beast.

Theo didn't want to agree with the *ton's* assessment. So what if Dash was unnaturally gifted in appearance? Witty and amiable, the sly glimmer in his indigo eyes calling to every female in the country. In the world. She palmed the squab, the velvety nap caressing her fingertips, her belly scrambling the closer he got to her.

Basically, she didn't want to *want*.

His hair was clipped in a fashionable style, the damp giving the black-as-midnight strands a delicate curl that softened his glower. She'd tried not to record a blessed thing about him since her engagement. Certainly not when he was her student. It went against her sincere vow to teach.

Now, however, with her life gone to Hades in a handbasket, she supposed it didn't hurt to look. Take note of the fact that he'd gained a stone of what looked to be muscle, his brawls with the Leighton Cluster forcing him to bulk up. His build was still on the edge of lanky, much leaner than Xander Macauley or Tobias Streeter, a preferable construct to her mind. Who needed to resemble a boxer waiting to step into the ring? Truthfully, Dash could have passed for a scholar if not for the teasing glint in his gaze. The perpetual card shoved up his sleeve.

She chewed on her bottom lip, preparing for the fight. He had nice fingers. Long, slim. She couldn't help but notice. His fidgets with dice brought her attention repeatedly to them. Recently, at another of his mindless literary presentations, he'd ripped his gloves off with his *teeth* before going into a demonstration about marking cards. She'd spent the evening fantasizing about his hands trailing over her skin, those glove-ripping teeth, straight where hers were crooked, nipping parts of her no one had seen outside her maid. Areas she wasn't even sure how to soothe herself, though they burned of late.

And in her darkened bedchamber, in the dim of the night, she'd tried.

She hadn't heard a word of his blasted book that night. Which was fine because she knew every single line by heart. Come to think of it, she'd spent half the time in her brother's study staring at his hands. *Psst, silly girl.*

The lanterns mounted on the carriage's postern lit his beauty and his anger. When he reached her, Dash didn't go for a chivalrous presentation, merely yanked the door open, and let it thump back against the carriage. His signet ring, the most mysterious thing about his attire, glinting in the sconce's glow. Then his head was inside the vehicle, his shoulders, the rest of his long body as he climbed in. The carriage rocked with his weight as he threw himself—thank heavens not right beside her—on the seat across. His scent claimed the space as surely as the man, rain, leather, and something that smelled unbelievably like cinnamon.

Theo sat up straight. Took a fortifying breath. Clenched and unclenched her fingers. Nudged the pup between her slippered feet and settled her skirt over him.

She wasn't going to plead, explain, *apologize*. For anything, ever again. Her brother, if he'd sent Dash while he cleaned up the mess in town, could go hang. Every man in London, no, in *England*, could jump off the Westminster Bridge for all she cared. One woman was never enough. Promises never kept. Love never returned. Rogues and cheats, the lot. She frowned, picking at a loose thread on her glove. Except Roan. He'd kept every promise he'd made to his duchess, Helena. And Xander Macauley to Pippa. Tobias Streeter to his wife, Hildy. The Duke of Markham to Georgiana. The Earl of Stanford, Ollie, to his new wife, Nessie. Chance Allerton, Viscount Remington, to his wife, Franny.

The Leighton Cluster loved their wives to absolute distraction. They were known for it.

She cursed softly. Well, *still*....

She was preparing her speech when Dash did the teeth-ripping-off-glove show again and vaporized her argument like mist in the sun. *Oh*, he had a beautiful mouth. What man needed a bottom lip as plump and rosy as a cherry?

He glanced at her then, truly, for the first time in months, the length of kidskin tumbling to his lap. With decided nonchalance, he removed the other glove with savage intent, his cheeks hollowing while her heart skipped in her chest. When his eyes met hers, they were as vivid as the azurite she'd seen in the British Museum's geological section. Intensely blue and hotly bothered. Unaware of her indecision, he groaned and shifted his injured leg, stretching it out, his boot coming alongside her hip.

Every ounce a man of leisure and crude elegance. Arrogant toad. Nothing surprising from someone the *ton* called the Gambling God.

"What a mess you've created, lass," he finally said, digging in his waistcoat pocket and coming out with a pair of the ever-present dice. Flipping them between his hands, his canny gaze fixed on her. "Dinnae want to be involved in this, I can tell you. You could have stayed put in that doty ballroom, played the broken-hearted betrothed, milked them like cows for sympathy, and done us all a favor. Did you learn nothing about playing people from a year spent working on my book? Not as if you're suffering to lose that fop. Even I can see your lack of misery."

"Well, I didn't stay and play anyone. So get out and ride away. Forget you found me. I'll make sure your gleaming conveyance is returned to you, good as new." She sank back against the seat with a ragged exhalation, spent to her *bones*. "Edward's merely a charlatan. A dirty, filthy liar. I would never have agreed to marry a fop."

Sinking his fingers in the tousled strands hanging over his brow, Dash shook out the damp. Raindrops dusted his cheeks, glistening pinpricks on sun-kissed skin. "Ride away, eh, that it? And have your brother murder me upon my return without you? I'll nae take that bet. He doesna know where I am, where *you* are, but he will. Dukes have eyes in every damned place I'm finding. A missing carriage and a missing girl, the grandest carriage in London at the moment, won't be long gone without notice."

His accent, with assistance from the Duchess Society, had transformed into the lilting tones of the Scottish upper classes. When Dashiell Campbell hadn't a lick of proper breeding, refinement, or education shading his backstory. He hid his gracelessness well, his past only brutalizing his speech when he'd had too much to drink or was angry. Both events she'd witnessed. His temper wasn't as explosive as her Roan's, but it ran hot often enough.

When he moved to strike the roof and alert the driver to return them to Mayfair, she caught his wrist, her fingers circling and holding.

Their gazes clashed, the sudden rush of his pulse beneath her fingertips a revelation.

Maybe, she thought in silent wonder. *Maybe*.

She'd always questioned if she was the only one who experienced a steady and unwelcome heat when they were together. Tangled up in her role in society and the expectations given it, she'd never tried to solve the mystery. Consider Dash in another manner. It had been enough to convince her brother to allow her to tutor the scoundrel, much less anything else.

Dash extracted his hand from her clutch, curled his fingers around his dice, and rested back against the squabs. A gambler to his core, his expression unreadable. At least he'd deigned to place his muddy boot back on the floor, away from her skirt. "Five minutes, *leannan*, then we're circling around the way we came. Out with your story."

Oot with yer story.

You still sound like a heathen, she wanted to tell him. A gorgeous, hulking, arrogant heathen. Instead, she asked, "Leannan?"

He cut his eyes her way, then toward the ceiling. Shrugged a broad shoulder. "Gaelic for troublemaker." He kissed the dice and gave them a spin on his palm. "A pest. A nuisance in satin."

Acting on impulse, the only way Theo could imagine provoking him, she grasped the dog-eared copy of *Proper Etiquette for Deception* from the carriage floor and tossed it out the window. It hit the cobblestones with a satisfying thud.

With a snarl, he shoved his dice in his pocket, smacked the roof, and sent the carriage jerking into motion. "Time's up, *leannan*. Back to the West End for you."

"I tried to find a companion but there wasn't time," she said in a rush, her skin prickling in alarm. "I never meant to venture out alone. But there was Edward looking like he'd been clobbered with a brick, and that woman shrieking that he couldn't marry me and..." With a huff, she blew a lock of hair out of her eyes. The damp was doing riotous things to her chignon. "I would have located Vivette if I'd had time to *think*."

"That hapless maid of Pippa's? How well did she protect her charge? Macauley stole in like a thief and snatched Pippa away. What's to thinking with that plan?"

"We could engage Vivette's grandmother, Nanna. I can wait in your carriage in another part of town, a safer part, whilst you work on that arrangement."

Dash scrubbed his fist across his eyes, clearly fatigued. "Nanna did a piss-poor job, too. The woman doesna speak English, lass. Why do you think Macauley's torment hired her in the first place? If she was warning Leighton about Pippa's antics, no one knew."

Theo picked at the seam of her glove, the grubby section of London bleeding into the posher section she didn't want to return to. The scent of the docks leaving the air to be replaced with coal smoke and roasted meat from the carts lining the roadway. She belonged in the former district not the latter—but no one cared what she wanted. "Pippa is not Macauley's *torment*, she's the love of his life. And I knew exactly what Nanna was saying. I simply chose to ignore her. I speak German as well as a smattering of Italian and French."

"Of course you do," he whispered under his breath.

Theo scooted forward, upsetting the pup who chose that moment to peek from beneath the frilled edge of her skirt with a muffled *woof*. "You owe me, Dashiell Campbell."

Dash eyed the hound with an expression of incredulous revulsion. "I fookin' what?"

"Remember what you told me the first time we talked? In Leighton's garden? 'Then I'll owe ye. Someday, lass, that owing will be worth something'," she mimicked in a fair imitation of his heavier brogue. "I won't go back there, not now. Not yet. So, here I am, calling in my marker. I need your assistance. Not with a book but with my *life*."

He opened his mouth, closed it. Glanced at the pup who'd jumped on the seat to nestle against his thigh. Fiddled with the glove in his lap. Patted the dice in his pocket, twice. Looking anywhere but at her.

"Why do you smell like cinnamon?" Theo asked and balanced her hand on the wall as the carriage took a wild turn. Dash was going to help her if the driver didn't crash the vehicle and send them into the streets. She could tell from the stiff set of his lovely mouth, the line of displeasure settling between his brows, that he was thinking. Of a way out more than likely.

When she wasn't going to allow him to find a way out.

She hated to tell him, but between the two of them, she was the most tenacious. She'd been denied a thousand times more than he had and come out on top. She'd had lots of practice at losing.

With his looks and undeniable charm, *everyone* told him yes.

"I was having a biscuit, lass, must you know. One of those luscious nibbles from the baker on Curzon your brother employs when Edward's torment"—he glanced at her, his gaze amused and frustrated —"can I use torment to describe the expectant chit who stormed your engagement gala?" He tunneled his fingers into the pup's snarled coat and gave him a gentle rub. "I was having a snack whilst deciding who I might seduce this evening when I found myself on this adventure instead. I canna countenance my choice."

Theo's heart took a precarious tumble. He'd chosen her. Over security. Over sense. Over the possibility of getting another woman in his bed. "Do they know you came after me?"

"*Nae*." The word shot from his lips like a bullet.

"Then why did you?"

He thumped the roof again with his fist. The carriage lurched to a stop, and he vaulted to the cobbles without reply. His conversation with his driver was brief, held in hushed tones that kept her outside it. When he returned, his expression was cross. The rain had increased, rivulets running down his locked jaw to soak his shirt collar.

Against his will, a decision made in her favor.

Uneasy, Theo patted her chest. Hiccupped like she did when she was nervous. Much more of this mad journey, and she was going to cast up her accounts. "Perhaps you'd better discuss proper driving techniques with your coachman? Our chances of making it anywhere safely are slim if he keeps this up."

Shutting the door with a curt snick, Dash threw himself on the opposite seat and began to loosen his cravat with indignant yanks while the pup whined and burrowed against his hip. "The lad's a groom, not a coachman. Meekins was recently released from the workhouse. My driver has a case of influenza." Dash released a mournful hum and used his rumpled cravat to dry his face. "He'll slow now because he has to. The rain is coming down steady enough to make a muddle of the roads. I'll climb up when we meet the post road. He won't ken the way."

"One of Pippa's foundlings," she murmured. After wedding Xander Macauley, a reprobate she'd wanted that no one expected her to catch, Pippa had started a charitable endeavor to locate employment in the *ton's* households for rookery adolescents. Her husband was a long-standing benefactor of Limehouse's orphanage and workhouse, as he'd lived for a time in both. Places she wondered if Dash had lived, too, in Scotland. A suspicion on her part, nothing to back it up.

Yet, he never said a word about his past. Not one peep.

Post road. Theo glanced at a watercress seller lugging her handcart down an alley, at the rows of townhouses clipping by in the rainy wash. The dwellings were getting smaller, the bits of land around them more expansive. They were headed east, not west. "You're not taking me back."

"I've gone daft, *aye*. Time not on my side. I have business in Bury St Edmunds. Meeting a team of workers there Monday morning. A cottage I purchased from a baron with extremely ill luck at the tables. Macauley said I should find a place of me—"

He halted and rubbed his fist across his chin, his cheeks tingeing. "My own. Establish *my* own place. Roots, he calls it. Permanence. Heritage for those of us born without. Which I reckon he's doing with all those children he and Pippa are having. I'd planned to stable my horses at a coaching inn for the night instead of changing mounts, the Hare and Billet which is about halfway between. It's a suitable guesthouse, respectable food with a cozy pub. Now this." He fired an irate glance her way. "*You.*"

She exhaled, relieved, her mind spinning through her options. She and Dash could work this out without her reputation being entirely demolished. He was cunning, a cheat at heart. As she was, even if she concealed it well. No two could devise a better plan than Theo Astley and Dash Campbell. "I thought you were going to say you'd purchased a property in Glasgow, and we had to travel there. Which would be a bit far for me to run. Bury St Edmunds isn't, what, forty miles outside London proper? We can hire a temporary chaperone at your inn for my return to London. As soon as tomorrow morning perhaps, once the fervor dies down. I'll repay you for any expense. I've saved almost ten pounds in pin money. No one in the city will have to know. They'll assume I've been crying in my bedchamber since the debacle at the ball."

"Sixty-three miles to my cottage from the Devil's Lair, to be exact. A delightful spot you aren't going to see." He reached to grab the remaining copy of his book from the carriage floor, his frown increasing when he noted the gnawed cover. "I'm nae living in Scotland again, *leannan,* so you know. There's nothing there for me. I visit Oban for the distillery enterprise with Macauley and Tobias Streeter, a native talking business to other Scotsmen, but that's it. For blunt, I go back. The old Scottish saying about small investments paying big dividends, *mony a mickle maks a muckle.* But it's not home. Will never again be home." He slapped the book to his thigh, his jaw hard as marble. "Don't ask, lass. Because I won't tell."

Her curiosity was apparently poorly disguised, but she forged ahead. "I didn't have a choice. I *had* to escape that ballroom, those people. The *ton* looks down on me because of my 'unfortunate lineage.' My sister leaving the docks to marry her duke is enough for them to allow me into their parlors but not enough for them to accept me. Even Leighton can't erase the stain of the stews from my skin. You know this. My love of books and wish to be educated push me even further away. Absurd dreams, but I hold on to them. I'm worse than a wallflower, Dash. I'm an intellectual!"

With an oath, he tossed *Proper Etiquette for Deception* to the seat.

"You bring up these humble beginnings because you think it binds us, which hell, maybe it does. It's one of the suggestions I posed in chapter five, remember? Find familiar ground before you run a con. The punch packs more when no one sees it coming. Only, there's a missing element to your grand plan."

Theo raised a brow in silent rebuke, a trick she'd perfected in the mirror because her face, she'd admit, was the least intimidating in her family.

"What's missing in your wee mind is Leighton taking a whip to me when he finds out I've left London with you. You may not have been born amongst them, but Helena married deep and dragged you down with her. A duke is a never-ending society commitment, lass. Rule upon rule you're required to follow for *life*. You, me, and my tawdry reputation in a carriage bound for Bury St Edmunds isn't the answer."

His voice dropped so low she barely heard him, "Even if he imagines I think of you as a sister."

Theo leaned in, eager to catch this last piece. "What did you say?"

Dash dug out his dice and gave them a ferocious spin on his palm. "*Nae*, forget it. I'm barmy. Tetched in the head."

"Delusional," she provided, knowing how much he appreciated learning unfamiliar words. His mood always improved when they played this game.

His gaze sharpened, his interest keen. He wrapped the phrase around his tongue like a sweet. His study took her in from head to toe, a leisurely perusal that lit her up inside while his lips moved in hushed appreciation. "De-lu-sion-al. I like the sound of it. Delusional. Quite bonnie, in fact."

"Has more of a ring, truthfully."

"That it does, *leannan*, that it does." Then he grinned, his eyes glowing, reminding her why this scheme of hers *was* a disaster. The most charming rascal in England sitting across from her, with nothing but a stray hound and an orphaned groom-cum-coachman between them. Thoughts of a long-ago kiss filling her mind, if not his. Thoughts of how, if she had more time, she might be able to pick the lock that was Dashiell Campbell.

Casually, Theo flicked at the lace trimming her sleeve, striving to disarm. "How about we discuss your next book over dinner at the inn, then I'll retire to my room? *After* sending a note to Leighton about my whereabouts. In the morning, I'll arrange for transport with a companion and be back in town in a flash. While you'll continue to your new property with none the wiser."

She smiled, confident about the strategy. What could go wrong?

Eyeing her, he sprawled on the bench, his jacket flopping open, giving her a stellar view of a lean body swathed in attire created by the finest tailor in London. She knew this because her brother, Roan, had introduced Dash to John Weston, who typically outfitted no title lower than earl. Per his style, a plaid waistcoat was the only splash of color among crisp, refined black. He might not plan to return to Scotland, but he never denied the opportunity to proclaim his connection. Or his increasing wealth. "Who says I'm writing another when this one has flown to the heavens? Padding my financial accounts every day, more blunt than I know what to do with. Combined with my investments with Macauley and Streeter and my partnership in the Devil's Lair, I'm set for life. Invited into homes I'd not have before except as a footman."

He buffed his nails on his knee, gave the pup an insolent scratch, yawned. Less indifferent than he appeared, a quiver of awareness zipping about the small enclosure, stinging her skin and making her breath catch. "Frankly, I canna see the need. Writing is demanding work when I've got enough of it elsewhere."

A spark of resentment ignited in her throat. Nothing made her angrier than a missed opportunity. One she would have killed to have. "You're wasting your talent, your gift, if you don't write another. Something real this time. You mentioned it to me once, turning your journals into a novel."

Cheeks flushing, he came up in a flurry of motion, rapping his head on the ceiling. The hound released a high, piercing yip and started to dance in excited circles on the squab. "I was foxed! Blinded by booze. The Duke of Markham and that blasted trip to White's before my lesson with you, such a brilliant idea. My first time getting tossed outta there, but not the last. A tradition I wish I'd never started. I told you to ignore what I said that day, *everything* I said. Those were dreams talking. Fantasies fueled by a gallon of brandy and a dash of absinthe, courtesy of the Earl of Stanford before he tidied up his life."

The carriage swerved, sending him bouncing to his seat. Rubbing his temple, he said through gritted teeth, "At least now I ken why you've been vexed for months. More hopes of my creating *literature* when what I've published is flying off shelves faster than the printer in Islington can keep up with. I've paid me dues, given talks in every deadly dull salon while suffering through enough cucumber sandwiches for three lifetimes."

"Yes, I've seen your marked card presentation at two assemblies this month. Fascinating, even in repetition."

Dash pointed in her direction, more a vicious jab. The pup yelped and settled in next to the person he'd decided was his new master. "I've been invited to a private showing of that very display with George if I choose to do it. Nutty as a cake, but not someone I can ignore, I suppose. How about that?"

Theo tangled her hands in her skirt and rocked forward. "*King* George?"

He had the good grace to blush, though he kept that blue-bright gaze fixed and steady. "*Aye*, that's the laddie. Tosses blunt about like fairy dust. I've heard he has a stack of my books, gives them out as presents to envoys and such. Known to be a fair hand at hazard."

"A Scottish ne'er-do-well invited to Carlton House," Theo breathed before she remembered to keep her opinion to herself.

"Tell me how you really feel, lass. I'm aware I'm a chancer in this life. Risen above my intended means."

Theo struggled to be honest without hurting his feelings. Or exposing too much of hers. "You're the luckiest of men, Dashiell Campbell."

The dice stilled in his hand. "How's that?"

"You have dreams you can actually achieve."

He gestured to her with the dice, weakly, because they both knew what he was about to say wasn't true. "As do you."

She rolled her eyes and patted the seat next to her, but the mongrel she'd rescued didn't look up from his snug spot wedged against Dash's strapping thigh. Theo couldn't blame him. "*Pishposh*, what tomfoolery and you know it. I want a formal education at a university and to one day open a school, which is not possible in this world. It's a shock I was allowed to tutor you and only then under lock and key. I'm grateful for what my sister's marriage to Leighton has given me, don't think I'm not. I recall the empty cupboards and icy hearth during the winter, the gnawing hunger, the fear, before Helena found out about me. You see, her father never told her about his relationship, and my mother died having no idea Helena would welcome me, would *want* me, when she found out she had a half-sister. What daughter of a shipping magnate, set to marry a man with the highest title in the land, wants to be burdened with a bookish orphan from the stews?"

"*Leannan,*" he breathed, ready to comfort her in a way he'd comforted a thousand women, using the same words and the same molten gaze. After all, he rarely strayed from his approach. She'd seen him work many a ballroom with that liquid smile.

Theo cut him off because his brand of solace wasn't what she needed. "You're a gifted writer, Dash. A true writer. I helped you edit, suggested words and phrases, but the narrative, the flow, the hint of *magic* is all you. Because there is magic on those pages or no king would think to give away copies as gifts. You're the talk of this town for a reason."

"I'm an entertainer, *nae* more," he whispered after a poignant pause, a flush still riding his cheeks. When she'd never known him to show a lick of unease. It was charming and softened her heart in ways she didn't wish it to be softened.

Then the halfwit ruined any tender feelings by adding, "I dinnae suppose your double-dealing professor is wasting *his* promise."

Theo's fingers curled into fists. If not for the fact that she'd promised the Duchess Society she would try to be an actual *lady* this year, she would have leaped across the carriage, climbed atop Dash Campbell and—

Oh. Theo sat back, stunned. Brought her fist to her mouth and let a slow breath leak through her fingers. The vision that streaked across her mind was blistering. So clear she could almost taste it.

Taste *him.*

Dash's lips beneath hers. His tongue engaging her in play, which had happened twice, not pleasantly either time, with Edward. But, oh, *heaven*, this was pleasant. Vivid enough of a fantasy to have the secret nook between her thighs igniting. Softening like her heart had earlier. Warm, warm, warm. Toast fresh from the oven. Flagstones beneath your bare feet on a sunny day. A warmed brick beneath the counterpane.

She frowned and shook herself back to reality. She'd known studying the illustrations in that erotic French text at the Rose Emporium was going to cause trouble. Before she'd seen those pictures, she'd not known there were so many *choices*. Tangled limbs and malleable bodies. Expressions of pleasure on faces alight with a brand of knowledge she'd thus far been denied. Society kept women outside that chamber until marriage. Or tried to.

"Whatever is in your bonnie head right now, *leannan*, get it out," Dash murmured from across the way. "It's turning your eyes the color of lochs with bottomless waters. Places men are tempted to discover. I'm a gambler, you ken. Attracted to provocations even if I shouldn't be."

She glanced up, praying her cheeks weren't as ruddy as his. "I'm not marrying him. Not ever. Even if you take me back." Which it appeared, from the rural scenery flashing past in scattered moonlit bits, he wasn't.

Dash grumbled and sank his fingers into the pup's fur, then lifted his hand to his nose with a grimace. "Your wee mutt needs a bath. And if your professor is still breathing after the beating Leighton was giving him when I left his ballroom, lass, no one, and I mean no one, thinks the next step is walking the bruised sod down the aisle to you."

"He won't kill him," Theo said, though she wasn't completely sure.

Dash hummed, spinning his dice, not sure, either.

"Edward didn't want me. Not really. I got swept into the romance of a romance that was no romance. Carried away with less, with planning my future than fulfilling a promise I made when Helena married Roan. To fit in. If you'd seen me when I came to her in a tattered gown a scullery maid wouldn't dare sport, holes in my stockings, and my slippers."

"Lass, if you'd seen me when I arrived in London, you'd have run shrieking down the lane." He tapped his knuckle to the windowpane in remembrance. "Holes in me boots was the least of my concerns."

Theo shoved aside her pity; a sentiment Dash wouldn't accept. "I knew Edward didn't look at me the way... the way he should. The way Tobias Streeter looks at Hildy, Macauley at Pippa. Roan at Helena." The statement arrived for no reason she could fathom, too personal in nature to share with another man. Although Dash made her feel like she could tell him anything. Dangerous, indeed. "He desired my connection to the dukedom more than he desired me. My dowry didn't hurt, either. Fact is fact."

Dash's cheeks expanded with a tight exhalation. His jaw was covered in dense stubble, giving him a curiously swarthy appearance when he usually looked fresh off the press. Irked a bit, she realized he'd not thought to shave for her ball.

Staring out the window, he spun his dice until the moment demanded a response. "Edward Biggerstaff's a dobber, *leannan*. A fool. I tried to tell you. Or I wanted to. But you had him built up in your mind, head full of mince. Women can't be reasoned with in that condition. Anyway, who am I to judge about love?"

Love? She hadn't loved Edward.

"I never imagined he was perfect for me," she said instead of admitting the truth. That he'd been the perfect *solution* to the problem of what to do about Theo Astley. Every rotation of Dash's carriage wheel was taking her farther from one life and deeper into another, and she wasn't panicked by the thought. She was an academic at heart even if her world didn't allow it. A planner. A strategist. She liked telling jokes, pulling pranks even, and was entertaining with those she trusted, but she didn't like change or games of chance.

This journey was outrageous, hopping into a stranger's carriage unlike her.

Unless she didn't know herself as well as she thought she did.

It was something her beloved sister, Pippa, would do. An *actual* duke's sister but wild as they came. And look how wonderful her adventure, unplanned and courageously executed, had turned out? Married to a former reprobate, the love of her life. A man now tame as a kitten. Putty in her hands. She wanted a man to be putty in her hands someday.

Putty in her *bed*.

"Get the stars out of your eyes, lass. This isn't the Earl of Stanford's prime view from one of his bloody telescopes. Do you have anna' idea what getting into this carriage with me means for you if you're found out?"

"I do." She swallowed and repeated the oath with more vigor, "I do." Bizarrely, the vows she was supposed to repeat to Edward in twenty-four hours.

"*Aye*, like hell you do. The poshest piece of my life is running a gambling den that titled men favor most days, recouping blunt they squandered the night before at another club down the way. Add to that, my popularity over a notorious manuscript amusing them at the moment. You want to be the scandal that surpasses my notoriety?" He tipped his head against the squab, jaw flexing. Shoving his dice away, he wrestled out of his coat and tossed it aside. Rolled his sleeves to his elbows, exposing skin dusted with fine, dark hair. She squinted at the tattoo of a Celtic knot on his forearm, as round as a penny but delicately mastered while her body caught fire.

His provocative behavior was a demonstration, she understood, to confirm the perilous intimacy of the situation she'd placed herself in.

When his gaze met hers, his eyes were a frigid, icy blue. "I was born in a brothel, Theodosia Astley. Moved from there to a filthy flat above a flash house when I was nine or so. It was a sluggish lifetime of near misses until I got out, escaped with nothing but the clothing on me back. A laddie who spent his childhood cowering beneath staircases, learning to steal rather than starve, isna meant for a chit who's dipped her toe in a fashionable pond and is never, no matter her will against walking that path, yanking it out." He fingered the cover of the book at his side, angrily creasing it. "I dinnae cheat anymore aside from counting cards, which I can't help but do in my sleep. But I'm gifted at calculating odds, lass. I ken a sour bet when I see one."

Theo hesitated, recognizing the importance of Dash's admission even if he didn't. Brothel. Flash house. Hidden stairways and starvation. She wasn't going to ruin this by asking for more information when it was the first time he'd opened the door to his past. Or by being insulted that he considered her a sour bet. Her heart took a tumble imagining him in such circumstances, and nothing he said in begrudging wrath was going to change that.

"Save your charitable beliefs, lass." His voice was a harsh echo bouncing about the carriage, overriding the stormy gusts slapping the windowpanes. "I'm not waiting to be rescued. You're the lass struggling to hold herself above the waves." He tapped his knee, three hard pops. "Remember that."

When rescuing was exactly what Xander Macauley had done for Dash years ago, but it would only vex him to hear it. Provoked when she should have been repentant, Theo gave the seam on her gloves a yank and counted to five to calm her temper. "Thank you for so bluntly asserting my circumstances."

"You're welcome," Dash muttered and gestured inanely to the pup nestled against him.

She released a bland smile, knowing when it was best to hang up her bonnet.

With dice back in his hand, the notorious writer and gaming hell owner, who Theo suspected secretly wished to be known for more than his beauty, his escapades, and his book, turned to stare out the window, a shimmery twilight reflected in his eyes.

Chapter Three

If you suspect the wager is stacked, don't take it. Go with your
gut in these matters.

    Dashiell M. Campbell, *Proper Etiquette for Deception*

Naturally, there was only one room at the inn.

One room and one *bed*.

A wedding celebration in the Hare and Billet's public
house—Dash wouldn't have dared write such a ridiculous coincidence
—leaving sparse lodging to be had. Add to this the calamity of an
overly intrusive publican who'd studied Theo with a crooked grin,
forcing the fabrication to roll past Dash's lips like cheroot smoke.

"Newlyweds," he found himself saying, gesturing to his carriage,
which made a bold statement he now wished it didn't make. "My bride,
she's on the delicate side. Touch of asthma lingering from childhood.
The air was too damp for us to continue, and the roads are becoming

perilous." When Theo was the least fragile woman he knew. She was like that smelly little bulldog she'd rescued. Hanging on to his coattails by her teeth.

The publican gave the tin cup he was cleaning a vicious swipe with his rag. "Scottish, are ye?"

Dash exhaled softly, pride and remorse rushing through him. Mentions of Scotland tweaked his last emotion, every time. A festive roar from the pub echoed past the kitchen entranceway he stood in. He'd gone to the service entrance for discretion's sake, an effort blown to hell and back when Theo followed him, though he'd shooed her out but not in time. "I reckon my blunt spends as well as an Englishman's. You have a room, guv, and I'm willing to pay twice the normal rate to secure it. Three times plus expenses if you toss in a chit agreeable to escorting my wife to London on the morrow."

He gave the mug another violent buff, his face lighting at the prospect of negotiation. "It's a proper chamber, the right best in the establishment. Faces west with a tidy bathing nook. Ideal for fainting females. Too costly for local folk, you see. Alice would be willing to serve a proper maid for a time as long as she's seen back here safe and sound. My niece, she's a divine gel."

"Done. You don't have to sell me." Dash dug in his waistcoat pocket for the scuffed pouch he'd had since the hungry Glasgow days. Filched from one in a long line of loathsome bastards he'd encountered as a lad, he wasn't giving it up even if the cracked leather sack didn't represent his improved situation. "I didnae say fainting. I said delicate. A wee cough now and then, nothing more."

Being insulted over a ridiculous lie about a bogus wife only added to the depth of his insanity.

Without blinking, Dash paid an outrageous sum for the proper bedchamber, a scullery lass who'd likely never served as a maid in her life, and lodging for Meekins and his horses in the stables. Calculating figures in his head, money he'd earn with the sale of twenty books. Another musicale and one of his idiotic lectures—and that would be that.

When he headed back, his limp pronounced from the racing

debacle last week, Theo was standing outside the Wourch though he'd explicitly told her to stay *in*side, her slim shoulder angled against the doorjamb. Looking like she belonged with the splendid transport when he certainly didn't. The grungy hound she'd begun to call Wordsworth, after some dreary poet, was dancing about her skirts, yipping and making a general nuisance of himself.

With a weary sigh, Dash halted beneath the portico, in the shadows still, pinching a minute to collect himself without her clever eyes trained on him. Stealing his breath and half his mind.

His little secret? Theodosia Astley unnerved him. He could admit it in the dusky countryside miles from Town, just him and the bloody birds. He wouldn't go so far as to say *intimidated*, a word he'd discovered recently that he loved, but definitely unnerved.

The brilliant girl who wasn't allowed to be brilliant.

He recorded the stray golden whisper from the carriage sconce rippling over her skin, across her rounded cheek, and down her stubborn jaw, flowing into the rumpled neck of her cloak. He buried the flash of want telling him to follow the path with his fingers, with his *teeth*. If she liked when he ripped his gloves off with them, he'd noticed that piece, she'd explode when he used them on her.

A path of pleasure.

He'd gotten used to, or at the very least good at, hiding his desire for unattainable things. Like that silly mutt at her feet, getting kicked repeatedly brought quick learning.

But Theo wasn't an easy lass to overlook.

Generous, unguarded, torn hems, ink-stained fingers, ripped stockings. Sly looks and even a wink now and then when he wasn't expecting it. Book in her hand, witticisms on her tongue. Delectable, charming Theo. The most intelligent person he knew.

He laughed faintly into the night.

The woman the Duke of Leighton, his friend, believed was a sister to Dash's mind. A bloody *sister*. When he longed to toss her across the nearest bed and make her scream into the rafters. Tease every silken moan she owned from her throat. Make her thighs quiver while he settled quite happily between them. A fantasy, the lass. He'd only wanted her more after she'd played teacher to his student. A spill of books beneath her luscious body, shards of a shattered inkwell beneath his boot. Their bodies destroying that desk of Leighton's.

God, the fantasies he'd had about her in that dismal ducal chamber. Watching her chew on her lip, her ragged thumbnail, the tip of her braid. He was only a man, a weak one at that, and if he'd pictured her gnawing on him, it couldn't be helped. He'd hidden his response beneath any number of her tedious texts, his rigid shaft threatening to punch a hole through paper.

A gust snatched at her cloak, tossed her hood back to reveal hair the color of gold-leaf tumbling down her back. Another wretched coiffure that had lost the battle with its willful owner. She smiled at something Meekins said, and Dash shoved aside a nasty spark of what he prayed wasn't jealousy.

The dooming catch, a secret he'd carry to his grave, is that he'd thought about interrupting her wedding. A time or two. Like the dreams he'd had the one instance, *one*, he tried opium. Delusions all bleeding night in that den in Whitechapel. Until Xander Macauley dragged him home.

Never again, he'd promised.

Dash Campbell kept his promises, hence the quandary he found himself in.

Should he have chosen to storm the ceremony, what could he have said? Before all of society, his rough-though-he'd-tried-to-soften-it brogue echoing through the church.

I saw her first?

Across the inn's stable yard, Theo laughed as if she'd heard him, her cloak falling open to reveal a reed-slim figure, just enough of a view, bonnie actually, to force the remaining air from his lungs. Her gown was the loveliest he'd ever seen her wear. Ivory similar to the inside of seashell flowing over her body like rainwater. Shaking himself free of her, Dash swore and stomped through a puddle in his path, drenching his trouser legs.

Leighton's sister was a sweet he had no intention of sampling.

As he neared her, she glanced back with a devious tilt of her lips, exposing that crooked tooth he'd imagined grazing the head of his cock.

There it was. An image of Theo on her knees before him swimming down his spine to land in places it shouldn't. Spilling hidden cravings into the open, where everyone knew, if acknowledged, they grew in power.

His wrath, internally directed, was there—but more powerful was the longing.

Aye, he was a devil. A miscreant (another favored word new to his vocabulary) to picture such indecencies with an innocent, no matter the diabolical glimmer that often slipped into her eyes. Only three years older than the lass, true, but three hundred in *experience*.

During the months they'd worked together, a change had occurred. He'd found himself striving to be a better man. Had tried valiantly, for a bit. No carriage races. No brawls. Celibacy, simply to see if he could —and because his need for Theo was a sharper blade at his throat. Less carousing and the rest. He'd not filched a wallet or pocket watch for fun once. Point of fact, he'd told a lot of women *nae* that year. Although the gutter press hadn't let up for a second, making up exploits when he wasn't providing actual ones. Then Theo found Edward lounging about on some library pew in scholarly attire, his skin parched from lack of sunlight, but his accent pure Queen's English.

She'd gotten engaged weeks later.

Aye, the situation had presented too much of a fight when Dash had an easy life filled with easy women. None of them giving him that calculating stare, making him feel less because he didn't wish to conquer the world. When he didn't understand how unless it involved a transaction employing his face.

Beauty he employed to his benefit, brains, not so much.

Even if he did, in secret, want to conquer the world. The literary one. Filling folios every night until he had a chest of them. Enough for ten novels should he think to untangle the mess of his memories. Something a *real* writer might do. A writer as ugly as a goose, handsome visage not required.

Sadly, puzzling over this validated what Theo thought of him (gifted) but betrayed what he thought of himself (sneaky bastard lucky to have stumbled upon such good fortune).

Her high hopes made him edgy, anxious, and unfamiliarly needy.

Sidestepping a pile of horse droppings, Dash worked the signet ring from his pinkie, the single item he owned from his past. He closed his fingers around it as he approached his former teacher, the emerald cutting into his palm.

Meekins was shifting from foot to foot beside the carriage, snickering, his cheeks as rosy as his hair, the carriage ribbons dangling forgotten from his fingers. A youthful version of flirting. Wordsworth was dancing around them, seemingly thrilled to belong to someone. The horses were stamping and blowing fast breaths through their nostrils. The air was sodden from the lingering storm, heavy as Dash drew it into his lungs. The sky opening up, clouds lifting, moonlight muscling through to strike his boot.

"Ain't the first female stowaway in this conveyance and likely not the last," the lad was saying as he arrived.

Fookin' hell. Dash patted the dice in his pocket and imagined the tumbler of whisky in his near future. He was going to drown himself in drink once he got his "wife" settled in that proper chamber. "Take the horses to the stable, Meekins. The groom will help you rub them down. There's a spare room in back you can use, best I could secure with this *ceilidh* going on. It has a bed and a working hearth, or so I'm told. Dinner in the pub when you're ready. We'll head out in the morning for Bury St Edmunds as planned. Miss Astley and her companion, heading back to London through other arrangements."

Meekins swallowed, noting the exasperation in his employer's speech.

Dash tightened his grip on the ring, remembering being this young. With a past as black as coal staining everything, hopelessness a pit he was always trying to climb from. "You did a fine job, lad, with the driving. I appreciate you stepping in for Paulie during his malady. I'd appreciate it even more"—he glanced at Theo, daring her to challenge him—"if you didnae mention this incident. His Grace, the duke, Miss Astley's brother, he'd appreciate it as well. I know you've come to me by way of Leighton's other sister, Pippa. Consider discretion a favor, if you will."

"Don't forget about Wordsworth. He'll be traveling to London as well." Theo crouched down to give the stinky hound a scratch behind his ear, uncaring of the muck staining her hem. "I've decided to keep him."

Dash swallowed his curse but couldn't quiet the click of his jaw as he clenched his teeth together.

Meekins's eyes rounded as he realized Theo wasn't one of Dash's typical ladybirds but the sister of a duke who'd run off from the city. An *almost* lady he'd been flirting with. Nodding and bowing, he backed away, tipping his cap. He even did a twitchy salute before he turned to unhitch the team from their harnesses.

"You're a soft touch," Theo whispered, laughter threading her voice. "Although you scared the wits from the boy. Threatening him with a duke. When I was born not five streets from the workhouse myself and don't deserve such special treatment."

Dash grasped her elbow rather than reply, afraid of what might come out, guiding her toward the kitchen entrance. Even with their supposed "marriage," he needed to keep Theo under wraps until he escorted her from the inn at dawn. God knows what she might say if given too much freedom. When he reached the portico, he ducked under it, pulling her into the shadows. Her body, slender yet bountiful, bumping his. A snug fit, her head topping out at his shoulder. The riotous curls unleashed by the rain catching hints of starlight. "Hold up, lass."

She turned, lips parting, a whispery breath sliding free. Her teeth caught on the bottom and held, sending a shudder through his belly. A move he'd seen her make a hundred times, her indecision clear while his hunger plunged deep. He struggled there in the darkness, debating the choice to tell her more lies.

Or shove her against the rough-hewn wall and unleash the truth.

"I had to tell a wee fib, *leannan*."

A crease settled between her brows.

"One room, lass. I had no choice." He jerked a shoulder toward the inn and the merriment spilling out around them. Woodsmoke and the hazy mist a shroud. He pushed on, her composure making him wonder if she understood what he was saying. "There's a revel being held here, and most of the chambers are taken. I'll sleep in the public house when the goings-on calm down. Willna be the first. If not, then the carriage. Not a first that, either. I've arranged for the innkeeper's niece to accompany you to London tomorrow morning. I'll get a message to Leighton if I can without alerting the entire village to the news of a runaway bride. Channels of communication in the backwoods aren't always private."

Theo tipped her head, gazing at the sky, then into his eyes. Hers were bright. Clear. Accepting. The serenest gray-blue of the loveliest loch in Scotland. "What's the wee fib?"

With a fretful exhale, he uncurled his fingers. The signet ring's emerald glistened, shooting facets over the grooves chalked in his palm. "For this night, you're"—*mine*—"Mrs. Campbell. Although the innkeeper disna have any idea your actual name or connections, so keep that to yourself. There was no mention made of a duke."

She held out a hand that trembled too little for the jam they found themselves in. Wiggled her ring finger. "It goes on *this* one."

"I know which it goes on," he snapped and worked the lone treasure from the once grand Campbell dynasty into place.

Of course, it fit. Near perfect. Leaving his heart to drop somewhere to the vicinity of his knees. He stepped away so quickly he banged his head on the portico's roof. The sting at the back of his eyes was appalling, and it wasn't from the knock to his skull. Seeing his grandfather's signet ring on her hand... any hand but his...

He needed that whisky, and he needed it *now*.

Unknowing, she brought the ring close to try to read the insignia. "We can roll dice to see who gets the bed. I'll happily take a pallet on the floor if I lose. As long as you promise not to use one of the techniques from your book. Fair and square."

Dash was done with mollycoddling. Finished, over, with this insensible chit and her ridiculous belief that they could be *friends*. That he could sleep on the floor next to a bed she occupied and not be expiring from the desire to climb in there with her. "Theodosia bloody Astley, you don't ken the mire you've thrown yourself into. You and your slaphappy choices."

Temper flashed across her face, turning her smile to stone. Finally. Enchanting, compelling, wondrous *anger*. He hoped the emotion carried her away in a vicious tide. "You bet I *ken*, Dashiell bloody Campbell. Those rules have been beaten into my head for years. I'm simply not afraid of the consequence of breaking them."

"That makes one of us," he murmured and hustled her into the inn.

Scandal #2

One misdeed you can recover from but never two.
Lessons from London Society, *Volume II, May 1817*

Chapter Four

Don't let overconfidence spoil your approach before the game's
even begun.

Dashiell M. Campbell, *Proper Etiquette for Deception*

T heo knew she was trouble. An incorrigible mix of curiosity,
intellect, and what her sister, Helena, called careless
happiness.

Which meant you were delighted when you shouldn't be. Blasé
about the deadly societal consequences if you stepped outside the lines
the world had drawn, for example. Imagine trying to break free of
those tiny little boxes that women were forced into? Theo understood
the risks and knew all about those boxes.

She'd been trapped in one since the day she arrived on a Mayfair
doorstep seven years ago.

But she wasn't willing to be trapped anymore. Not when she'd given
it a go, thought to marry a suitable gentleman, followed the

predictable path, and the entire situation had turned out to be as rotten as a piece of cherry pie left baking in the sun.

She'd never expressed outright defiance with anyone but Pippa. Certainly not with the tolerant but hard-hitting ladies of the Duchess Society after they'd tried in earnest to reform her. Hildy Streeter and Georgiana, the Duchess of Markham, had taught her how to prepare tea for a chamber full of affluent nincompoops, stitch crooked patterns on handkerchiefs no one wanted, and play *one* jangling tune on the pianoforte in the event she was pressed into service. They'd ensured she understood the topics to avoid during parlor discussions—politics and women's rights—and those appropriate in any circumstance. (Weather.) They'd given up on watercolors when the majority of the paint ended up on the floor, not the canvas.

She'd put in the effort to change, she really had. There were four stages in the metamorphosis of a caterpillar to a butterfly.

Theo had gotten caught somewhere around stage three, transition.

Her family didn't appreciate how much of herself she'd suppressed to fit into the mold. For instance, at a musicale last week, she'd pretended not to know that Napoleon had been elected the First Consul of France in 1800, when the Marquess of Blandon said 1805. A typical male, the marquess thought he knew everything. Pippa had told her many times that men, even ones who loved you, didn't appreciate being corrected. And that she'd best get used to keeping mum about it.

Well, Theo Astley had news for the world. She was finished being the obedient, retiring miss. A wallflower because it was the only society label that fit. Letting men mispronounce words, toss out incorrect historical facts, and have her say nothing because it was presumed they were the superior sex. Being forced to talk about *weather* while the blokes discussed political affairs.

So here she was, causing more trouble because her room at the Hare and Billet had begun to feel like that tiny box.

Theo peeked through the slats of the railing from her perch on the top step. The bedchamber they'd been given was located in a late addition to the medieval dwelling. Jacobite, if she had to guess. The brick didn't match, the lines were oddly drawn. Tobias Streeter, who'd become something of a sensation as an architect after leaving his smuggling career behind, would have loathed it. She loathed it. She'd been deposited like a sack in a hallway, housing no other chambers, just two dusty storage rooms. She could sit here all night if she wanted to, watching Dash work his magic in the public house below, and no one would even see her.

With that gorgeous face, magic occurred without his lifting so much as a pinkie. The arrogant knave. Mix in spirits and the chances of mayhem tripled.

Pinkie. Theo flexed her fingers, staring at his signet ring. She'd about choked when he slipped it on, a sensation unlike any she recalled experiencing sweeping her. Like foreshadowing in a novel, a significant clue to the mystery. His mystery. And hers. A weighty moment that seemed innocuous from first glance.

She knew well not to trust simple manifestations.

Sure enough, the innkeeper had zeroed in on the ring like a hawk searching for food. Its appearance confirming Dash's fabricated story and giving it credence. *Newlyweds*. She shouldn't have been surprised.

After all, he was an expert at running a con.

Theo leaned her head against the banister and blew a whistling breath through her teeth. Now her phony husband was down there surrounded by women, drink, laughter, and music from a fiddler on a makeshift wooden stage in the corner. While she was sequestered on a deserted staircase, awaiting her return to a decorous life.

Theo had debated for a half hour and decided merely to observe. A wallflower with no wall. Her mind busy planning things she'd never have the nerve to actually do. Waiting for the next pregnant mistress to stumble in and ruin her day.

Until...

The woman was tall, dark, and dangerous. Everything Theo, in fact, was not. She had a swagger not unlike the scoundrel she approached. Voluptuous with a knowing smile. She grasped things Theo had only read about in books, scandalous writings she hid beneath her mattress.

However, Theo had an excellent imagination, one she'd yet to unleash.

Dash observed the vixen's approach without expression, a cheroot dangling from his lips, smoke trailing across his cheek and over a well-formed left ear revealed by a recent haircut. In shirtsleeves, his coat long gone, untied cravat dangling around his neck. He didn't even blink. Theo snorted. Not a flicker of surprise or anticipation, this happened so often. He rolled his dice across the table, picked them up, and did it again. He had a card shoved in his waistcoat pocket. To announce his profession, she supposed.

If the lethal chit was seeking encouragement, Dash Campbell wasn't going to give it.

Theo glanced at the ring. Wiggled her fingers. The emerald shimmered against her skin, a fierce glow. For one night, he'd said she was his. Or he hers.

This was all the encouragement she needed.

Conversely, at her approach, down the stairs and across the public house's main room, weaving through the raucous crowd, dodging spilled liquor and rubbish, sentiment flashed across Dash's face. Surprise, admiration, displeasure. Which was leagues better than indifference, she'd remind the bold tart if she had a chance.

When Theo was five feet away, a man stepped into her path, swaying from drink. His breath smelled of brandy and rot. He sought to touch, and Dash was there immediately, his chair skidding behind him in his haste to get to her. "Leave her, guv, or I'll dislocate your arm," he growled and stubbed his cheroot beneath his boot. "Dinnae test me on this."

The vixen who'd been on a quest to seduce him faded into the crowd, her opportunity evaporating like mist in the night.

The innkeeper rushed over, an excellent judge of a situation about to spin into a brawl. He grasped the boozy bloke's shoulder, preparing to lead him away. "Newlyweds, Arch, don't you know. Still bound up in each other. And the fella's a Scot. You know they're the most mulish heads in the kingdom. Thoughts of independence and such bunk filling their minds since Culloden. He won't allow for no funny business with the missus, not yet anyway."

"Not *ever*," Dash murmured in as vicious a tone as she'd ever heard from him.

The innkeeper grimaced, his smile dying. "Oh, so that's the way."

He dipped his head, a humble bow. "I feel for you, sir, I do. When the heart is involved, the path is littered with stones."

Dash opened his mouth to say something dreadful. He'd ruin their bogus love story in seconds if she didn't stop him. Theo recognized a man in high temper as she was surrounded by the moody beasts every day. Her brother by marriage, the Duke of Leighton, being the worst.

Theo stepped in, assuming the close confidence of a wife. Reaching to cradle Dash's jaw, she guided his gaze to hers. His eyes were dark with emotion, depth-of-the-sea dark. His breath shot from his lips in a gust. It was a mistake, of course, the touch. The closeness. The arm he'd braced on her hip tightened like the string of a bow before settling into a slight quiver.

Her heart kicked in response, and she was breathless when she spoke, "Darling, don't be vexed with me. I couldn't sleep."

"She missed you, mate," their foxed friend said, patting his chest with a sluggish burp. "Sweet, it is, young love. Abject devotion." Happily, he broke into a rambling tune unsuitable for any salon unless it was located in a bawdy house, though his voice was quite nice. Another drunken soul joined in until the room was swept up in a vulgar song about misplaced affection.

With this spectacle raging around them, Theo and Dash became the focus.

The crowd was at her back, at his, surrounding them. Laughter, nudges to the shoulder, winks, the scent of whisky and garlic fairly choking her. Behind her, a fiddle warbled into play, another sentimental song rippling through the air. It was like a carnival.

Heavens, what had she started?

"Kiss her, you randy Scot," someone shouted. "Unless you want to talk yer country's sovereignty instead!"

The mob roared in reply as glasses clanked in toasting cheers.

Theo sought Dash's attention as he glanced wildly about the room, his hand clenching on her hip, his jaw doing that thing it did—flex, shift, flex—when he was perturbed. Perturbed. He might enjoy that word. A new one would take his mind off the tangle she'd embroiled them in.

"It's not as if we haven't kissed before," she whispered instead, hushed, for his ears only. It was a solid rationalization featuring an experience that was never far from her mind.

His gaze shot to hers. "We have *not*."

Oh, oh, oh, she silently raged, *you vain peacock! You dirty cheat!* Her first kiss, the only decent one she'd received thus far as kissing hadn't been Edward's talent, and this oaf, London's answer to Casanova, didn't remember. Heat rose from Theo's toes to her brain, cooking her senses.

He only recalled that he'd begged her to help him write his bloody book!

The guidance she'd given Pippa when she was chasing Xander Macauley, Shakespeare's advice in summary, rippled through her mind.

The right kiss can tame the man.

Show him a kiss to end all kisses.

This, Dashiell Campbell will remember, Theo vowed before every soul in the Hare and Billet.

"What's one kiss," she shouted to the crowd, "between man and wife?" Plucking his card—queen of hearts—from his waistcoat pocket, she let it flutter to the floor.

"*Leannan,*" Dash whispered, a slice of panic entering his voice, "this will change things."

"Maybe I want change."

He shook his head, his fingers tensing at her hip. "You dinnae understand."

Decided, she lifted on her toes, the Duchess Society's dance lessons paying off, slipped her hand around the nape of his neck, and drew him to her. His gaze struck her before their mouths touched, his lids sliding low, his breath a vaporous mist across her jaw.

Then she closed her mind to everything.

Until there was only Dash.

Dense stubble abrading her cheek. The teasing caress of his unbelievably supple lips. Long fingers curling around her waist, drawing her close, pushing her away.

"Show me, Dash," she urged as she swallowed his taut breath. "Teach me this time."

"*Mo ghràdh,*" he murmured, lowering his head as he sank in.

49

The skilled gambler started with practiced control, playing to the crowd. Patient, while her blood thrummed in steady, impatient beats. His hand rose to cradle her jaw, tilting her face to his. His lips were anything but urgent, his touch impish. A show for the audience surrounding them.

Not a real kiss.

Frustrated, she knocked against him, and Dash had no choice but to claim a firmer hold to keep them standing, his arm coming around her waist to bring their bodies closer. Their heat mingled, their fast breaths, driving out everything standing between them. Her hand fisted in her skirt; the other Theo let have its way. Sliding her fingers up his chest, over his shoulder, and into the silken hair tickling the nape of his neck. Tangling in the strands, fingertips pressed to his scalp, guiding the kiss. Asking for more. Encouraging a man with unspent passion for the first time.

It was there she began to exert control.

Minute, feminine *control.*

Parting her lips, she tasted his with her tongue as his low groan washed over her. His bottom lip was plump and chapped at the edges. Extraordinary. The bow at the top, a philtrum, flawlessly formed. Like sculpted stone. Philtrum. She stored this word in the back of her mind to share with him.

It was a languid exploration that, as he'd predicted, changed everything.

He surrendered as her power grew, his mouth seizing hers, demonstrating how he'd only been playing before. Accepting her invitation, the ragged moan he uttered nearly took her down with it. His tongue stroked, circled, luring hers into battle. Challenging, daring.

Teaching.

Drawing her into a caress she'd never dreamed could be this remarkable. Shift the earth beneath her feet, stop the clocks on the wall, trap the air in her lungs.

Two wicked souls meeting on equal ground, not as far apart as they'd imagined.

To anyone situated outside her heart, it was a gorgeous catastrophe. An infamous gambler's ring on a near-lady's finger, his form molding quite superbly to hers in the middle of a public house den. An unplanned kiss gone too far, too far, spinning out on a life of its own. Everything inside her flourished in that moment, brilliant bursts of sunlight against her eyelids. Her breasts heavy, her nipples peaked, the space between her legs awakening with desire. They reached for each other in grasping, scandalous pursuit.

This instant, if nothing else, proved the path she'd thought to take with Edward hadn't been the correct path after all. No man except the one she was meant for should make her feel this way.

The air smelled of Dash—rain, leather, and brandy—and she drank freely. The exchange fierce and lusty. Hips bumping, hands seeking, mouths imposing. A dip and sway, their bodies colliding as they nearly danced in place. Animalistic and ribald, the erotic conversation fit the crude space they occupied. The swelling cries from the crowd disappeared like vapor on the senses. Tension from avoiding him the past year and suppressing her attraction incinerated beneath the desire rushing through her. *Finally*, she thought. She fisted her hand in his hair and gave it a yank, having no idea where she was going, only knowing she had to get there.

Get closer, dive deeper. Take all of him, give all of herself. *More.*

Somehow, the world eventually broke through her bewilderment. Clapping, whistling, crude directives, and shouts abounded about the space. Stinging pricks of awareness, recognition of the fact that they weren't alone an icy flush through her. *A thousand kisses buy my heart*, floated through her mind. Shakespeare, who knew passion far too well.

Bewildered, Dash lifted his head, breaths firing from his mouth. He gazed at her through indigo eyes gone misty, his pupils spilling into blue. His fingers dug painfully into her hip as if she were his only solid connection. He opened his mouth to speak, shook his head, perplexed. He had a thin line of freckles marching across his cheek. How many women had been allowed to see them? How many had taken the time to notice?

Theo strategized while he continued to simmer like a kettle on high heat, his hands on her but his body sliding away. His mind caught somewhere in between. She wanted more of him than anyone else had received, and she meant to have more. She was, if nothing else, an opportunist. "What does the M stand for?"

Dashiell *M.* Campbell. She'd always wondered as had the rest of England.

He blinked, his throat pulling in a taut swallow. Confusion, then clarity, lighting his features. "Malcom," he whispered before he regained his wits, though it wasn't long before he did. Cheeks flushing, he shoved her back a step. "Sneaky tosser, you did that on purpose. When a lad's at his weakest."

She laughed and dusted the back of her wrist across her lips. They'd never felt this abused. Titillatingly exploited. "Maybe."

"Talk about dishonest," he snapped, the softening elements of the kiss bleeding away.

"Perhaps my skill in that arena helped me help *you* write a world-famous book about it."

With an oath, he glanced around the room, dropping his hands as if her skin scalded. Chaos surrounded them. The throng was cheering, chanting, singing. Tossing glasses to the floor. She noted two other couples engaged in kisses not nearly as fierce as theirs.

When Dash's gaze returned to her, it glowed with banked anger and—she was sorry to silently point out—*hunger*. "Now you've gone and done it."

Before she could ask what he meant, her brother, the Duke of Leighton, plowed through the crowd, fury on his face and murder in his eyes.

Chapter Five

You win some, you lose some.

Dashiell M. Campbell, *Proper Etiquette for Deception*

Everyone was talking at once.

The men shouting, the women consoling. Someone was weeping, and Dash only kent with absolute certainty that it was not Theodosia Astley, troublemaker extraordinaire. Perhaps it was Leighton. Dash could sympathize as he nearly wanted to cry himself. There were tots of various ages underfoot. Jam-stained hands and gap-toothed grins. Napping on the settee, playing with dolls, snacking on biscuits. He wasn't yet able to connect every child to every parent. It was simply impossible with so many. The stray pup, Wordsworth, was tangled in a young girl's arms. A talkative chit of about eight or so he thought belonged to a duke.

A man without siblings, children warmed his heart but also scared the breath from him.

Mind still whirling like a top from that astounding kiss, he gazed at the people who'd come to be his family these past four years, pondering if this was a nightmare or a dream.

Why had they *all* come to Theo's rescue?

The dukes Leighton and Markham and their duchesses, Helena and Georgie. Tobias Streeter and his wife, Hildy. Xander Macauley and his wife, Pippa. Chance Allerton, who was a viscount or marquess or something, and his American torment, Franny. Jasper Noble, a competitor of Macauley and Streeter's shipping venture and a new member of the group for no reason Dash could identify. Only missing was the latest to walk the marriage plank, Ollie, the Earl of Stanford, half-brother to Xander Macauley. His wife, Necessity, was expecting, and they'd apparently chosen not to travel. Ollie was taking the news with the fragility of a first-time father—with unlimited amounts of joy and terror.

Ninety-five percent of the Leighton Cluster jammed in the dining parlor of the Hare and Billet was a sight to behold. The innkeeper had instantly recognized he needed to secure private space when a duke—not one but *two*—deigned to show up at his establishment. They'd broken down the door to get inside the public house, actually, but certainly in elegant ducal form.

They traveled, society said, in a pack. Like dogs. Dash grunted beneath his breath, dice clicking in his hand. He agreed with the *ton's* assessment for once.

"Speak up, boy-o." This from His Grace, the Duke of Leighton, who arguably had the most to be enraged about. Although, there was more than one glare being directed his way. Dash *had* sought to dally with the youngest member of their group aside from the actual children. Theo was a decided favorite. Leighton had thus far kept from throwing a punch, which considering his legendary temper, was surprising. Helena's hand had been on her husband's arm the entire time, holding him in place across the room. "If you have an explanation, I'm ready to hear it."

The parlor quieted, all eyes turning to him.

Georgie, the Duchess of Markham, thankfully interrupted the tribunal by gently coughing and holding up her hand. Always calm in a crisis, Her Grace. "Let me take the children for milk and biscuits. The kitchen staff has prepared snacks and pallets in a parlor down the hallway. This seems a conversation for the adults in the room."

Excited to be up past their bedtimes, the tots trooped out with waves and giggles, Wordsworth racing along behind them. Georgie directed a forgiving smile his way before she closed the door behind her.

Thinking fast, Dash took a breath, but before he could fashion an explanation that didn't get him killed, Theo chimed in. "It's my fault."

Dash cracked his dice together, shoulders slumping. Theo's stance on the settee was unperturbed, legs swinging, a volume of poetry she'd somehow managed to obtain in this literary wasteland clutched in her fist. Rosy-cheeked and swollen-lipped, she looked well-kissed. "I stole his fancy German carriage. Sprinted from the ball and hopped into the first available without any idea whose conveyance it was until I saw *Proper Etiquette for Deception* on the floorboard. I tried to locate Vivette—"

Leighton snorted at this and tossed back the contents of his tumbler. Everyone knew what a wretched maid Vivette was, though no one had the good sense—or nerve—to sack her.

"I tried to locate a companion on the way out, but instead, I ended up with a stray hound and the most infamous rascal in the East End." She shrugged, glanced down, paging through the volume of poetry as if her future *wasn't* on the hook. "In the end, I think the Gambling God kissed me to shut me up."

Shite, Dash thought and dropped his head to his hands.

Jasper Noble, the scoundrel, his reputation even worse than Dash's, sputtered a laugh. "This weekend is turning out to be the most fun I've had in years, when I honestly wasn't looking forward to another mind-numbing wedding."

"Shut it, Noble, or I'll shut it for ye." Dash jammed his dice in his pocket and rose to his feet. A brawl might be just what he needed to clear his head of that damned kiss. The heavy weight of his brogue showed the room where his temper was heading.

Helena, the Duchess of Leighton, the only female shipping magnate the city had ever known, left her husband's side to step into the middle of the parlor. "We're not solving this problem by bruising fists and faces. Gentlemen, in this family, you'll have to work out your aggression at Gentleman Jackson's. This issue will be handled with minds, not muscle."

"I don't believe it. The Cluster leaves a discussion without blood on their clothing," Pippa piped in from her spot against the hearth, her husband, Xander Macauley, as always, close by.

Leighton gestured with his glass. "Theo, what's that ring you're wearing? I begin to see why the intoxicated crowd was chanting 'newly-weds' when we stumbled in."

Dash's heart sank. Glancing up, he watched Theo trail her finger across the emerald's facets. For the first time since the kiss, she looked directly at him. It wasn't as powerful as the blind instant in the pub when the entire universe slid away, leaving only her scent and body and mouth beneath his. Her hair tangled in his fingers, her taste soaking his tongue. That crooked tooth wedged against his lip.

But it was something. There was *something* between them, no need to lie about what that was. A vexing needle beneath his skin, a silken-thread bond with someone he admired above all others.

A connection to an upper-crust lass he had no business being connected to.

Lust, he assured himself, *doesna have to make the decisions, lad.*

He could manage this.

Then Dash realized, with that insane itch you got when someone was staring at you, that his entire family had witnessed the sparks flying between him and Theo.

"The ring was my grandfather's, Your Grace," he found himself admitting to Leighton. "Not a high-stepper like some in this room but a Lord of Parliament, nonetheless. Ruthven of Paisley being the title. I dinnae ken the entire grim story, because the letters patent creating the peerage burnt with the House of Freeland in 1750, but in his time, Alexander Campbell made enemies, powerful ones. Trouble bleeding down to me once I came along. A distant cousin to the first King of Scots if the tale's faithful. Even that couldn't save him from the gallows, or those who wanted anyone in his line gone."

"Rex Scottorum," Theo murmured, her fingers curling tight to secure the ring. *King of Scots*. Of course, she knew Latin. Probably more than he did about Scottish history.

Xander Macauley, who'd adopted him as a near brother when Dash had been a lad of fifteen and was by then running a thriving business teaching aristocrats how to cheat at dice and cards, rose from his careless slump against the hearth. "Is this why you left Scotland? Is it still dangerous for you there?" Macauley's grimace split the hard lines of face. His eyes shone gunmetal gray, flashing furiously. "When we've been sending you back to Oban on the regular to manage the agreements with the distilleries? You could have told me, mate. I would never have sent you. Trust. A basic element of partnership, innit?"

Dash flicked away Macauley's babble. The man liked to keep his chicks close and Dash, whether he appreciated it or not, was one of the chicks. "There are heaps of Campbells running about, guv. Calm down. Everyone concerned is dead and buried." Rubbing his temple, he wished away the headache coming on strong. He wasn't up to discussing the story of his mother's heartbreaking choices or his bleak childhood.

Helena paced to the hearth and back, sweeping her hair, a startling mix of shades of auburn, from her face. She was fierce, a force to be reckoned with. She'd inherited her father's shipping company, run it better than any bloke could, then landed a duke. The *ton* gleefully called her Lady Hell behind her back but cowered when she walked into a room. Dash was actually a touch afraid of her himself. "I'm presuming this gallows business means we can't use the Lord of Parliament story to polish up your image? Ruthven of Paisley being a crook doesn't help you much."

Dash sank back to the armchair, his knees weak. He'd known what was coming since he'd told Meekins to continue on to the Hare and Billet with a bride on the run. Tangled himself up with Theo Astley for *life*, it appeared. "Best not. Me mum worked hard to snuff out that line of Campbells. Let it lie." He smoothed his hand down his chest, wishing he'd left his coat on. His impressive waistcoat. His cravat. He could tie the sharpest one in Town. If he'd known two dukes and the by-blow of an earl were in his near future, he would have. "You'll have to continue on with what we have. Author, con artist, gaming hell proprietor, entrepreneur."

"At least it's a captivating list," Theo added, her thumbnail jammed between her pert, pink lips. A mouth he could still taste if he tried hard enough.

Helena appeared less than certain. Twisting her silk skirt in her fist, she turned to Hildy Streeter, co-owner of the Duchess Society. "His file was clean?"

Hildy shrugged, the smile she directed his way tender. She adored Dash and had been incredibly caring when he'd decided to improve himself. "The standard debaucheries. Most of his escapades hit the scandal rags. Right there, under society's noses. No surprise to anyone. Nothing like this tangle with Edward. His paramour didn't show up on any of our inquiries. His excesses were well hidden."

Dash yanked his dice free, forcing himself to remain seated, and not sprint from the room. "Tell me you didnae research me." The Duchess Society investigated prospective grooms, usually finding things—hidden debt, wives, mistresses, children—that meant their marriage proposals were not going to be accepted. Their services were in-demand with so many men being swindlers. The fathers who hired the Duchess Society were often tricksters themselves. They understood the breed. "No more lessons if you canna be trusted. I'll take my half-polished accent and be on my merry way."

"I saw you staring at her one day when you were working on *Proper Etiquette for Deception*. The way she looked at you in return shot a little spark in the air. One that can't be contained. Or controlled. I should know." Hildy spread her hands, helpless. "So, yes, I did. In the event we encountered a situation like this, I wanted to be prepared."

Dash traced a crimson thread in the carpet with the toe of his boot, his stomach clenching. How had Theo looked at him? How had he looked at her?

"What's this about some hidden attraction after I let them spend a bloody year together in my study?" Leighton frowned, fingers clenching around his glass. "I thought Campbell considered her a sister!"

"*Sister*." Macauley hooted, earning a scorching glare from the duke.

"Better to be prepared, mate, your file at the ready. Saves time. You know these chits run a tight operation. They've a superior nose for matchmaking. It's in their blood."

"We're not matchmakers," Hildy and Georgie said at the same time.

Theo huffed in distress and came to her feet, her poetry hitting the carpet with a *thump*. "I'm not marrying him. Not unless I want to! And I don't want to. I've decided matrimony is not for me. I want an education. I want to *teach*. Mr. Darcy and I shall retire to Hertfordshire for the next, oh, ten years or so. I can do better with those blasted watercolors given the time. Won't my face never being seen in London again solve this problem?"

"Look where the single student you've been allowed to have has gotten us." Leighton paced across the room, his eyes turning the color of the emerald in Dash's ring, a warning sign. "After that kiss, blistering enough to scorch timber, by the by, I know because I unfortunately witnessed the tail end of it. You're marrying him, beloved sister. You can champion women's rights, open a school, teach a thousand lessons about maths or geography. It will be the young Scot's predicament, won't it?"

"But—"

Leighton cut her off with a slicing jab as practiced as if he held a saber. "The decision was made the moment you stepped into that absurd carriage of his, the most conspicuous vehicle in England for a couple on the run. You see, this fiasco is traveling faster than the post stage, from scullery maid to footman to groom to coachman until it lands like that putrid pup's shite on our Mayfair doorstep. One bedchamber, no chaperone. The innkeeper was only too happy to give me the details. Forget about a kiss hot enough to burn the hair off one's head." He groaned and pinched the bridge of his nose. "In a tavern, no less."

"I didn't even make it to the bedchamber," Dash murmured, not helping his case in the least.

Leighton stalked to the sideboard and poured himself a glass of liquid reinforcement, throwing it back with a curse. "The only consolation is arriving before you rolled your dice to see who got the bed.

Helena and I won't have you ruined, Theo." Dragging his hand through his hair, he aimed a flinty glance at Dash. "Or *him*. Since Macauley's adopted him, and he's apparently here to stay."

Dash wasn't going to argue this because he *was* here to stay.

Helena draped her arm around Theo's shoulders and pulled her close, their brows touching. They were devoted to each other, the fact that Helena hadn't known she had a sister until Theo was thirteen never making a difference to either of them. "Reforming a rake can be a fascinating project, darling. If the man's heart is within reach, which I think Dash's is underneath the Scots bluster. I will never again allow you to be attached to anyone whose heart is sealed. I almost made that mistake with Edward, and for that, I apologize." She lowered her voice, but not enough. "He is the most desirable man in the country. You'll be the envy of London, and your children will be gorgeous. Besides, he's already family."

Slightly gratified to hear a duchess found him attractive, Dash popped his knuckles, nerves racing through him at the mention of children. They talked about him like he wasn't sitting in the same parlor. However, the familial care and concern, things he'd never had, warmed him to his bones. "Hellie, luv, she prefers an *academic*."

"I took care of her anemic scholar. He won't be reading a straight line for weeks." Leighton flexed his injured fingers, wincing. "In any case, we're not going that route again. No more professors."

Theo reached to scoop her poetry volume from the floor. "Better a professor than a Lothario."

Dash glanced at her, his brow winging high.

"Rake," she explained. "Flirtatious cad."

"*Aye*, well..." Nothing to argue there, but at least, he had a new word to add to the pile.

The parlor was, sorry to tell the exasperated Miss Astley, full of former Lotharios. Why, Tobias Streeter he thought it was, had once leaped from a two-story window to get away from the clutches of a desperate countess. Nearly broken his neck. Macauley's antics had been a wash of ink across the scandal sheets. The dukes, Leighton and Markham, no better. Dash was merely the youngest and most appealing in a long line of Leighton Cluster ne'er-do-wells.

Honestly, he couldn't help it if his bonnie face caused such strife.

Leighton gestured to Dash with his empty tumbler. "You were wearing your finest rigging earlier. Get it back. Coat and cravat if you please. Theo is rumpled but suitable. I've never seen her have a hem that wasn't muddy, so why start now? The innkeeper is summoning the village vicar, five pounds in his pocket to secure his silence. We can hold the service here. Cut this scandal off at the pass. Hold a ball to commemorate the marriage once we have our stories straight and Town forgets about the disastrous celebration we just held."

Pippa, sensing her sister's distress, shouldered past Leighton, forcing herself into the conversation. Dash rolled his eyes and sank low in the armchair. *This should be good.*

Throwing a pleading, hidden-meaning-between-sisters glance at Theo, Pippa hopped from slipper to slipper, devising a plan. Heaven help them. "What about Bury St Edmunds?"

"*Nae,*" Dash said, but Pippa shushed away his objection.

"We'll have Ollie and Nessie meet us. Ollie must be close to grasping that his wife can travel while under confinement. Which will mean we're all in one place for the first time in ages! It will be delightful. Theo, I'll have them bring Mr. Darcy. Cats travel well, don't they?"

Dash clicked his dice together. *Fookin' felines.* "What if cats give me a case of the hives?"

Pippa flicked this nonsense away, too. "Nessie will be in charge of the flowers since she's famous for them. A week or two giving us time to plan a proper wedding, private, just family, while crafting a message for Dash's staff to pass *discreetly* to the vultures in London. Where the narrative we want delivered will ooze like a contagion through society. That the couple is in love, and Theo had been planning to call off her engagement, anyway. Before the expectant problem arrived at her ball." Pippa clapped her hands and began a mad search for quill and paper while everyone stood with stunned expressions, fearing the worst.

The worst being, following Pippa's advice.

Except for Macauley, Dash noted with a sneer. Mac was grinning, heart in his eyes. Lovesick dupe.

Pippa plopped into the chair behind the escritoire, licked the tip of her quill, and began scribbling notes. "We need to reveal part of the actual story, which a ballroom of people witnessed, to ensure Edward looks horrible and Dash the hero. Saving the damsel in distress. That's a popular theme. Love conquers all." She thrust her quill at him. "He can craft the narrative, he's the writer."

Closing his eyes, Dash dropped his head back. This was torture. Absolute torture.

"Wait, wait, Pippa! Hold up. Everyone, please."

Dash lifted his head, relieved. Theo was finally, *finally*, stepping into battle. She was, or could be, as formidable as Pippa. With the Leighton Cluster, anyway. She certainly was a termagant with him. She only acted the wallflower in society, self-preservation Dash couldn't blame her for.

But he didn't trust it, either.

Theo turned in a snug circle, touching everyone's gaze but his. He wished he didn't think she was a vision. Wished his body didn't react to the way silk clung to her hips, flowing over her slender body like cream. Her hair a glossy luster down her back, curling more than he'd ever seen it be allowed to do. Her scent—citrus and a hint of something floral he couldn't define—captivating above every aroma in the space. The memory of their kiss, the hottest of his lengthy history, raced through him like a runaway stallion. Her taste was there, close by if he wished to retrieve it. In his bed, his hand stroking his cock to completion.

Bloody hell, this wasn't good.

Sitting up, he crossed his legs to hide the evidence of his longing. This was madness. What were he and Theo, anyway? Friends? Enemies? He'd been running the odds, counting possibilities instead of cards since Leighton dragged him into the parlor.

He was losing this bet, sure as shite.

Beseeching, Theo spread her arms like she was preparing to make a speech in the House of Lords about women's equality or something similarly daft. "Let's take a breath, take a moment. We can return to London, and I'll hide out while the dust settles. Or perhaps Hertford-shire. Or Markham's estate in Ireland. We'll discuss this tomorrow morning when we've had a night's sleep. Dash can't accommodate this gathering. He has a cottage certainly in need of repair. A tiny dwelling without staff. Dusty and damp. A bachelor's residence."

She turned to him, looped her hand in a tight circle. *Come on, tell them. Stop this train, will you!*

He scratched his chin with the beveled corner of the die. "*Aye*, well, it might be a wee bit more than a cottage. Fully staffed, too."

Besides, he couldn't tell her, would *never* tell her, that he wasn't sure he wanted to stop the train.

"How many bedchambers?" she asked, getting right to the heart of it. He was impressed, always, every second he spent with her, by her intellect. Such a fierce mind the lass had. If she turned that cleverness on a man beneath the sheets, he'd go off like a pyrotechnic.

She stamped her foot, her wee slippered foot, against the flagstone. "How many, Campbell?"

Dash blew out a sluggish sigh, shifting his gaze away from that crooked tooth of hers. Hand cocked on her hip, frown twisting her lips. Her feistiness appealed to his base instincts and always had. "Twelve, at last count."

Grumbling, she slumped to the desk Pippa had by this time covered with notes. "*Twelve*. And how could there possibly be more than one count, you Scottish fiend?"

"It's Queen Anne period construction, but the timberwork is definitely Tudor. The cellars are medieval. Georgian door casings and architraves. It's charming and well-built, not a pit to toss money into. Or not more blunt than it's worth." This spot of architectural information rolled out from Tobias Streeter, who observed the proceedings from a shadowed corner, his preference, a toothpick twirling between his fingers. Remarkably, he was a renowned architect, self-trained, a rookery boy like Dash. Part-Romany and a viscount's unacknowledged by-blow, he was the least probable man of any to be a success. "Owning a spread such as this could be seen as fairly respectable, Dash, my boy. Here you are growing up right before our eyes, like the rest of the children."

Dexter Munro, the Duke of Markham, finally found a reason to enter the conversation. He was the quiet one, the least temperamental of the pack. "I read they found Roman coins in the area. Leighton, you and I might have to poke around a bit." An amateur geologist, his duchess, Georgie, had once told anyone that would listen that Dex only cares for rocks. Leighton held similar interests, and they often traveled to ecological sites together.

Dash sought to catch Theo's gaze. Soothe her temper using one of his well-tested smiles. "It's merely an investment. Tee-tiny compared to Ollie's spread. Markham's castle. Half the size of Macauley's fortress." He'd only hired Streeter to assess the property before he settled with the baron. Dash understood nothing of estates, had never owned anything substantial in his life. His terrace on Bruton was a dump in comparison.

However, Southgate was admittedly more than a cottage. Once again, he'd stooped to trickery. Utterly discomfited, the only justification he came up with was, "I'm not respectable."

"Theodosia Astley is," Leighton said in a stark tone brooking no argument. "You've cut to the chase as she already has your bloody ring on her finger. Since I'm in a charitable mood, Campbell, we'll plan the rest at your *cottage* in Bury St Edmunds. My family and I will require three of the twelve rooms."

And that, Dash realized with a jarring kick to his chest, was that.

The knock on the carriage door was hard enough to rock the vehicle on its axle.

Dash lowered his legs to the floor and elbowed to a sit. He patted his hip, still aching from the curricle race through the streets last week. Reckless idiocy, when he was getting too old for such rubbish. Hours earlier, the Leighton Cluster had disbanded as swiftly as they'd come together. Theo, Pippa, and Helena taking his original chamber at the inn. Another two rooms having been obtained, members of the village's wedding celebration were booted at a duke's request. The children, Georgie, and Hildy were bunking there. He'd never seen such overjoyed tots, sleeping on floors and settees the most excitement to date in their young lives.

That left the men to find other quarters. Hence, Dash sleeping in his carriage. The dukes in the stable. He'd no idea where the rest had landed.

Because he had no choice, he opened the door, unsurprised when Xander Macauley climbed inside. Ripping off his beaver hat, his friend settled his long body on the opposite seat. Working inside his great-coat, he came out with a dented silver flask. Thumbing the cork off, he took a drink, then extended his arm. "I imagine you can use it. Take me up on it. Once Ollie shows, I try to go dry. No need to provide additional temptation."

Dash accepted the offer, the whisky burning a path to his gut. Everyone in society knew about the Earl of Stanford's battle with opium after the war. And his older brother's effort to save him.

When a man had to solve his problems on his own, Dash was coming to find.

It was excellent whisky, Macauley and Streeter's concoction. *His* concoction. *Campbell* going on the label next month. The prideful jolt was unexpected, the sting at the back of Dash's eyes unwelcome. He was growing up, damn Tobias and his mocking comment. About to make a bloody husband of himself, in fact.

"Guessing I ruined things, Mac. I dinnae ken how I got here exactly." His words were tripping with Scots, so he took a breath and slowed his pace. "I should have brought her back straightaway. Instead, I thought to save her. What a skiddle." He tapped the mouth of the flask against his teeth with a ragged exhalation. "Theo Astley has me doing the barmiest things. Out of me mind, spinning like dice across baize when I'm with her."

Macauley laughed and wedged a cheroot he had no intention of smoking between his lips. He'd given up the habit for good with the birth of his first child, Kit. A father on a mission. "I'm presuming a 'skiddle' is a disaster in your native tongue."

Dash shrugged, shifting the flask in the glimmer shooting from the carriage sconce.

"Your situation sounds like mine at the beginning, mate. I was dotty with love but fighting it with every breath. Pippa was so certain, staring me down, telling me we were meant for each other. Mad, innit, for a man with my grisly reputation to fear an eight-stone chit who's head barely topped out at my elbow? We waltzed once in the moonlight and..." He cleared his throat, gesturing with the smoke, his lips kicking in a crooked smile. "Pippa's a force, much like her sister. So alike, you'd think they shared blood instead of being joined by the whims of marriage and fate. Theo has more patience, clever about keeping her deviousness hidden. Which, frankly, is worse for you. At least my darling wife puts her wishes out there for everyone to see. No surprises."

Dash tipped his head, gazing at a scratch on the ceiling he'd never noticed before. He took another sip, the whisky soothing his mood a fraction. "Yours was love."

"Admitted, it is. A deeper connection than I'd imagine having in a thousand lifetimes, but it didn't start that way. It started as it does most often for men. Lust. Attraction. A mongrel trailing after a treat. Eyes crossed from need, want. You have that, don't you, for Theo? The scene I interrupted in the pub was hot enough to fry an egg, mate. I thought Leighton was going to detonate when he saw you."

Dash found Macauley's calculating gray gaze in the dimly lit space. He wasn't admitting anything that would make its way back to her brother. "This between us?"

Macauley nodded. "It is."

Dash swished whisky around his teeth, swallowed. "Theo Astley's a pot of gold, an unseen treasure. The wallflower routine throwing society off until they couldn't see the real woman. Like a wager you think is trifling until it turns big. I write about this type of ploy in chapter nine. The meek bet. That was Theo's suggested word, meek, during the editing, and it fits. Imagine what she could do if she set her mind to something... and what she set her mind to is *you*. It's terrifying."

And thrilling. There, he'd admitted it. Not so hard. *Thrilling*.

Macauley fought his amusement, but it took over, sweeping his face. Spilling out in laughter he bent into, curling his arm over his belly. "Ah, wee laddie, I fear you're done for."

Dash's temper sparked. He hated being told what he didn't want to hear even if he agreed with what he'd heard. "I didnae say I want to *marry* the pot of gold, guv. I simply like looking at it."

"It's never the one you think it'll be. Streeter shared that wisdom during a weak moment with Pippa's siege, and I've never forgotten. I tell every man caught in misery of his making the same. Ollie, the last poor soul to hear it, and look how nicely that turned out? Necessity Byrne, gardener extraordinaire and soon-to-be mother. Blimey, I played matchmaker better than the Duchess Society chits and *won*."

Dash grunted and drained the flask, unimpressed.

"My advice? Marry the girl and be done with it. Take her to bed every day, twice a day. That'll keep her quiet." Macauley slapped his hat against his thigh, sending dust motes swirling. "Leighton saved you from the agony of seeing her wed to that ashen milksop. Always looked like he was seconds from fainting or correcting your grammar. Did you really want to sit by and watch that happen? Theo and the limp professorial biscuit?"

Dash stilled his mind, a trick he used when he was fixing to cheat and cheat big. A spark of sentiment was there, buried deep where he'd shoved it. He hadn't wanted Theo to marry Edward Biggerstaff and have a family of little Biggerstaffs. Help the elitist nob climb society's ladder on the back of a duke.

Kiss him like she'd kissed Dash, with everything in her.

The most exhilarating five minutes of his life, hands down. Not knowing what planet he'd been standing on when he came up for air.

He'd told her his middle name, for God's sake.

"Another benefit of marriage is having someone to help you manage your enchanting, twelve-bed cottage," Macauley added, seeing he was making progress. He wasn't known as the canniest negotiator in Limehouse for nothing. "You're set to spend a lot of time there, so why spend it alone? I wager Theo will be a crack hand at organizing. I see her managing a staff and tenants like a general. Leaving you time to work on your writing."

Dash patted his pocket, checking that his dice were there, getting cagey with this conversation. He wasn't talking about the books. "I wouldn't be alone. Not if I didnae want to be. Not with this face."

Cursing, Macauley yanked the flask from his protégé's hand. "Leighton would never give her to you if he didn't respect you, figure you were up to the job. Which is making his sister happy, not being the cutest crook in the room. Clear your head, boy-o. If he didn't, she'd be in Hertfordshire, and you'd be nursing broken bones right now. I'd like, seeing as I've invested years in you, to see you happy as well. If I didn't think Theo was up to the job, I'd step in. Not too much to ask for my loyal service."

Dash's throat closed, another salty sting hitting the back of his eyes. He dragged his fist across them to stop it. What in the bleeding hell was *wrong* with him? "London's calling, isn't that a famous saying, guv? I have tariffs to review, croupiers to train, swindlers to corral. The gaming hell isn't gonna run itself. Into the ground without me."

Macauley exhaled in relief, damn him, sensing capitulation. "I have the Devil's Lair in hand. The Macauleys will return to Limehouse the minute after I serve as best man. Scottish tradition, innit? Figured you'd want to follow."

Dash coughed, sitting up straight, his boots hitting the floor with a thump. "You'll stand up with me during this charade?"

Macauley pocketed the flask and the cheroot. "Not a charade if you want it, even with so much as your little toe. Want *her*, that is. But I'd wait on the bed sport, mate. Until you marry so Leighton doesn't come after you."

"She has a wretched temper," Dash felt he should add. A man trying to keep his head above water, gasping and flailing. "She's dogged, more than Pippa even. You've probably never seen it because she smiles so much, but her stubbornness is there. Arguments locked in a steel-trap mind, like this magistrate I was unfortunately associated with in Glasgow. I scrapped with her for a year, losing every argument. She has grand dreams, outsized, this lass, meaning she'll be impossible to please. She wants chits to have the vote. *Voting*, Mac. She longs for things no woman can have. She's going to spend me out of house and home, too. Reads three books a *week*. I'll have to sell more of me own, attend more of those eye-bleeding musicales to keep up." He slumped back, spent.

Also, wonderfully, disturbingly, she kissed like a goddess. This striking fact he left out of the list. "How does *that* sound, best man?"

Macauley grinned. "What it sounds like, lad, is you've found a keeper."

Chapter Six

Beware the meek bet. Those are the wagers that leave a sting that lasts.

      Dashiell M. Campbell, *Proper Etiquette for Deception*

I n the end, because her brother was an early riser, she and Dash weren't given a two-week reprieve after all. Roan bumped into a laundry maid in the courtyard who gave him a meticulous accounting of her kiss in the pub the evening prior. Hours before her fake husband bribed the staff for their silence as he was still slumbering in his carriage.

The scene was infamous, now the stuff of village legend, according to Roan. The romance of it encouraging two men on the brink of committing to propose. The laundry maid, Janie, described in syrupy detail how achingly long the kiss had lasted. The way Theo and Dash had looked at each when they broke apart. Her dreamy smile. His greedy fingers clenching her hip. The magic. The *heat*.

Wagers were being placed on when the newlywed's first babe would arrive.

This last bit sealed the deal for the Duke of Leighton.

Damning proof of the need for swift action.

An acquaintance of Jasper Noble's had an estate—and a private chapel with an accompanying vicar—in the area. An uncommon coincidence, though the scoundrel gave absolutely no explanation beyond providing a venue and a contact who could secure the legal paperwork faster than a duke could. Theo bet her brother hated to take Noble up on his offer, but due to Xander Macauley and his charitable heart, the poor soul was now part of the group.

Consequently, the Leighton Cluster left the Hare and Billet for middle Suffolk immediately after breakfast. Dash and Theo in separate carriages to preserve the mystique, she supposed.

Or to keep them from fighting.

Two hours later and here she was. Stuck.

Theo frowned and trailed her thumb along a crack in the chapel's stone she could have shoved her pinkie in. They'd stowed her in a medieval chamber redolent of incense and dust, books she normally would have investigated stacked in every corner. Actually, she'd located a volume on Suffolk's history with an interesting description of Bury St Edmunds, the town that would be her new home. Her hand was currently clenched around the book's spine like the cracked leather was going to save her.

The only fortunate news this day was the chapel was twenty odd miles from Dash's twelve-chamber jewel of a cottage. Meaning they could continue there after the ceremony.

The unfortunate news? She was marrying a man who'd touched her with a depth of passion she'd never envisioned yet... she didn't know if he wanted to marry her. While she'd stated to anyone who would listen the day before that she didn't want to marry *him*. Which, come to think of it, might have been the reason they'd been kept apart all day. Two crafty minds better than one when figuring a way out.

Except the Duke of Leighton, with protective love for her, wasn't affording a way out.

Ollie and his new wife, Necessity Byrne, had arrived at the chapel in a slightly flustered state. Or perhaps it was merely Ollie who seemed unnerved now that he was preparing to be a papa. The most famous landscape architect in England, Necessity brought flowers and garland and trimmings and such, some of which Pippa had entwined in Theo's hair. They'd also fetched Mr. Darcy who, unperturbed by the chaos, was sleeping on a blanket by her feet and purring madly.

What are you doing, Theodosia Astley?

Theo dropped her chin to her fist and blew a neglected lock of hair from her eyes. Gave the signet ring on her finger a twist. She was marrying the Gambling God, that's what. She the brains, he the beauty. She the academic, he the creative.

Theo would be the envy of every woman in society if she and Dash didn't kill each other.

Though it felt good—or right—to have a scandal of her own to claim. Amused, Theo realized she was finally a woman with a past. Honestly, it was easier to fit into this family if one had a streak of grime on their reputation.

Theo turned at a scraping sound, gasping in shock to see her intended climbing through the room's ground-floor casement. Leaping down in an athletic move that made her heart seize, Dash brushed debris from his sleeves and yanked his plaid waistcoat into place before advancing upon her, a thief in the night. Or day, rather. *My,* she thought for the thousandth time, he was a dreamy beast no matter how little he tried to be.

"Isn't it bad luck to see the bride before the ceremony?" she whispered, throwing a swift glance at the door. Pippa and Helena were outside, going on about some disappointing aspect of the chapel. When Theo found it enchanting. Graying stone and grizzled ironwork. Ancient grooves chalked in the cobbles. Stained-glass tossing multicolored prisms about the space. Necessity's florals adding a delicate sweetness to the air.

What better place to wreck your life than this?

Dash halted before her, an expression she couldn't place marking his features. Studied indifference with an edge. Then he was down on one knee, reaching to bring her off the chair and into his lap, her Suffolk history text spilling to the floor. His mouth capturing hers, he curled his arm around her waist, fit his wide palm to her lower back, and guided her into bliss.

The kiss was deadly. Decisive.

Telling her, showing her, proving... *something*.

Her lips parted without hesitation, allowing him to stake his claim. She would gladly battle with him, but not about this. This she *wanted*. His tongue swept in to dance with hers, every additional moment spent showing her what he liked, what she liked.

She was going to be as good at kissing as he was if he gave her enough opportunities to practice.

As it was in the public house, she lost time, reason, breath, caught in the wonder of him. How unexpectedly delightful to stumble upon passion that had been missing before. Sensing her escalation, Dash gentled his pace, putting care in the handling. But his hunger ran rampant in the trembling in his arms, his fingers hard upon her skin, unveiling eagerness she guessed he rarely revealed.

A tell, a con's worst enemy.

"You want me," she whispered against his lips, a question as much as a statement.

Agreeing without words, he took her bottom lip between his teeth and nipped until she saw stars. Gasping, she clutched his shoulders to keep from tumbling to the floor. His body was hardening beneath her bottom, there was no way to hide it. As a test, she wiggled her bottom, and pleasure flooded her as he groaned deep in his throat. *Ah-ha.*

"I want you, lass. I couldn't allow you to walk down that aisle thinking I dinnae. That I'm forced into this, when no one's forcing. The Duchess ladies not letting me see you. I'll do what they ask, a family I want a part of, but you're *mine* now. This gamble comes down to you and me. Right here, right now."

Theo drew a breath, meaning to tell him she wanted him, too.

But his hand was trailing along her spine, leaving a path of sensation behind it. His fingertips burning through layers of satin, silk, and cotton. His lips gliding along her jaw and settling at a sensitive spot beneath her ear. His whisper swirled inside as he bit her earlobe, turning her legs to butter. "The wicked things I've dreamed of doing to you, *leannan*. Going back to our time battling my book across that desk. I'm starting to think, from the way we spark off each other, starting wee fires, you've thought them, too."

She had. But this...

Shoving off his lap, she stumbled to her feet. A length of ivy dangled before her eyes, and she yanked it free. Necessity's bridal crown was being destroyed by their enthusiasm. "Leighton will never believe we've not touched each other before last night if I stagger out of this room looking ravished. He searches for an excuse to start a brawl on any given day as it is, you know this. I'm amazed we've not had one so far."

Although, she wanted to be ravished.

When she'd never cared if Edward ravished her.

Dash glanced at her from his spot squatting on ancient flagstone, a stray beam of sunlight catching him across the brow. He appeared angelic, but she knew better. "We haven't. We *didn't*. I got the hell away from you anytime the stirrings started. Why do you suppose I bolted from our tutoring sessions an hour early on the regular?"

Theo snatched the history text from the floor and jammed it beneath her arm, filled with imaginings of where he'd gone after leaving her. To his countesses and actresses, widows and opera singers. The string of women up for soothing him, stretching to Westminster and back.

And he *still* didn't remember their kiss in the moonlight in her brother's garden.

Dash muttered a curse and shoved to a stand. "There you go getting cross again, not allowing my pre-wedding gift to curl your toes a bit. *Leannan*, I remember, I do. The night you agreed to help me write my book I brushed my lips across yours. Signing a verbal contract, lass, nothing more. That was no *kiss*. I'd have done better if I'd kent you considered it one." In a move that made her want to laugh, he patted his pocket to check on his blasted dice. "You see now, I'm predicting, since we've done the deed but good."

"Edward—"

"I dinnae want to bloody talk about him touching you. Not today. Not *ever*." Furious, the oath tumbled out in hard Scots. *Bluidy.* Yanking his hand through his hair, Dash paced to the window, possibly considered climbing through it, and sprinting across the fields. He didn't like when his past slipped into his speech, this she knew.

He was jealous. Dash Campbell, *jealous*.

Theo beamed, enjoying her first encounter with a man's possessiveness. She quite liked the sensation. "This is remarkable. Shakespeare called jealousy a green-eyed monster, yet your eyes are sapphire blue. When, if I stop to consider *your* peccadillos, I shall feel the need to finally become Leighton's sister in every sense and sock you in the nose."

He glanced back, dipped his chin to scratch it with a broad shoulder. His smile was sublime. Innocent *and* erotic, toe-curling he'd be happy to know. One he'd used a thousand times to get himself out of trouble. "I can't contend with you, *leannan*. My antics dinnae represent well, as the Duchess chits keep reminding me. Sounds like rubbish, a bloke's sad excuse, but those women dinnae mean anything. Not like you do. I can only promise that piece of my life is done. Over. I mean to be a proper husband. I swear it on the Scottish oath. I wouldn't think to swindle. You're the cleverest person in London. In England, perchance. Your mind makes me *vauntie*. Proud. I'm honored that such a canny lass will be my wife."

She laughed gently, undone by his sincerity. Warmed by it, honored herself. Understanding, nevertheless, that like a reformed cardsharp, he used what he had at his disposal to sway her.

He crossed the room until he stood before her, not touching, letting her decide, control she'd seldom been given. The line of freckles marching across his nose had deepened to the color of mahogany with his morning ride. His eyes were a bold indigo this day, making her wonder at the tie between shade and emotion. He was a conundrum. More than handsome, secrets and challenges, elements that tempted the curious soul swirling about him. Armed with gifts key to *her* attraction, his talent with prose one she desperately wished to help him unleash.

Methodically, during a night of contemplation, she'd decided she didn't want Dashiell Campbell to mean everything. It was too great a risk with a man with his looks and his past. No one should have the power to break her. Destroy her like Macauley could destroy Pippa.

She wanted sensualism. She wanted friendship. She wanted, with someone she could admit this to, *freedom*. She'd been set to enter into a marriage without either of those things when the man standing before her had rescued her.

Theo didn't require love. She'd enough cushion from her family to live on. Before Helena adopted her, she'd not expected to be offered another slice of affection again. She was grateful and satisfied. Asking for too much, scholars understood, angered the gods.

Friends who played at being lovers? This she would accept.

She stuck out her hand, a common gesture Viscount Allerton's American wife, Franny, employed much to society's dismay. Theo loved it. "Friends."

Dash rocked back on his heels, eyeing her in amusement. Running the odds. "I'll go with what you taught me. Define the meaning, lass. *Your* meaning."

She nodded to the main chamber of the chapel, where the din was rising. The vicar had arrived. She could hear Leighton's echoed instructions sliding beneath the door. Pippa and Helena laughing. The children shouting. "We don't need that."

He tilted his head, confused. She couldn't wait until it was her right to smooth away the pleat between his brows with her lips. "Dinnae need what?"

Theo searched for a word to describe her sister's connections to their husbands. Every marriage surrounding her, in fact. "Obsession," she returned without thinking. "Fascination. Absorption above all. Adoration. I want a steady relationship. Companionship. I want to read. I want to teach. I want to *learn*." She swallowed, her cheeks firing, but this last piece had to be spoken. "Have children. A family. But I don't want to lose control."

Left unspoken: I don't wish to fall in love with a man I cannot *trust*.

"Absorption," Dash murmured, rolling the word over his tongue in a way that made her thighs quiver. He loved language more than anyone she knew. "It sounds dicey, this obsession business. Not for our kind. We're far too shrewd to fall into that trap." Clicking his tongue against his teeth, he reached for her hand, turned it over to draw teasing circles on her palm while her heart banged out a song in her chest. "Children." His gaze touched hers, then returned to his task, the circles getting wider, creeping beneath the lace-edged sleeve of her gown. "Since we're bargaining, what if I propose the obsession bit stays in the bedchamber? The steady head, hard heart bit, ruling everywhere else."

"Of course, but... well, that is..."

He lifted her hand to his lips, and she watched like it was another's, certainly not hers. The Gambling God making love to a bookish wishful-scholar in painfully measured increments in the medieval chamber of a Suffolk chapel couldn't be real. Could not be where her story was going.

But it was.

When Dash sank his teeth into a distinctly vulnerable spot beneath her wrist like he would bite into a peach, her lids fluttered, a gasp of arousal she couldn't contain shooting free.

"We can agree, *leannan*, on living our own lives, in part. That independence you've been yammering about for years. Take it. Hold your wee life party and invite who you'd like. I'll be busy with my gaming hell and the distilleries, you with your lessons and your learnings. Use marriage like men do, claim every advantage. Go about without a chaperone if you have a wish to, attend lectures, visit bookstores. Wring the prospect of freedom dry. That daft situation Macauley and Pippa have, we won't go there. I dinnae want to go there, same as you. Do you see that poor sod most days, bewildered by feeling? You and I are *friends*."

Teasing, he blew a warm breath over the skin he'd moistened with his tongue, nipping the rounded edge of her thumb and sucking on the tip. "But I won't agree to holding back when it's the two of us. I mean to have you in each and every one of those twelve chambers. On the staircase of my Bruton terrace. In that bonnie carriage the Germans designed for just such an occurrence. Every way I can find and you beg for until you're right and fully sick of me, and I can't walk another step."

"*Oh*," she whispered, images from that naughty French manuscript sneaking into her mind.

He glanced at her from beneath lush, lowered lashes, his smile five shades of devious. The intriguing tickle between her legs was adding a rhythm to her pulse she felt sure he could hear. "That crafty brain of yours, I want that in my bed. In my life. I've dreamed of the things you'd ask me to do, curious, imaginative, bold Theo Astley. Study every filthy book you can get your hands on, lass, walk right into the shop as Mrs. Campbell and buy it, then come to me. I'll answer your questions until you can't remember what *day* it is. Scottish men take their time."

Her hand trembled in his, her body aflame from his suggestions, his words sufficient to provoke. She reviewed the benefits in her mind, to be certain. He wanted her. They'd agreed to avoid the love trap. He'd not argued about having children. She *liked* him. Respected him. Her family was over the moon with him already. Macauley his champion until the end of time.

Heaven knows, he was magnificent to look upon.

One element above any other was the deciding factor.

Freedom. No chaperones. No musicales. No balls. No Marriage Mart. No Vauxhall. She'd not have to paint another landscape in her blasted life. Disregard some silly nob who told her George III died at Carlton House when he died at Windsor Castle. Utter bliss, she could read *Frankenstein* in a public tearoom without hiding the cover beneath her handkerchief.

Indeed, she'd be taking a step back as a gambler's wife. A place closer to Shoreditch than Mayfair, but her connection to the Duke of Leighton adding an edge of fearful respect. No one would think to cross her because they didn't want to cross him. Too, Dash's current popularity meant the *ton* sought to seek his favor.

She tapped her slippered toe against the flagstones.

This could be a delightfully perfect storm. A scandalous married miss society had to accept. A curious, imaginative, bold *wife*.

Dash tipped her chin high, his sigh amused and strained, his body drawn up tight as a bow. Thankfully, she wasn't the only one affected by his lewd talk. "Look at you, plotting away. It does my shifty heart good to see it. You'd have made a bonnie Scottish lass, but a rookery lass is close. The question though, between us, not out there before the eyes of God and family is, are you ready to turn society on its ear, *leannan*? Take the biggest wager of your life? Because hooking yourself to me and a reputation as tarnished as a long-forgotten teapot is what you'll be doing. You'll have that freedom warming you like a cloak, but you'll have the nasty whispers, too."

She paused, adding substance to the moment when she already knew the answer. "I am. I do, Dashiell Malcom Campbell."

Grinning, adorably relieved, he pressed a tender kiss to her brow. "I do, too, lass."

Vows informally accepted, he shot across the room, nudged the faded velvet curtain aside, and hopped out the window, exiting in the same daring way he'd arrived.

At the last, he leaned back in and winked, leaving a breathless bride to wonder how long it would be before the groom made her forget what day it was.

Chapter Seven

Bury St Edmunds, originally called Beodericsworth, was built in 1080. Known for brewing and malting and the production of—
Theo shifted her book until candlelight hit the page. *Production of sugar. The town is now most often referred to as Bury.* She smiled. Bury. How charming.

She'd gotten her first glance at the village from Dash's carriage window, Helena and Pippa assuring her it was the loveliest parish they'd ever seen. Rows of thicket-roofed cottages leading to a main thoroughfare lined with mercantile shops, Bury seemed a decidedly vibrant community. A cathedral was located on the western side of the village, always an important aspect of commerce and viability. Perhaps there was a school she could inquire about supporting.

Mercifully, she would not be lost in the wilds here.

Between the gorgeous countryside and watching her fetching

husband ride alongside the carriage, his powerful thighs gripping his bay's flank, she hadn't needed reassurance. Or a heated brick. She was toasty warm from *life*. A natural whip, Dash rode like he'd been born to the sport, another characteristic to admire about him.

Giggling, she held the history book she'd pilfered from the chapel to her chest and rubbed her toes together beneath the counterpane. Wedding chapel. Home. Husband. Hound. So many bits being added at dizzying speed, her mind was blurred with sensation.

A sweet scent from the thatch of hydrangea situated beneath her window crept into the delightful chamber overlooking the parklands. Truly, she'd been surprised by the home and Dash's reaction when they arrived. She'd never seen him display anything resembling trepidation. Yet as he'd held the carriage door, shuffling his feet and humming beneath his breath, she'd realized he was nervous. When Southgate was beautiful. Two stories of stately red brick surrounded by gardens and lawns, overflowing urns, gravel footpaths snaking between sculpted hedges.

She'd made plans to explore the estate with Necessity Byrne Aspin-wall, the Countess of Stanford, before they headed back to London next week. Nessie would be able to label every bloom and tree on the property if her husband, Ollie, let her out of his sight. His wife's preg-nancy was a new development, and the normally relaxed earl was a bundle of raw energy and nerves.

On the way to Theo's bedchamber this evening, Dash had given her a brief tour—entrance hall, breakfast room, parlor, study, music room, library—his staff of eight surrounding them. Then he'd escorted her to a door trimmed in a pale shade of green, dusted a kiss across her cheek, and vanished down the hallway.

Dash was with the men. A Scottish custom to rabble-rouse the night of the wedding that no one had considered breaking.

Theo didn't want to break it. She didn't want to break *him*. Control Dash or have him control her. Certainly she was curious about this marriage venture, and she wanted her husband to touch her again. Snake his fingers into her hair and tug loose the pins. Ignite a fire in the pit of her belly, between her thighs. Kiss her senseless. Make that magical sense of abandonment sweep her away again.

As he'd promised he would.

She wanted those things. Was going to *have* them. With careful study and practice.

Nevertheless, she could wait while he celebrated. Act the man. The silly fool, more like it. Lose the tension that had had him chewing on the inside of his cheek, flipping his dice, and avoiding her gaze upon their arrival at his manor.

Patience was a talent she held in spades. Life was a lengthy race, not a sprint. Southgate would be the first true home she'd had since her mother died. Sadly, Mayfair had never fit. Protecting her, Helena hadn't allowed her to spend time at the shipping warehouse, close to the neighborhood where she'd grown up, which may have eased some of her angst. Therefore, Theo would give Dash—and herself—time to figure out the journey they'd embarked upon. To build a life together without losing their hearts or their minds.

Dash had saved her, liberated her, and she wouldn't overlook his generosity. He hadn't had to marry her, truly, he hadn't. Yet he'd stood at the end of the aisle in a sun-splashed chapel, clear-eyed and steady, waiting for her. Her loyal heart would never forget this gift.

It was only when the time came to share parts of himself that he withdrew.

This, too, she would work on. She tapped her chin thoughtfully. Like a research project—when Theo loved nothing more.

She was debating her plan of attack when Dash staggered into the room, making an unsteady entrance through the door adjoining their bedchambers. Pressing her hand to her lips, she smothered a gust of laughter behind it. Her husband was foxed. Hair standing on end, shirttail untucked, trouser braces hanging from his waist. Crossing the chamber in a loose-hipped stride, he tossed a crooked grin over his shoulder and wrestled with his coat one sleeve at a time, finally dropping the garment to the floor. Toeing off his boots, he stumbled and, with an oath, righted himself.

Dear me, she thought in delighted alarm, *he's going to disrobe right here.*

"Should you not be in your own bedchamber?" Wearing a shirt she'd filched from his wardrobe, as the trunks containing her trousseau weren't arriving until tomorrow, she wasn't suitably dressed for entertaining and hadn't expected to have to, quite yet.

"Theodosia Astley Campbell, I dinnae wish to follow society's practice of separate bedchambers. It's not the Scot's way." His brogue was as dense as the mud she'd been forced to wade through to get to the carriage this morning.

Of course, she didn't normally see him whilst he was in his cups.

Halting by the marble-topped vanity, he unpacked his arsenal—dice, deck of cards, two knives, pocket watch, coin purse—placing them in remarkably precise alignment for a man rosy-cheeked and wobbly from drink. "You scurried away from the meek mouse who'd let you sleep without him."

Theo started to stop the unveiling, then realized watching her husband shed every last stitch of his clothing, obviously an easier thing for him to do than share his secrets, was her right.

His right, when she was asked to do the same before him.

She might as well enjoy the show. After all, he'd performed the act for half the women in London. So, she plumped her pillow and rested against the headboard, striving to ignore the heat shimmering beneath her skin.

This could be considered educational if she didn't let lust get in the way.

Legs spread, Dash reached over his shoulder and grasped the back of his shirt, tugging it over his head until he stood stripped to the waist. The air in her lungs rushed out in a burst. *Oh. My.* Her book tumbled from her hand, landing on the floor with a *thump*. Theo's gaze roamed from his stockinged feet to somewhere in the vicinity of his mouth, a shuddering thrill racing through her. He was classically built, like the sculptures she'd seen in the British Museum. Not too broad, not too skinny. Perfection in form, his shoulders and arms leanly muscled with a faint shadow of dusky hair trailing from chest to belly to add balance to the portrait.

While he fiddled clumsily with the buttons on his trouser placket, she ravished him with her eyes, her appreciation not *entirely* of the physical nature. She respected his ready wit, his ravenous intellect, his enigmatic brilliance, but this—

This display held its own magnificence. She clenched her fingers in the counterpane, weak with the yearning she'd hoped to contain. She began to understand men's enthusiasm to watch women cavort around in improper clothing as they did in Covent Garden.

The buttons of his trousers undone, Dash stepped from them, kicking them away until he stood before her in nothing but thin cotton drawers riding low enough to show the rounded edge of his pelvic bones. He hooked his thumb in the waistband, his head rising sharply when she made a sound of what could only be termed veiled delight.

The gleam in his eyes, tinting them the color of a sizzling summer sky, was apparent from across the room. His gaze never leaving her, he swept his hand down his chest, recording how she followed the movement, knowing more about her in that second than she knew about herself.

Her breath caught as his hand lingered over the muscled ridge of his belly, close to the hardening protrusion beneath his drawers. She swallowed, her fingers tangling in the counterpane hard enough to tear the silk. His cock. She knew what to call it. Knew how to identify every part of one's body. She didn't believe in using ridiculous, sheltering terminology. Limbs instead of legs, for instance. She'd heard the men in the Leighton Cluster whispering the phrase during a drunken outing months ago, although they'd hushed up when she entered her brother's study. Additionally, the word had been mentioned in a risqué novel she'd found in the back room of the emporium on Grafton Street, one of those filthy texts her husband had asked her to read, then come to him for a graphic summary.

His gaze skated over her like he held charcoal and was putting her image to paper. The sconce tossed wavering layers of gilded illumination over him. "What's that you have on, *leannan*? Underneath the coverlet?"

She understood this was his way of asking to see her. His tender, across-the-chamber regard. Trusting him—because she did except for his impossible vow not to touch another woman when she'd never held a man's attention longer than the time it took to complete a waltz— she let the counterpane drop until it lay in a crumpled fold on her lap. Exposing herself as she'd never done before.

His fingers tensed on his belly, digging into his flesh. "My shirt," he whispered, his tone hoarse. "You're wearing my shirt."

"My trousseau is on the way from London. Arriving tomorrow, I've been told. I have... nothing else suitable for sleep."

She started to lift the blanket. The air had thickened, her breath coming out in shallow exhalations to break through it, and his following in rushed pulses just behind. She didn't understand what was happening, only that his vigilant study was making her feel as if she'd had a glass of brandy. Been struck in the chest. Shaken until she was dizzy.

He threw out his hand, moved to the end of the bed. "Dinnae cover yourself. I want to see ye like this, through a mist of cotton and candlelight." He licked his lips, leaning into the bedpost, his stare fiery. "Your nipples are the hue of those blooms outside Leighton's terrace, the ones below your bedchamber window. I canna wait to slip them between my lips, see if they taste as bonnie as they look. Suck them until you plead for more. Feast my way down your body and back up again."

As if he'd stroked his tongue across them, they tightened, hard as pebbles. "Hydrangea."

"Hydrangea," he repeated in his deliberate way. Sensual, the word rolling off his lips like chocolate.

She motioned with her body, an invitation as hushed delight whispered through her.

"Not tonight," he said in answer to her question.

"Why?" Her voice was breathless, the word exploding like an oath. Did he not want her?

He folded back the corner of the counterpane, trailed his calloused fingertip across her ankle. A simple caress that nonetheless echoed through her. "Because this isn't one night, lass. I have a thousand and one to give you pleasure, to take my own. To find what makes you lose track of that day, like I promised. Teaching takes time, does it not?" He traced his knuckle along the arch of her foot, laughing softly when she released a muted sigh, an indication of his success. "I've decided, after giving it thought, hell, the entire ride here my mind consumed with you, that a purposeful strategy is best. Similar to a game of *vingt-*

84

et-un with a master, we're going to make deliberate moves. Because I've only done the temporary myself, and this is more."

"More," she whispered, agreeing but a bit frightened of the admission.

He caught her gaze, making sure she understood. "*You're* more, Theo Campbell. Otherwise, I'd never have left you tonight to be with the men. That was a diversionary tactic on my part. There is nae Scottish tradition on this point, lass. Though I enjoyed fleecing Jasper Noble of ten pounds at the poker table. I didnae even have to cheat. For a smuggler, the guv is a middling speculator. I'm not sure I believe all he's told us."

Theo glanced to the untouched side of the bed. "You'll stay here, then?"

His gaze fondled her body as he renewed his casually erotic assault on her foot. "I want to. I've had plenty of sleeping alone in this life. Those ragged nights of me childhood. No more. Not with you here."

Theo couldn't deny his vulnerability, suspecting he'd never have admitted this much if not for the whisky flowing through him. When she was hungry for knowledge, would take what she could get, and he knew it.

She drew aside the counterpane. She'd had enough of being alone in this life, too.

Dash tucked her foot beneath the covers and crossed to his side of the bed. Climbed in and instead of letting her lie quietly beside him, pulled her into the warm nook of his body. His nose dropped to the crown of her head, his chest rising with his inhalation. "You smell like bloody heaven, lass." Covering them, he settled back, drawing circles on her back until she relaxed. He was long and lean, hard and sculpted where she was not. She nestled, finding they fit well. Finding herself aroused *and* comforted.

He lifted her hand, shifting his ring in the muted light. "I'll get you better."

"No, I like it. I... want it." The ring's weight added substance in a way she couldn't describe.

"It's yours, then. Teach me a new word, lass." He yawned, his voice drowsy. "To help me sleep."

From her spot atop his shoulder, she glanced at him. His jaw was covered with dense stubble, his lids riding low, lashes an ebony splash against his skin. Hand trembling, she brushed her finger over the delicate bow shaping his top lip. Heat unfurled inside her, today's lesson. That she could manipulate her own passion as easily as she stoked his.

"Philtrum."

The arm encircling her tensed. "Again, *leannan*."

She stroked his upper lip again, recording his sigh, his body's quiver. "Philtrum."

"Your voice, these words, your teasing, make me want to do remarkable things to ye, lass. Brand your skin with my touch. I'm nae a patient man, but I'm trying."

"How leisurely must one go when using deliberate moves?"

He blinked an eye open. "A lesson a night sounds reasonable to me. Or day. Dawn, twilight, midnight, take your wee pick. Inside, outside, upside down."

"One lesson," she agreed, having no idea what she agreed to. *Day?* Did people have relations in broad sunlight? Outside? Was he joking?

Puzzling over his promises, she forced herself to stay awake until he slipped into slumber, his breathing flattening out, his hold on her loosening. He'd let a thin beam of illumination into their conversation. His calculated disclosures were intimate and madly addictive.

Addiction was permitted, however, because Dashiell Malcom Campbell was hers.

With protectiveness and a simmering ardor brewing inside her, Theo tumbled to sleep in her husband's arms.

Chapter Eight

If you get caught with a card up your sleeve, make sure it's not an ace.

　　Dashiell M. Campbell, *Proper Etiquette for Deception*

N o man cleaned his body and his teeth at dawn unless he had notions of seduction on his mind. Seducing one's *wife*.

What a novel concept.

"Wife," Dash whispered into the darkened bedchamber, the word holding more power than a loaded pistol pressed to his temple. He glanced at Theo from his benign vantage point by the window, where he'd spent the past twenty minutes gazing sightlessly at the lawns surrounding Southgate. A bonnie morning was dawning, the horizon lit with veins of blue and gold while he felt a timid lad in search of escape.

Dash turned the dice in a tense circle in his hand.

What to do about her?

An arrangement he'd accepted, and perhaps even desired in modest measure, but one leaving him tied to a willful bit of baggage. Not his usual leave-them-without-a-qualm type, either. This chit hit him in the gut, holding rare sway over a man known for playing fast and loose. It was his secret that she did—never to be shared. Reckless smiles and that crooked tooth making his heart knock and his breath catch.

Especially since her happiness had been, for the past twenty-four hours at least, directed solely at him. Even when they'd been working on the book, Theo had held her affection in reserve.

Dash had waited at the end of the chapel aisle, watching her stroll confidently toward him, the memory of her, *any* memory, not serving for the real show. Muffled conversation and the laughter of children, the aroma of roses and sunlight barely reaching him. Only her, like he eyed her through one of Ollie's telescope barrels. Before she took control of herself, tears had shimmered in her eyes, turning them the color of the shutters on the lone home he remembered from a grim childhood. An effervescent blue. A new word he'd found recently and loved beyond measure.

Theo was steady, *aye*, while he was a bobbin of thread, unspooling, hidden fragments spilling out. It wasn't to be borne, the lass pulling confidences from his insides like she would pluck items from a sack. He needed to stop this right now.

Separate the need from the giving.

Dash tapped his knuckle to the chilled glass pane, three knocks to get himself on track. They'd agreed, he and Theo. Friendship. None of that madness Xander Macauley and Tobias Streeter, the dukes, Ollie, even that lovesick excuse for a viscount, Chance Allerton, were suffering under. He didn't want to be beaten with the same whip. Sad-eyed with longing. Scared to death when their wives were expecting. Talk of forevers, talk of home being wherever their womenfolk were.

Dash delighted in the seclusion of the Devil's Lair. Delighted in his time alone. Delighted in his choices being his own.

Already, life was changing. Theo's shawl on a hook in the entrance-way. A hair ribbon he'd found abandoned on the staircase. The stink of a scruffy hound, a mutt currently snoozing in a crate in the kitchen. A lazy feline, who seemed unconcerned as hell about anything, sprawled on a settee in this very bedchamber.

Dash glanced about, flipping dice, assessing. There were clues to Theo's character all over if a bloke was savvy enough to search for them. Statements a person unwittingly made, missteps Dash had devoted an entire chapter to in *Proper Etiquette for Deception*. A tell. Assertions the competent gambler ought not make to protect himself. He had no intention of disclosing too many of his own.

Philtrum, he thought, his lip tingling as her silky voice rang through his mind.

Despite his misgivings about his wife's obstinacy and how cagey she'd be to manage, he wanted her. Badly.

With a threadbare exhalation, he smoothed his fist over the front of his drawers, his shaft hard as wood. Rather strong need thrumming through his veins, in fact. Leaving his dice on the window ledge, he crossed to the bed to gaze down at her. Theo's hair was a cloud of spun gold, tangled, and half covering her lovely face. Her hand tucked beneath her cheek like a child's. He'd been jug-bitten last night, well and truly legless from drink, but the sight of her in his shirt, her dusky nipples straining against cotton, had about done him in.

Other men were blind to her delicate beauty, but he wasn't. A trained swindler, he knew to seek past the obvious.

Too innocent. Too kind. Too intelligent. She'd probably never seen a naked man before. Even with her birthright being tattered around the edges, she had two dukes on her side. A duchess for a sister. An earl hanging about, an insipid viscount. Rookery titans, the most powerful lads in London. When all he had was a middle name he'd given himself on his tenth birthday because he believed it important to have one.

Was he a horrible person if he considered this marriage an opportunity? Was he wrong to seize it? Seize *her*?

The timing was near perfect, actually. Dash was disillusioned by the path he'd been traveling. The women, the booze, the high jinks. And his wee wife was curious, only now starting her adventure. Besides, she'd gotten herself in a fix, and someone had had to come to the rescue. He relished the protective sense of stepping in, a knight in battle. He was a competitive sort; it couldn't be helped. All Scots were.

The lone confidence he'd keep, a part of his plan he hadn't

mentioned, is that he thought it would be a sounder bet if the lass believed she couldn't live without him.

Not that 'absorption above all' nonsense she'd described but...

Images stormed his mind, erotic and raw. He genuinely didn't know how to persuade a woman without it being of a physical nature. Using his face and his body. Certainly, no chit had ever appreciated more than this about him.

If Theo needed him enough in that way, she'd never leave, as everyone else in his life had. One achingly sensual step at a time until her mind was blinded to any man but him. As long as he endeavored, absolutely *mastered*, keeping his wits about him.

Resolute, he made his way to his side of the bed, slid beneath the coverlet, and drew her close until they faced each other. She murmured and snuggled against him, seeking his warmth.

Brushing her hair from her face, he trailed his nose down her cheek, along her jaw. She smelled of lavender and the faintest hint of spearmint from what he recognized as his tooth powder. His gratification over this minute detail was ridiculous, but there it was. Nibbling beneath her ear, he whispered nonsensical words to wake her gently. He would instantly retreat if he sensed he was moving too quickly.

Hoping he wasn't, he filled his hands with her astonishingly splendid body. Where had his lass been hiding this? Ample at the hip, slim as a reed at the waist. He didn't reach beneath her shirt—*his* shirt —to really touch her. Drape her leg over his hip and spread her wide as he wanted. Work those gorgeous nipples between his teeth and bring her home. The thought flashed across his mind that he didn't have to leave her during his release if they were planning on children, a first in his experience.

Simmer down, Dashiell, he warned himself, *you have all the time in the world.*

When he grazed his lips across hers, she exhaled softly, slid her hand over his shoulder and into the hair bordering the nape of his neck. Lips parting, tongue touching his. A decided *yes*. Groaning, he rolled her beneath him, hanging on to his plan by a thread. He tried to ignore that she had on nothing but a length of cotton, he in nothing but his drawers. Mismatched attire leaving a lot of exposed skin.

They were clumsy at first. Bumping chins, scraping teeth, bodies searching for an ideal fit. Hunger and a primal eagerness he'd not felt in ages bubbling beneath his skin, rushing through his veins.

Until they weren't.

Until it was a balanced mix of breathy moans, gliding tongues, seeking hands. Kissing and petting like he would have as a lad, no rush to get to the final step. Extending the pleasure, ripe but not ready, to the breaking point. Hips cresting, thighs flexing, a fundamental dance as old as time. Damp skin atop twisted sheets. Straining bodies fighting for release.

A faint breeze pushed their scent about the room, the fragrance new and fragile, an aroma he wanted forever lodged in his memories. Theo arched into him with a ragged sigh, and he responded, crowding her into the mattress, matching each push and pull. She learned quickly, taking control until it was a fevered exchange.

For perhaps the first time, he followed along, seeing where his *leannan* would take him.

When her hand curled around his hip, guiding him into a rhythm she had no clue was as natural as the stars, he lifted to see her face. He couldn't hide his state of arousal. Not with this close fit, his thigh wedged against her sex, the two of them tangled up like vines. He wasn't sure how to advise her to ignore his rigid shaft for now, that this experience was *hers*.

She opened eyes that had gone a cavernous blue, her lips curving in a knowing smile that should have scared him. "Is this the first lesson?"

He dusted a kiss inside the V of her shirt, above her collarbone. *Ah*, did he want to tup this lass. Plunge inside her until he lost himself and had her halfway to heaven. The lingering teasing and touching, a trick he didn't always employ, especially with the chits he wanted gone sooner rather than later, was becoming *his* lesson. "Maybe."

"Are you going to take"—she wiggled a finger, indicating his drawers—"those off?"

"Patience, lass," he whispered and began to unfasten the buttons of her shirt, spreading the material wide, exposing a river of bare skin and temptation running to her belly. A path he longed to follow with his lips to the very core of her. "That's another lesson. This one is all yours." He pressed a kiss between her breasts. "Some will be my pleasure, some your pleasure. Some our pleasure. We shall keep it fascinating with variety."

His mind full of erotic images, he leaped in before she could ask more questions or start reciting words from the dictionary to set him on fire. If not a writer, he'd have happily been an artist and sketched her until the end of time. Naked skin, nothing between them but air. Her atop him, beneath him, in front while he thrust, one of his favorite positions. His head settled between her thighs, where he'd remain until he broke her.

Because he didn't trust the lass to comply with his demands, he trapped the hand she had clenched on his hip, pressing her arm into the mattress. She made to complain, but the words were lost as soon as he wrapped his lips around her nipple, dampening cotton until it stuck.

Still, it wasn't enough. Nudging the material aside, he sucked the peaked nub between his teeth, his tongue circling. She tasted glorious, sweet and tart, that lavender scent reaching out to grab him by the throat. With his free hand, he cupped her other breast, palming, teasing, his thumb working her into a frenzy. Pausing, he gazed up at her, skin flushed, eyes closed, head thrown back in rapture. What a *fookin'* picture his wife made.

For a scholarly chit, a lass with a *spectacular* mind, she had an equally spectacular body.

A shape she'd been hiding beneath loose-fitting gowns of a distinctly unappealing style. The men of London should make more trips to Hatchards was all he could advise. Surrounded by books perhaps the place to be. Jamming Theo against a towering bookrack sounded like a dandy afternoon to him.

Releasing her nipple, he blew a breath across the silken bud, thinking the dusky color ideal. The loveliest teats in England. "How do you feel about begging, *leannan?*"

She moaned and arched, the tight blossom hitting his cheek. Urging his mouth back to her. "I won't."

He laughed, delighted. Cheeky girl. Had she no idea of his talents?

She wrestled her arm from his grip, tried to touch him as he was touching her. Below the waistband, a man's weakness. A dirty fighter, which he admired. "I want to win this time, Campbell."

"*Aye*, winner takes all, isn't that what I wrote in chapter twelve?" Lazily circling her nipple with his tongue but not latching on, he watched her squirm as his own body pulsed in delight.

"You and your blasted book," she murmured, her voice muffled against the counterpane. "Even here, it's in bed with us."

Smiling, carefree at a moment when he typically wasn't, he began a campaign unlike any he'd ever waged. He followed his heart.

Dash could chase the blush lighting her flesh to her toes and back, unfurl her sex like a bloom and feast. Make her explode before she got to the letter M in that alphabet she loved so much. His usual tactics. Mindless, they were so innate.

This was another effort altogether.

He wanted to win, too. His life. His wife. A woman he was finding he desired more than he should. More than was advisable for a gambler. A man who protected himself first.

Spontaneity spelled disaster, but he continued powerlessly along the path, reclaiming her nipple and suckling until she quieted, only her breathy whimpers released to the night, sounds set to drive a man mad. Once his fortitude was waning, and hers was gone, he traced a sluggish path down her body, over her waist, her hip, her thigh, his touch nimble. He glanced down, unable to help himself. The hair between her legs was a gilded shade darker than that on her head, his skin swarthy against it as he began to trace teasing rings around her sex.

"Shall I make you come?" he whispered thickly against the side of her breast. "Have you shatter into a thousand pieces while I watch? I ken exactly how to do it."

Bucking her hips, she bumped his hand, seeking. "You arrogant beast."

"Is that a yes, *leannan?*"

"Yes, yes, make me come, Dash Campbell, god of sexual congress." Her gaze was furiously dazzled when it met his. "If you think you can do a better job than I can on my own, go to it."

His breath left his lungs in a tear. Undone by the image of her touching herself, he captured her lips beneath his, spread her delicate folds, and dipped his finger inside. She was dewy, slick, her channel tight, her mons pulsing beneath the heel of his hand. Giving attention to the rigid nub topping her sex, he set a rhythm meant to ruin her, pleasure at his direction. Such grand pleasure that he'd wipe that taunting expression from her face.

Doing something no woman ever, ever had, she laid her hand atop his as he stroked. Not a controlling move, limiting or in any way forceful, merely *feeling* what he was doing to her. His shaft shifted in his drawers, nearing an embarrassing situation he'd not faced since he was thirteen years old.

The education he'd promised, the clever lass he'd desired in his bed stepping up.

Leaving the kiss so he could look at her, he marveled at his fortune. Cheeks flushed, lips parted, hand clenched in the coverlet, she was a delicious sight. Theo Astley, *no*, he corrected and dragged his teeth along her jaw, *Campbell*, was everything he'd not known he needed. Right there beneath his nose all this time. Now his wife was riding his hand, her thighs gripping his wrist, body shuddering around him. He buried his face in the wild abandon of her hair and thanked the stars.

She wasn't far from completion, and he could have spilled himself with a lingering caress. Working gradually, he slid another finger in deep, and gave it a twist.

Neck arching, body bowed, she lifted off the mattress, her climax arriving sooner than he'd expected. Her muscles milked his fingers, a series of pulsing contractions. Her cry was throat-deep, hoarse. And loud. His name interspersed with random bits of nonsense.

Shite, Dash thought, and smashed his lips over hers, swallowing the rest of her feral release. He had no clue who his housekeeper, Mrs. Irving, had placed in the next bedchamber. It could have been her bloody brother. Or Xander Macauley. Dash would jump out the window if he heard them making love.

Although this was mere play, the initial stage, a beginning he usually rushed through. He'd not realized he would like it so much, forget about the wild lass beneath him. Her orgasm had been explosive for only using his finger. What would she do when he used his tongue?

As he contemplated how responsive his wife was turning out to be, their kiss spun into deeper waters. Theo's sated body clinging to his in preparation for the next lesson. Her whispered, *what about you,* moments ago nearly bringing him to his knees. Until he was half a mind to tup her despite his plans. He could spend days like this, his fingers coated with her consent, the little ripples coursing through her body swimming into his.

If she'd been a rose, her petals would have been tumbling off.

Sexual congress, he recalled. Theo had referred to their lovemaking as sexual congress. Wasn't that the way of highbrows to make something splendid sound like maths?

Laughing, he rolled to his back, tossing his arm over his eyes to hide the vision beside him. A satiated goddess who'd freed her bliss to the heavens. Her power at that instant was extreme, her loveliness unmatched. Her scent drifted from his fingers to his nose, painfully hardening his cock. A moment alone in his bedchamber was an excellent idea. He didn't need long to spill his seed, then he could think clearly.

Being consumed by his wife wasn't part of the bargain.

He heard her shift, bed ropes creaking. Opened one eye to find her lying on her side, cheek balanced on her hand, gaze drinking him in from head to toe. "That's not going to fit."

He followed her observation to his shaft, which was currently testing the seams of his drawers. He tilted his head, trying to see it like she did. *Impressive.*

"It'll fit, *leannan,* trust me," he confirmed, tucking her into his side when he could tell she was starting to think. Thinking being the drawback to her brilliance. About the women he'd been with and how he'd gotten so bloody talented at this.

Wide beams of dawning light scattered across the bed, the echo of a waking house sounding around them. They were due at breakfast soon; they had guests. Dashiell M. Campbell had a country home and *guests.* A situation he had nil experience with and less training for. Who needed two dukes underfoot with an earl thrown in, anyway? His belly twitched at the thought of what he should have done that he hadn't for this production to be successful. He didn't know how to manage a staff as large as Southgate's. Make sure chambers were readied and foodstuff appropriate, not for such high-steppers as these. What had he been thinking, purchasing a spread as significant as this? "Try not to appear too content at breakfast, lass. Not with your brother here. I'm up the brook with the laddie. Frankly, in over my head with the whole tangle."

Theo snorted, half laugh, half sigh. Shoving away from him, she sat up, clutching the rumpled lapels of her shirt together. Breasts bouncing, she presented a bonnie picture. "You're the most arrogant man I've ever met! Who cares what my brother thinks? What if I'm *not* content?"

"Ever come that hard by yourself, Mrs. Campbell? Next time, it'll be my tongue inside you, not my fingers, do you ken?"

Riveted despite her annoyance, she tossed another glance at his cock, a pout twisting her gorgeous mouth. *Ah, lass,* he wished to tell her, *arousal is shimmering across your fine features like you tossed a pebble in a pond.*

Debating her next move, her tongue came out to lick her lips, exposing the crooked tooth he loved. Her tenacity captivated him. "Truthfully," she finally said in response to his question, "I didn't come that hard alone."

"I dinnae think so." Wishing to bring back the playful mood, he dragged her to the mattress, kissing her until they were breathless. Where they snuggled and laughed and petted as if they'd been sharing a bed for eons.

They were fortunate souls, he and Theo. They had chemistry, when that was not always the way of it. They more than fit. They were sparks set to dry kindling, an uncontrollable blaze if he allowed it to rage. Similar curiosities about life. Able minds, nimble, attentive bodies.

Wonder of all wonders, Dash had found a wee wife who made him burn.

Aye, they were going to destroy this bedchamber.

Destroy every single chamber in the place.

He didn't know how long he could wait, how many lessons he could *honestly* make it through before going all the way, but it would be the most fun he'd had in years finding out.

Chapter Nine

Don't assume you have the full count of the cards too early in the game.

     Dashiell M. Campbell, *Proper Etiquette for Deception*

T heo decided after determined study on a sun-dappled Suffolk afternoon that her husband was a Renaissance man.

He wouldn't be comfortable with the romance of the description, yet it was true.

The men of the society-dubbed Leighton Cluster were gathered around Xander Macauley's borrowed carriage parked on Southgate's circular gravel drive. The conveyance was nothing as ostentatious as Dash's German model, rather a new standard Lord Brougham was trifling with. Untested and conceivably dangerous, is how Tobias Streeter had skeptically described it. The Lord High Chancellor wanted Macauley to test the setup, believing a rookery thug being tossed to the cobbles was better than a peer of the realm.

Dash circled the vehicle, running his hands over the axle and leaf springs, a groove of concentration centered between his brows. Going to his knee, he pointed to the wheel with a shake of his head, his fingers held two inches apart to represent a shortfall in the design. A glow of pride lit her. His intellect was such a revelation, buried beneath a crude accent society discounted in seconds flat. When he was a gifted writer, astute gambler, able entrepreneur, and now it seemed, an engineer, able to fathom the inner workings of carriages and the like.

He ran his hand along the carriage step, following the spiraling metal arch. Theo squirmed and palmed her flaming cheek. Those fingers had been inside her, two to be exact. Doing wicked things, delicious things. Accomplished skill she was jealous of—and wanted more of. He'd done this slight twist of his wrist that had set her off like a pyrotechnic. She'd only recognized the move because her hand had been atop his, recording everything, two lifetimes of amorousness occurring in one.

The conceited cad was right. She could never have come so hard by herself. There was talent, and there was *talent*.

He knew she was staring from her perch on the main entrance's marble steps, had recently flashed her a cunning smile, but she couldn't stop herself. Her pleasure at his guidance had connected her to him in a mysterious way, a length of twine attached and hauling her closer.

Always the academic, her observations from the morning's activities were numerous and detailed.

One. Dash had freckles not only on his cheeks but his chest, mixed with the ideal smattering of hair trailing to his nether region. Not too much, not too little, the hair and the freckles. Two. His eyes were scattered with specks of gold and when aroused, they glowed. Or appeared to, in her fanciful accounting. Three. He hummed beneath his breath at crucial moments, like when he'd slid finger number one inside her, a muted rumble that had come close to sending her over the edge before the contest began. Four. He was going to be glorious in bed. He understood how to pleasure her in more ways than she could contemplate. *Upside-down*, he'd said, and she rather believed him. (This talent born of experience angered and provoked her at the same time. The women in his past were legendary, but she was his wife, so she was going to strive to forget them.) Five. Her plan, because she knew *he* had one, was to make him beg. Soon. She'd not read those erotic French texts at great risk to her reputation for nothing.

In fact, she had a filthy idea taking shape in her mind this very second.

"What are you sighing about over there?"

Theo startled, turning to her sister, Pippa, whom she'd forgotten sat on the stair above her. "Um, if you must know, I was considering what directives to give Mrs. Irving about dinner."

Pippa rolled her eyes and took a bite from the cinnamon biscuit in her hand. "Not thinking about that adorable husband who keeps flashing us a triumphant smile? Dash Campbell looking more the proud peacock than usual. My beloved Theo, whatever did you do to put such a shameless expression on his face? He's practically strutting."

"Not enough," Theo whispered for her ears only. But her victory was coming. *He* was coming, she should say. He thought to be the only one doling out pleasure, dealing the cards so to speak. Simply because he had knowledge about the subject, and she did not.

She would show him.

"Did you see him when you started coordinating breakfast with his housekeeper? I feared he was going to expire with relief. You'll win his affection from that partnership alone. Poor devil has never dealt with the trials and tribulations of running an estate. Walks around like he's filched someone's home from their back pocket. It took years for my darling Xander to free himself of that thinking."

Theo had noticed. Which made her heart clinch, a sensation she was extremely wary of. Her sister, however, didn't understand what it meant to have no home, then be presented with one you'd only dreamed of. The contradiction in life station was shocking.

"I wonder if Bury has a proper school," Theo said in an effort to lead her inquisitive sister down another path of discussion. "Perhaps I can assist if they do. Add a subject I'm qualified to teach to their curriculum. I'm having books sent from London. I was about to start *Principles of Political Economy* by Malthus. Surely, the older students might benefit from a dialogue about the book."

"*Gads*, That sounds horrid." Pippa chewed, wiping the corner of her mouth with her fist. "Will you have time to teach with an attentive husband and two properties to maintain? Children, please, *please*, on the way? Then we'll be in loving misery together. I only have this moment with you because Hildy took pity on me and is teaching the children to make honey cake."

Theo waved Pippa's concern away, watching Dash brace his hands on his muscular thighs, and rise to his feet. Tunnel his fingers through his hair, leaving it in tousled disarray. *My, my, my, he was a fantasy.* And she knew what he looked like in nothing but a pair of thin drawers. "Dash will be in London part of the time running the Devil's Lair. I'll stay here. I never cared for Mayfair, so I won't miss it."

Pippa swallowed, choking. "Won't you miss him? You plan to spend nights apart? What about the strumpets in town who'll only see his marriage as a challenge? You can't wed a man with his reputation and turn your back, Theo. Not until you have him eating from your hand."

Theo snatched up an elm leaf and twirled it between her fingers. She'd known she would face this line of questioning at some point. "We're not in love, Pippa. We were forced to marry, Leighton's saber pricking Dash's jugular as we walked down the aisle. We have an agreement. We've discussed this." She let the leaf drift away in a gust where it landed atop her slipper. The leaden weight in her belly she was prepared to ignore. She wasn't going to be possessive of a man who was comelier than any in England; she simply wasn't. It was a waste of time and thought. "We worked it out. Relax."

"*What?*"

Pippa ground her back teeth together. People in love never understood people *not* in love. "We're friends."

"Friends?"

Theo nodded. Friends.

"I understand you had to marry after the stolen carriage debacle." Pippa dusted crumbs from her hands, clearly distressed. "But I wouldn't spend a night apart from Xander if I didn't infrequently, and I mean infrequently, have to. I like waking to his smiles and his frowns. He isn't what I'd call a morning person, and he can be grouchy."

Theo shrugged, defeated if it came down to wishing for the kind of relationship Pippa and Macauley had. "I don't think I loved Edward, and this match is beneficial for so many reasons. I'm satisfied. Grateful, even. Ecstatic Edward's pregnant paramour showed up at our engagement party. Anyway, aside from our peculiar family"—she gestured to the group inspecting the Brougham, with the exception of Dash, men who enjoyed being obsessed with their wives—"love isn't a requirement."

Pippa grimaced. "For society marriages, you mean."

"We're a part of that dreadful class whether we like it or not." She knocked the leaf off her slipper, recalling Dash's sage advice. She hadn't wanted to hear it, but he was right. She was stuck with the aristocrats. "Did you forget our brother the duke?"

Pippa grasped her forearm, dragging Theo's gaze to hers. "Love isn't a science experiment. Like mathematics, where everything adds up. Sometimes it doesn't, but it still works and is wonderful. Xander drives me mad, absolutely raving *mad*, but I love him more than life. On paper, we're not a good match. A rookery smuggler and a wallflower who wasn't actually a wallflower. Who would have imagined such a thing? But I'm blissfully happy." She grinned, her contentment breathtaking. "I think he is, too."

"Dash and I are an excellent match, Pippa. We worked for a year on his book and got along famously—"

"Except for the time you threw a vase at his head. And the months of barely talking. Remember the argument at Lord Chamber's ball? The Gambling God was furious for a week."

"For once, we're speaking the same words, and they're not ones from his blasted book. Love is off the table. Let us settle into what we've determined we *want*. Our freedom. We're actually being very contemporary in our thinking. I've read about a similar marital experiment being conducted in France."

Pippa snorted and fished another biscuit from her pocket. "Then why is he heading this way atop his horse, looking every bit the knight-errant riding to your rescue? He's gone medieval, darling."

Theo's heart turned over before she had the chance to hold it steady. Knight-errant's love for the heroine was a celebrated fictional theme. Theo had given up fairy tales when her mother died penniless and broken, her heart crushed beneath her father's polished boot.

Fairy tales were for lost girls and lonely women.

Although it was hard to deny Dash's magnificence as he crossed to her. Alleged to be a superb whip, perhaps the finest in the city, he sat astride his mount like a prince, his muscular thighs gripping the flanks with ease. She knew it was his habit to ride along Rotten Row each morning. It was conceivably the reason he was asked to race carriages through the streets at dawn. Antics he'd said would cease now that they were married.

Though Theo wasn't sure she believed any of his promises.

Halting at the bottom of the staircase, his smile was filled with every wicked lick and kiss from their bedchamber. Diabolical. She wondered if he knew the word, and if he'd like her to whisper it in his ear the next time he had his hands on her.

"What's that look, *leannan?* Fearsome, it is. Smoky at the edges, ready to smolder."

She gestured toward the parklands, struggling to appear nonchalant when her pulse was thumping like mad in her veins. "Take me for a ride, a brief tour of the estate. Right here, right now."

"*Theo,*" Pippa whispered, "maybe this isn't a good idea. Leighton is watching."

Dash caught the cusp of his glove in his teeth and pulled it on tighter. She suspected he knew this action sent her belly into a spiral. His eyes flashed, the indigo orbs meeting hers above scuffed kidskin. "This a dare? For me or your brother? I'm not a wee puppet to be dancing at the end of your string."

She rose from the step, smoothing her skirt. "It's for all of them. To prove we won't do this any way but ours. Cut the lead my brother has us secured by."

Looping the reins around his fist, Dash squinted at the Leighton Cluster gathered around a carriage that was almost certainly going to spill Xander Macauley upon the cobbles in the near future. Laughing, he shook his head ruefully. "*Aye,* you have the rookery hellion in you still. Society hasn't been able to beat it out. I hope your brother understands I'm not going to try."

Theo pressed her lips together to hide her pleasure at his avowal. He didn't want to change her.

How long had it been since someone *wasn't* trying to change her?

Scowling at her cheeriness, Dash indicated the low stone wall bordering the stairs. "Up with you, then, lass, if we're going to spawn another scandal. This will be the third if I'm not losing count along with me mind."

Raising her skirt to her knees, she hopped atop the wall as Pippa sighed gustily behind her. Angling his mount close, Dash held out his arm, his sleeve lifting to reveal a hint of the Celtic knot inked on his forearm. Soon, she was going to take a bite out of that piece of him. "No astride business, Theodosia. Side-saddle or nothing. I stake my own rule there. Leighton will pound my comely face into the dirt if I push this stunt too far."

The world stilled, a moment she'd remember her entire life.

Dashiell Campbell atop a dappled gray mare, sunlight a muted, misty shimmer at his back. A Suffolk breeze ripping past, carrying the scent of her new home and her new husband. His gaze demanding more than either of them were willing to entertain or even understood they wanted. It was confirmation, a stronger vow than those they'd repeated in a medieval chapel.

It was *acceptance.*

No breaking of spirits occurring this day.

When Theo let him know she was ready with a slight nod of her head, Dash lifted her as if she weighed less than a sack of vegetables, settling her in front of him, the pommel at her hip. Her legs covered and off to one side, showing only a tinge of ankle, a trivial concern as this was family. Before they moved, he tunneled his arm around her waist, and pulled her against his broad body.

His strength enveloping her, they broke into a carefree gallop, as if they had no one to answer to but each other.

Which was today's wondrous lesson outside the bedchamber.

If Dash's heart was beating faster than he wished to communicate, Theo made no mention of it. If she pressed her cheek lovingly into his superfine coat as they surged over ancient grasslands, she could only pray he didn't notice.

Chapter Ten

The later the hour, the riskier the wager.
Dashiell M. Campbell, *Proper Etiquette for Deception*

Dash was late with his words.

He tried to write a precise number of pages per day—two—and he was stuck at a measly half page of scrawled nonsense.

Sitting back, he stretched his legs beneath the beaten butcher's block he'd fashioned as a desk, and took a sip of whisky, the finest in England rolling down his throat. Not in Scotland, *nae*, he, Macauley, and Streeter weren't that far along in the distilling process, but this batch was good. Commendable, if he used a word from his burgeoning vocabulary. Dash had established an association, United Distillers, with brewer members in England, Wales, Ireland, and Scotland. They shared recipes, techniques, and engineering advice. It wasn't that they trusted each other, but the enemy you kept closer often became an ally, if not a friend. This description made Dash think of Jasper Noble, and he laughed into his glass.

He glanced out the lone window in the scullery at the rain streaking the glass. A storm had rolled through after dinner, bringing howling gusts, and a curious sense of seclusion. If the roads were too pitted, the houseguests who'd been set to depart on the morn would be staying another day.

Inexplicably, because Dash was suited to the dearth of privacy associated with city life, he wanted to be alone with his wife. Preferably naked. Or enmeshed in quiet companionship across the breakfast table. Reading together in bed. Trotting through the fields surrounding Southgate. Situations he'd never invited another person to share with him. Certainly not needed or longed for. Their ride earlier today, his wife in his arms, their heartbeats seeking each other's rhythm, had altered something deep inside him. A shift he felt to his bones. The incident had tossed in a hidden element, a complicated element.

He didn't know how to describe it, only understood it *was*.

Sighing, he wrapped the hair ribbon he'd been using as a bookmark around his finger and gave it a tug. It was the palest of blues, not far from the icy hue of Theo's eyes. It had been looped through her hair in the chapel, then later ended up on Southgate's main staircase. So *Theo* to lose her bits all over. Amusing lass.

He caressed the satin with his fingertip. One yank and a cascade of gold would tumble to her waist.

Or so it was in his fantasies.

He wasn't surprised in the least to hear a delicate footstep he knew to be hers in the kitchen beyond. She wanted her lesson as much as he wanted to give it. It was cowardly to hide in the servant's quarters for reasons he couldn't yet face. Tucking the ribbon in his trouser pocket, Dash fixed an indecipherable expression on his face, thinking of cards and dice to steady himself.

Theo's head popped around the door casing, the riot of curls he desired there, in part. A messy presentation, true form for his wife. Half-up, half-down. Disheveled was the word for it. A lace-edged, too virtuous nightgown covered her from head to toe. Her smile was hesitant even if her step was not. Dragging a chair from the dark corner, she settled into it, the book she held deposited between them as a sorrowful chaperone. "So, this is where you've taken off to. A place no one in the Cluster will think to look for you. Making the scullery your office. Brilliant."

It was the warmest area of the manor and close to foodstuff when he required a midnight nibble. Besides, he didn't see himself seated behind the massive mahogany beast in his study. He felt like an imposter there. Oftentimes, an imposter in this entire place. Scowling, he nudged his glass her way. "One question, *leannan*." He could give her that much.

Ignoring the whisky, she picked up his dice, and rolled them across the block. Double threes. "How do you know I have questions?"

Chuckling, he gathered the dice, rolled. Double threes.

She gasped, pointed. "How did you do that?"

"Luck, lass, pure luck." Which was a lie. The dice were weighted. But these kinds of fibs, gambling and the like, the only kind he'd be telling her, were harmless.

Fiddling with the cover of her book, some drudgery about economics that was surely the most boring text in the house, she captured her bottom lip between her teeth, the crooked front one doing its best to distract him. "How did you get the scar?"

"Scar," he murmured, searching his mind. Had she seen that nasty one on his lower back? He didn't think so.

She reached, *aye*, she had to go and touch him when he was tangled up, brushing her fingertip across his chin.

Stop, he wanted to say, *your concern is bloody confusing*.

"What's that you're reading?" he asked instead of going to a place he wasn't sure he ever wanted to go again. His past.

Frowning at his evasion, Theo circled her book into view.

He squinted until the gold lettering on the spine popped into focus. "*Principles of Political Economy*." His leaden tone showed his enthusiasm for the topic.

Embarrassment lit her face. "It's more interesting than it sounds. The author is a Fellow of the Royal Society, and he wrote it in rebuttal to Ricardo's text on economics and taxation."

Dash gave the tome a cautious poke. His wife was brilliant, the flash of pride that went clear to his toes a warning sign. *Troubled waters ahead, Dashiell.*

"You need spectacles, Husband."

He reached for his glass since the lass wasn't partaking. "We covered this during the writing of me book, wife. In nagging, exhaustive detail. I suppose you figure you have the right now, is that it?" Grunting, he tossed back the remaining whisky. "I've gone and gotten me own torment. How is that for irony?"

"They'll reduce your headaches. And only *add* to your attractiveness if that's what you're worried about."

This topic he could discuss. Grinning, he sprawled in the chair, running the lip of the tumbler across his mouth. "You think I'm attractive?"

Theo growled and braced her hands on the block, set to rise.

"It happened at the workhouse. The injury. Split my chin near open, it did." He scrubbed his fist over his face, expecting it to come away covered in blood. Denying his wife the pieces he longed to hide wasn't fair to either of them. "I'm left-handed, as you well ken." He flexed his fingers, then brought them into a tight fist. "That's something typically beaten out of a lad when I wasn't a lad to be beaten."

Theo stilled, searching for a response when she always had one at the ready. "You're writing again," she finally said, redirecting the topic. She nodded to the folio at his side. "Two pages a day?"

With a leaden thud in his belly, he nudged the notebook toward her. *Take a look.*

She moved her lips while she read, a habit she wasn't aware of. It was enchanting, her earnestness. Cute, if he used the word that came immediately to mind. A description his little rebel would loathe being associated with. He'd known few decent people. Didn't expect such in the world they were so rare. Rescuers of lost pups like that hound snoozing away in the corner of the kitchen. Next, her damned cat would be sleeping on his *bed*. While he, Dash Campbell, crooked con, lone wolf, writer of double-dealing manuals, was left to safeguard one of those true souls for the rest of his given time on this earth.

What a muddle.

It wasn't long that she read. Three minutes, maybe five. But it felt like eternity when you were letting someone into your life. Exposing the ugly pieces to bright view. When he had the strength, he was going to bleed her dry about *her* past—because he knew she had one.

Theo flipped a page, exhaled softly, his signet ring sparking in the candlelight. "Oh, Dash, is this true?"

He rubbed his temple, the headache she'd mentioned brewing. "*Aye*, it's true."

"Nanna?"

He tilted his empty glass and peered into it. "She ran the bordello, a distant auntie of me mum's. A useful place to disappear that turned into a home of sorts. I was there until I was nine. The ladies were kind to me, sharing affection they couldn't share on their backs, I suppose. Nanna went a bad way the year after my mother died from cholera, a tumble down the domestic's staircase. A guv who dinnae want to pay, a daily occurrence in a bawdy. When I entered the workhouse, no one cared anything about my past. About me."

"London," she said, urging him on when he stalled.

"That was five years later, and by then, I had my own business, Sharps and Flats. Admittedly, there were certain enterprising gaming hell owners who didnae appreciate my sharing techniques to defraud them. Macauley being one. Though he went a step further, thinking to relieve me of my enterprise by offering me a better opportunity. He believed overconfidence and base connections were a risky mix. When I had men traveling hundreds of miles to sit in the frigid back room of a rookery boarding house for instruction."

She leaned in, her voice dropping to a whisper. "How good a thief are you?"

He thought of the thousands of cards floating around England with razor-marked edges. The rippled baize on hazard tables in at least three countries, a distinctive skill he'd not *dared* include in *Proper Etiquette for Deception*. The off-balance roulette tables. None of which were used at the Devil's Lair. In a move only a higher power could muster, the gaming hell he managed was first class, legit. In part, because he knew every despicable trick of the trade.

He had to give an answer, just not these. "Counting the smuggling with Macauley?"

"I thought... that is, he's respectable now that he's married."

Dash shrugged, not *about* to tread that path. "Let's just say he and I are on fair enough terms with God."

"Why continue working at the gaming hell? Isn't it dangerous? You have enough funds from your publishing ventures. Giving talks in every parlor in London."

"I earn enough from the distilleries without dipping into the publishing monies, lass." Dash rested his elbow on the block, ignoring the urge to pull her onto his lap and kiss away her need for information. This was more than he'd promised to give, but with Theo, life was an inquisition. "You see, every able body employed at the Devil's Lair was born in the district. Streeter, Macauley, and I are funneling money, lawfully, back into the stews. Improving the streets, providing medical care, foodstuff for the aged. The posh toffs spending their blunt in the hell saw how much faster they could get to Limehouse if they supported better roadways in the House of Lords. We've turned their greed against them."

"You're a philanthropist." Theo's lips parted, shooting a blast of awareness through him.

She had a fetching mouth, skin the color of rose petals. Plump and temptingly kissable. Alas, he couldn't scrub the idea of her on her knees before him from his mind lately. He scooted forward, dragging the chair's legs across the floor. "Have a care, *leannan*. I've taken down hulking dockworkers for less."

She laughed, delighted. It was a weakness that however he'd pleased her pleased *him*. "Oh, no, Dash. It's a compliment. It means you support the care of those in need through your generosity."

Huh. That was a new one. He gestured to his notebook, hoping she didn't notice the heat hitting his cheeks. "Write it down. That's high praise I want to remember."

Grasping his quill, she did as he asked, bowed over his makeshift desk in his makeshift office. He didn't understand how *she* didn't understand that he was an urchin and would never be anything but no matter how many shillings he gave away. How fine his accent or his clothes.

"Your rookery districts could certainly use better schools. Something I could assist with." Her gaze stayed glued to the folio, her suggestion as offhand as any she would make. Her indifferent tone didn't fool him.

He filed it away, an idea for a future gift. Maybe someday. *Maybe.*

She lifted her head, revealing a wash of smoldering heat in her eyes. "When is our next lesson?"

He released a relieved sigh to leave his past behind.

Vacating his chair, he crossed to the door and flipped the tumblers, powerfully glad this chamber had a lock. Turning, he leaned against it, his heart knocking so hard it was ringing in his ears. "Now, if you want it."

She rose but remained in place, impossibly beautiful in her demure nightgown, candlelight threading through her hair and glinting off her creamy skin. "We could roll the dice. Highest number fulfills a fantasy."

He drew a tense breath. "Do you have fantasies, *leannan?*"

She only smiled.

Shoving off the door, in seconds he had her about the waist, backing her into the block, his mouth seizing hers. Fingers tangled in her hair, sending pins to the granite slabs. They were well-matched in hunger, in need. Her lips parted, letting him in, *pulling* him in. Tongues tangling, bodies pressed, they grappled there in the middle of a deserted scullery. The air in the room thickened, her teasing scent whipping out to power desire through him. Her hands were traveling over him, exploring. Igniting fires as rain lashed the glass panes.

She gave him a shove, sending him back a step. "Into the chair."

He blinked, bringing her image swimming into view. "*What?*" They hadn't even rolled the dice. He'd been thinking they'd go another round with his fingers inside her, maybe, *possibly* his tongue. He could control who won, of course. Control the whole damned episode if it came down to it.

"I want to touch you." She rushed the next out like her courage was fading by the second. "I want to taste you. I read about something in a book at the emporium last spring, one of those filthy texts we discussed. I have ideas."

"Ideas," he murmured. *Ideas.* About taking him into her mouth? In a spare nook off his kitchen? Was that what she was saying? His cock hardened absurdly in reaction, his vision spotting. *Fookin' hell.* She was his dream lass.

"Last time was for me. This time is for you. You said that's how it would be." She smiled, flirtatious, gaining her mettle while he watched with hot eyes. "I think I'll like it. I may be able to... arrive, somehow, too. Again."

"I—" He was lost at this turn, dumbfounded. "*Leannan.*" Such play was skipping from step one to step twenty when they'd only shared one orgasm between them. They were still baby stepping. Doing this with him was serious business.

She sulked, huffing out a breath. "You don't like oral sport. I should have known."

He gestured to his rock-hard shaft. *Try again.*

She gave him another push, and he let her win, stumbling into the chair. She was on her knees before he could get out a warning about the end game. Did she know what would happen, him spilling his seed all over her? Not long after she wrapped those rosy lips around him?

"*Leannan,*" he tried again, "listen to me."

She glanced up, wide-eyed and lovely, running her finger along the tented front of his trouser close. His body jerked, his concern doing nothing to soften his erection. His mind might object to her schemes, but his cock sure as hell wasn't. "I *want* to."

He hesitated, speechless. When blathering on, at least about ways to swindle, was part of his profession.

He dropped his head back when she began to unbutton his trousers, closed his eyes to the torrid picture of her kneeling before him. Fantasy mixed with reality meant he'd last no longer than two seconds. Her crooked tooth and gloriously sky-blue eyes. Hair a tangle about her shoulders. Breasts swaying while she sucked him. His studious, clever, daring *wife* on her knees, doing delicious things.

She obviously wanted him to twist his lust like that signet ring around her finger.

When she tunneled past his drawers and her breath hit his shaft, he wrapped his fingers around the chair's spindles until his knuckles popped. His hips lifted, a deadly sign, as her tongue met his swollen crown. Tentative, she was not. The metal of his ring was cool where it grazed him. Thank the gods, her touch was gentle. He could handle himself for a time if she kept to this pace.

Aye, but then she didn't keep the pace.

And she was good. Talented. A natural. Born to pleasure him. Sucking, but not too hard. Kissing, teasing bites striking him like lightning. Using her fingers, her closed fist. Her hair a shroud, the silky ends dancing across his tender skin. Tongue, teeth merely a caress.

What had she read in those bloody French books?

He couldn't stop it. Her. Him. Mind racing out into the night, he plunged his fingers into her hair, guiding her. More, deeper. Ah, *there*. Her mouth stroking just so, imitating the act. His breath and body struggled for relief, the ground falling away until he floated on a wave of ecstasy.

Why had nothing been this amazing before? This perfect?

"*Leannan*," he whispered, ragged caution threading his speech. He shifted, the chair rocking beneath him. "I'm close. I can't... if you don't want... maybe you should stop now."

She laughed, her exhalation washing over him. Her confidence was entrancing. "When I said I wanted to taste you, I meant I wanted to taste everything. I'm not frightened of what's happening. At heart, I'm a scientist. Testing all parts of the process." She traced her fingernail down his shaft, and his sight dimmed. "Although you can beg now if you'd like."

"I won't," he whispered, repeating her vow from the night before.

But he would have—and they both knew it.

Smiling, she returned to her task, her steady focus shattering him into a thousand pieces seconds later. His release swelled from the area where she knelt to encompass his entire being. Every sense, every inch of him. His fingertips, his toes, his earlobes. Blood pounding in his ears, his heartbeat scattered. Hips lifting, lifting, thighs tensing.

The rest of the encounter was a blur.

Desire wrapped in sensation wrapped in bliss. His groans echoing off aged stone. Her hands, her mouth, *aye*, her glorious lips tormenting him beyond measure. *Advantageous* torment this time. His release was prolonged by her persistence, even as he pleaded. But she didn't stop sucking his cock until he was wrung like a wet rag, sitting upright in the chair a proper test of his endurance.

A disturbance in the kitchen sounded. Voices, laughter, a stool sliding across the floor. Dash recognized Pippa and Macauley, teasing and giggling. He had a good idea what they'd been doing. Activity leading them to search for an after-lovemaking snack.

Without explaining, panic streaking through him, his mind an absolute scramble, he grasped Theo's hand, yanked her up, and hauled her across the room. Shoved her into a closet hardly big enough to fit one person, much less two.

Bodies pressed from hip to chest, a narrow band of light swimming across them, Theo murmured into his shoulder, "What are we doing?" Her question was layered with glee.

Dash yanked his hand through his hair, banging his elbow on the wall. His body had not found its normal rhythm yet. "*Fookin'* hiding in me own house, with me own wife. I dinnae ken. I failed to recall I can touch you anytime I want and you me. New rules, this marriage venture." Dipping his head, he sank his nose into her hair, and breathed past his mad heartbeat. She smelled of lavender and the faintest hint of woodsmoke—sweet scents when this naughty chit had almost killed him.

She bounced on her toes, finding his lips with hers. "Did you like it? I used what I read and added some of my own inventiveness."

Dash cradled her jaw, tilting her gaze to his in the meager light. "I'm swayin' where I stand, woman. My brogue thick as syrup you've got me so worked up. I canna feel my fingers. Do you ken? Your cunning trick to hold at the end, until the wee end, and not let me go." He shrugged, astounded by her mastery of a brand-new skill. "I've nae experienced the like."

She trembled in his arms, the first clue that she was similarly affected. "It was the most..." She sighed faintly, rubbing her cheek on his chest. "You were..."

"I was gone for you, lass. Out of me mind gone."

"I loved it," she murmured dreamily. "I can't wait to do it again. Where you went there at the end, it was thrilling. Breathtaking.

Crude, but in the best way. No words in any book in any language can match the real thing."

His body vibrated like a plucked guitar string. What damned luck to marry a woman who liked doing *that*. Who wasn't offended by raw, feral passion. She found it *breathtaking* that'd he nearly lost his mind, dangling by a thread in a rickety chair in his scullery.

He could have her whenever he wanted, whenever she wanted.

Dizzy with longing, he brought her into the sheltering curve of his body, marveling at the fit.

"How long are we hiding?"

Dash grinned, his heart as weightless as a wee feather. "Until my knees quit shaking, lass. Until my knees quit shaking."

Chapter Eleven

If you step back from the gaming table, the grander picture often presents itself.

    Dashiell M. Campbell, *Proper Etiquette for Deception*

The next day, Theo began to see the rest of her life spilling out before her. Although it could have been the mug of ale she sipped, giving her a heady feeling and such fanciful illusions.

Surrounded by children, townsfolk, and a salty sting from the nearby crumbling cliffs and sandy beaches of the Suffolk coast, her future seemed secure. On a stable path with a scoundrel most considered out of her league in looks, he out of hers in station. A destination she'd not realized was possible with a man who was coming to fascinate her more than he should.

Across the crowded churchyard, Dash laughed at something Macauley said, the ever-present dice in his hand, a graceful rotation around his fingers. His skin was sun-kissed from his ride this morning, a subtle glow gracing the high sweep of his cheekbones. His clothing was casual as was his stance. His expression typically unreadable. Cool elegance. A knight among mere soldiers. A young woman in a flowing crimson frock stumbled over a tree root as she passed him, lost to his beauty.

Theo understood her predicament.

Because as she stood there, staring through a haze of woodsmoke, harmonies from the trio of musicians situated beneath a soaring elm flowing past, everything ceased to exist but *him*. As if Theo viewed the scene through one of the Earl of Stanford's telescopes, narrow but with extreme focus. The scar on her husband's chin, his slim fingers, curls formed from the damp air hitting his jaw. Those striking indigo eyes.

And the rest.

Theo expelled a hint of agitation, her body catching fire at the remembrance.

What she'd done to him in the scullery, his fervent reaction, the raw beauty of his release, would never leave her. Never. Her grand design to remain friends, to retain a measure of independence, to separate marriage from her ambitions and his, hadn't taken into account the intimacy of pleasure.

The tenderness, the familiarity. The primal want. Untidy, slightly embarrassing, and *oh*, so enticing.

She'd been remiss and foolish to ignore these elements, but she'd not known. The sounds he'd made when his orgasm claimed him, his thighs quivering, his head tossed back in rapture, weren't images an illustration could suitably bring forth. His hips lifting from the chair, fingers tangled in her hair. The encounter had been explosive, arousing them both to a fever pitch. Making her crave the next lesson.

So potent was her lust that she'd considered dragging him from the breakfast room this morning and into the closest salon housing a lock on the door.

When they'd yet to be naked and fully engaged in sexual congress as he was giving her time to adapt. The vision of him sliding inside her terrified her and conversely sent streamers of fire racing along her skin. She'd slept the previous night burrowed against his body, his arms tight about her. This, too, more profound than she'd anticipated. Listening to Dash's breathing, recording the rise and fall of his chest, marking the freckles on his cheeks in the muted moonlight, were uncommon delights. Sunlight and wonder as they woke in the same bed, unsure of next steps. How far to go, how much to share.

It pleased her, or at least reduced the pain of his sordid reputation, that he seemed unsure, too.

This morning's next step had been lingering kisses and roving hands before being interrupted with a knock on the door from a maid unaware of the correct procedure for newlyweds: to leave them alone.

A wish, her husband and no one else in the world, circling her mind for days.

There was danger in such raptness, precisely the sentiment she wanted to avoid.

Theo nibbled on her braid, her chest tight. Her heart didn't need to belong to Dashiell Campbell for her to be happy. Nor did her body, though it seemed to be racing to his side.

The question was, how to keep a part of herself *for* herself? And, subsequently, keep him?

Theo was forced from her musing when a gap-toothed girl of seven or so tugged on her skirt, reminding her of her promise to read the children *Cinderella*. The light would be gone before long as would the opportunity. She'd brought the Grimm brother's book in the event the chance arose.

If she wanted to be a teacher, she must begin to teach.

If his wife didn't stop staring at him with a half-starved gaze, Dash was going to haul her behind the nearest pine and tup her soundly against it. Her hair ribbon was burning a hole in his trouser pocket, a silly spot of whimsy utterly unlike him. A reminder, *aye, hell,* of every wicked thing they'd done in the scullery.

To date, the fieriest ten minutes of his existence.

Her lips wrapped around him and hanging on for bloody *life*.

Or maybe it was like him, the far-fetched gesture with her ribbon. The man he'd have grown into had he not been raised in a brothel—

the workhouse, scheming, surviving, always alone, always running—could have been a tender lad indeed. A bloke who'd let himself fall in love without five hundred shades of fear riding along beside it.

But, why? Except for his family of pining misfits, no one in society adored their wife. It was unheard of and not in any shape or form required. The difference was, he noted as Theo gathered a group of dancing tots around her, dropping to the ground without a care for her gown or her status, he respected her. Admired her. Envied her brilliance and her compassion.

He cared. Desired. *Liked*.

Dammit, he wasn't going to love. He stuck to his promises and the deals he made—to others and himself. He and Theo had an arrangement, and he meant to abide by it to the letter.

If she was more of a hellion than he'd imagined, climbing the oak tree outside her bedchamber this morning to retrieve Mr. Darcy, scraping her wrist and ripping a hole in her stockings in the process, that was merely part of the gorgeous burden of Theo Campbell. If her talent in the bedchamber was turning out to be keener than anticipated, more the winner him. If his heart skipped, just a tad, when she waltzed into a room, he *fookin'* couldn't help it.

Grumbling beneath his breath, he left the remaining Leighton Cluster—the Duke of Leighton and Tobias Streeter and family had returned to London—and headed in the direction of the village vicar.

The gent was stooped, drab gray hair a jumble about his head, his gaze biting. Luckily, Dash was acquainted with being unjustly evaluated and knew exactly how to handle tetchy old men.

"Vicar," Dash said and took up a relaxed stance by the dessert table. Selecting a slice of rum cake, he bit into it with relish, the syrupy flavor rolling down his throat. It was damned tasty.

"Campbell," the vicar returned, his steely gaze focused on Theo and the excited children circling her. His lips tightened when she showed a flash of ankle while reaching to open her book. Judgmental bugger.

Dash struggled to ignore what seeing his wife with a ginger-haired lass perched on her lap was doing to his insides. A melting sensation similar to the gooey mixture in the cake he held. He and Theo would be working on a similar project of their own soon. And surprise of surprises, Dash *wanted* children.

He chewed, waiting for the perfect moment. It was often a feeling when one chose to toss the dice. "I noticed the church roof is in a state of disrepair. New pews wouldn't be remiss, either."

The vicar came alive in his tedious way. His shoulders rising, half a foot shorter than Dash's impressive height at full stance, but it was a reaction at least. "I didn't realize you'd attended service."

Dash swallowed, licked his lips, and reached for another slice. He needed to get this bloody recipe. Could Theo cook? He'd no idea. Probably not something society chits were supposed to do, dawdling in the kitchen like a servant. He'd ask Mrs. Irving about it. "My responsibility now in a manner, innit? The baron I acquired Southgate from assisted in repairs and the like, I'm guessing. I've seen notes in his study. Village roads, church, school."

The vicar shot a furious breath through his nostrils. "*Stole* the property, you mean. Your brand of trade, isn't it? Lord Jackley was an upstanding citizen, Southgate in his family for generations. Your reputation, *her* reputation, frankly, which is equally disgraceful from what's swirling about, aren't welcome here."

Aye, so that's the way of it. Dash appreciated the haughty bastard getting to the meat of the message so quickly. He chewed slowly, letting his temper cool. If not for the pristine white dog collar circling the man's neck, Dash would have tossed him into the dirt for his snide comment about Theo. As it was, he was going to make this man of God pay in a manner worse than being placed on the rack and stretched until your bones popped.

He was going to unleash Theodosia Astley Campbell in all her scholarly splendor.

"Laddie," Dash said, knocking a spot of mud from his boot, "I'll have my solicitor, one of the three I employ, send funds for the roof and the pews next week, wrapped tidy as a bow. I'm happy to contribute to the well-being of the community. Families I plan to live amongst for years to come." Not that this horse's arse would know it, but he'd funded repairs of this kind in Limehouse and Shoreditch many times over.

"No strings are attached to the offering, is that what you're proposing? You? Owner of the most infamous gaming hell in London?"

Dash swallowed a laugh. Wiped his lips roughly with his fist. Gamesters always attached strings. "Point of fact, there is a modest favor you can do for me. To keep the business channels open for future needs you may have. An addition to the vicar's cottage is a grand idea now that I think on it. In the spring, we could meet again to discuss."

The vicar swayed back on his heels, his hands going behind his back and clasping, a meditative pose Dash bet the man employed every Sunday. And the world thought *he* was a charlatan. "Go on."

Dash poured a concoction smelling of orange juice and the faintest trace of liquor in a chipped glass. "My wife, Mrs. Theodosia Campbell, would like to teach."

The vicar's arms loosened from behind his back and spilled wide in fury. "We *have* an educator. Mr. Crumkins attended Cambridge for one term, I'll have you know. He's well versed in every subject a rural community demands. This is not London, Mr. Campbell. These are children of tenants who don't typically have more than a year or two of schooling available to them before they move to work on their land. Girls generally have no schooling, as you might imagine."

Dash didn't wish to tell the vicar what he imagined. Or thought should occur. As life wasn't fair, and he understood that as well as any. "Point him out," Dash murmured and sipped the foul mixture, "this Mr. Crumkins."

The vicar sighed but did as requested. The man he indicated leaned heavily on his cane as well as the side of the church's portico. A head of shockingly silver hair flowed past his jaw, his face overwhelmed by crags and wrinkles. He appeared to be nearly eighty years old and in danger of expiring before the festival.

"Cambridge?" Dash snorted. "When? The dark ages?"

The vicar turned to him, cheeks firing, his coat flapping about his bony hips. "I overheard Mrs. Campbell telling a young mother, Mrs. Stuart, her husband is Bury's cobbler so they are quite decent people, that women should be able to *vote*! That they'll have no voice in Parliament until they do."

Dash shrugged, thinking the drink was the horrid brew the *ton* called ratafia. "Well, they won't. You can't argue with her. Good luck, if you feel you must."

The vicar sputtered, his voice cracking. "Who in England, in the universe, thinks women should have a *voice?*"

Dash wished for a pair of dice but thought that might be dragging in the spotty pieces of his reputation. "Let's move to the negotiations, shall we? I have a wife in need of a vocation, no matter how unusual that is. *She's* unusual." Exceptional, he would say but that bit was his and his alone. "You have a village in need of funds. And children"—he gestured to Theo and the joyful group surrounding her—"who will benefit from her knowledge. Why not work every angle? I admit this when most days I almost wish it weren't so, but Mrs. Campbell is the brightest candle on the mantel. Her intellect is too vast to be wasted on normal female pursuits, watercolors and stitching and the like. Have her teach history to the older students. She has a volume on economics as big as her arm. Say you have a need in that subject."

The vicar shrunk inside himself, shoulders slumping, chin dipping to his chest. "Economics? Holy mercy, she's a radical. And her husband, the sensible partner in the relationship, is offering the clergy a bribe."

Dash howled, unable to contain it. Ratafia hopped from the glass to his fingers. "*Aye*, vicar, but only if you refuse to call it a donation."

Dash tucked his slumbering wife against his chest and climbed Southgate's grand stairway, a sprawling flight Tobias Streeter had told him was Georgian in design. It was beautiful, this house, and he was coming to adore it. Too, having a woman in residence was creating instantaneous change. Vases of daffodils in the entranceway, banister and railings gleaming, the scent of beeswax stinging his nose. Theo was taking the servants in hand, kindly but with sure confidence, in a way he hadn't known how to do.

He chuckled, pressing the sound into her mass of curls so as not to wake her. Who at the Paisley Workhouse for Conditional Improvement would have guessed the boy they knew as Malcom Campbell would someday own a house of Georgian design? Have two dukes, a viscount, and an earl as fast friends. Claim the most formidable smugglers in London as partners. Hold interests in distillation and shipping enterprises.

The biggest boon? Wed to a gorgeous, clever bit of baggage.

Dash halted at the top of the staircase and gazed down at her. Her lashes were delicate slashes against her creamy skin. Her lips parted with shallow breaths. He placed a kiss there, harmless but full of meaning. She was light as a clothing bundle in his arms, and he was hard-pressed to deny the protective impulses marching through him. Like a brother's. Dash frowned, his eyes dropping to the plump curve of her breast.

Exhaling, he continued down the corridor. *Not* like a brother.

He'd decided this evening while watching her with the village children, emotions he wasn't up to receiving knocking on his heart's door, that he'd protect this against-all-odds celestial occurrence, his marriage, with his life should it come to it.

He wanted the union; he wanted the woman. Case closed.

He nudged her bedchamber door open with the tip of his boot. Pulled the counterpane free and placed her gently on the bed. Allowing for breathing room, he unbuttoned her gown to the waist, rolled her back over, and tucked the coverlet around her. She woke, her lids fluttering, reaching for his hand before he could rise.

"I'm going to teach," she whispered into the hushed night.

Perching on the mattress, Dash slipped a lock of hair behind her ear. Teased a soft breath free as he traced a Celtic knot, similar in design to his, on her earlobe. "I heard the vicar ask for your assistance. It's a bonnie plan. You'll be quite the scholar, what you've always wanted."

"Bonnie, indeed." Laughing, delighted, she hiccupped at the end of it. "Let's talk about how you got that tattoo. I've never asked."

"Let's not." Rising, Dash crossed the room, coming back with a rubbish bin, which he placed by the bed. "If you feel unwell, lass, use this. I'll put a glass of water on the side table. Take my advice and drink it. I've impressive experience in such matters."

She hiccupped again, her smile crooked. "It was only a wee"—she held her fingers an inch apart—"dram meant to celebrate my teaching position."

He pulled the coverlet to her chin, sneaking his hand away when she tried to touch him. She had a look about her, one he knew led down dangerous paths. He wasn't tupping her for the first time with her mind muddled from brandy even if his cock was stiff as a candlestick from holding her close, her sweet scent clinging to his skin even now. She'd roused briefly in the carriage and kissed the air from his lungs. "You and Pippa finished the entire flask. Macauley had to carry her back as well. Singing that lewd song as their carriage rolled away. Adding another individual in this family to the vicar's unsuitable list."

Theo rolled toward him, cushioning her cheek on her hand. Her yawn was robust and indelicate. He wanted her mouth on him again. Soon. "Stay here." She jerked her shoulder to the other bedchamber. "Not there."

He kissed her brow, trailed his knuckle over each eyelid until she closed them. "I'm not going anywhere, *leannan.*"

The words reverberated through him, meaning more than she knew. More than he liked. More than he'd anticipated. Every second he was with her drawing him into what felt like a loving trap.

Bloody blasted hell.

Chapter Twelve

The longer the hand plays out, the trickier the game is to secure.
Dashiell M. Campbell, *Proper Etiquette for Deception*

Her husband was a very heavy sleeper.

He was lying on his stomach in the middle of the tester bed, arms wrapped around a pillow, the silk sheet bunched low, exposing the roped muscles of his back. There was a nasty scar below his ribs that, when the time was right, she planned to ask him about. She'd learned during her short tenure as his wife that Dash answered questions more readily if approached with caution. Like a stray dog, you couldn't creep up on him. He was leagues from the bookmaking crook he presented to the world, his impenetrable expression sheltering a rare and delicate vulnerability.

There was a boy behind his eyes, his laughter occasionally catching the man by surprise. Realizations that broke her heart. How someone could be beautiful *and* tender astonished her. Generous, kind. She had a sneaking suspicion her husband had worked his crafty magic with the sour village vicar, arranging for a teaching position she had no intention of refusing. His compassion was unexpected.

In her experience, beautiful people were callous creatures.

Her raging desire to unleash his secrets and find the man beneath wouldn't surprise anyone who knew her. She'd always been labeled as more inquisitive a chit than any situation called for.

Theo sighed and gave her shoulders a scrub with the linen rag. Bringing it to her nose, she sniffed. Definitely honeysuckle. She'd woken to the biting scent of brandy and realized with a start that the aroma was coming from *her*. Now, submerged in the chamber's massive copper tub, she splashed to no avail. Whistled. Even talked to Dash about the shoots of gold lighting the dawn horizon, the undeniable charm of the home he'd acquired for himself. For her.

He wasn't waking, dead to the world. Had not stirred as his staff carried in the tub and enough steaming pails to fill it. While she'd lingered by the bed, the protective spouse, even going so far as to lower the velvet drapes to shield him from view. She couldn't blame the maids who glanced his way with flushed cheeks and giggling titters. This spot of theater was part and parcel of being wed to such a handsome scoundrel. Everyone wanted a taste.

She feared her existence was going to be centered on safeguarding him from the reach of grasping women. Watching his back and hers.

Theo drew her finger through a bubble on the surface of the water. *Illusion is the first of all pleasures,* Voltaire had famously said. This portrait —woman lounging in bath awaiting husband's ravishment—fit that depiction. She wanted to give Dash more than he'd ever been given. With his "one-nighters" as he'd called them. Not significant, he'd also claimed, these ladies with experience she didn't have. Bold creatures with knowing gazes and welcoming bodies.

Theo could only hope that sharing the pieces they'd agree they *could* share would bring her to the forefront and erase the others. Those connections had been shallow while theirs was miles deep.

She didn't realize she had a competitive spirit until Dash walked her down a medieval chapel aisle and gave her his name. Claimed her with his sensual touch, his cautious smiles, his keen wit. From this feast, she was left wanting him for herself. Not love, perhaps, but *desire*. She needed him to feel as covetous as she did.

Wasn't that a reasonable wish?

Rising from the bath, she hopped from the tub, hurriedly wrapped a towel around her body, and raced across the room. A gust from the open window danced over her damp skin, making her shiver. Reaching his side, she let a rivulet of water running down her arm drop to his cheek. Another and another, until he roused, scrubbing his hand across his face, grumbling.

Giggling, she dashed back to the tub. Rising to his forearm, he yanked his hand through his hair, disoriented. Theo splashed for effect, sang a little ditty appropriate for bathing.

He glanced over his shoulder. "Why am I wet?"

Theo shrugged, her body lifting above the water to show the sloping rise of her breasts. He sat up straighter, exhaling softly. He liked her breasts. She'd seen him eyeing them many, many times. Even before their marriage.

He licked his lips, his chest hitching. "Is this an invitation, *leannan?*"

She skimmed the washcloth over her collarbone and down her body, her gaze fixed on him. She didn't know what to say, bewildered action her solution.

How did one go about seducing one's husband?

"*Aye*, then it is," he murmured and rose from the bed.

He removed his clothing across the short distance. His trousers hit the Axminster carpet, his shirt landing in the puddle she'd created while prancing about. Leaving him in thin cotton drawers. Gazing at the evidence of his arousal, her body lit from the inside out, nothing to do with the warm water. Anticipation a quiver between her thighs, a vibration in her chest, her fingertips. The expression on his face was lethal.

Halting by the tub, he stepped from his drawers, and tossed them aside.

A rush of air shot between her teeth. *Oh, my.*

She'd never seen her husband completely naked. Any man naked.

Her toes curled, fingers clenching around the linen rag. He had a classically sculpted form, the ideal balance of muscle and bone with a delicious scattering of hair on his arms and legs. Lean, yet not. Strapping, but not too. Dark skin. Swarthy, if she'd been asked to define it. An aristocrat's bearing with the torrid gaze of a swindler and the body of an athlete.

And the rest of him...

Her heart dropped. His shaft rigid and leaning at a slight angle to the left, a glorious, mysterious piece of him she wondered how she'd accept into her body.

Even with her study, he didn't hesitate, climbing into the tub at the opposite end from where she sat. Stunning her, he dunked beneath the surface and came up sputtering, swinging his sodden hair from his eyes. Water leaped over the curled rim and hit the floor with a splash. Laughing, he crooked his index finger—*come here*. When she didn't immediately comply—this wasn't duplicity on her part but astonishment that her plan was working—he reached beneath the rippling waves for her ankle and dragged her the short distance to him. Waves lapped over the sides as he circled her waist and brought her to his lap. Astride as she would ride a horse.

Where she found him hard and ready as he captured her lips in a searing kiss that foretold every filthy thing they'd not yet said to each other.

It was an encounter that traveled past the phase of discovery. This was a meeting of lovers, secure in their shared passion, no unwillingness between them. Eagerness, excitement, and longing, yes, but not reluctance. His fingers tweaked her nipple, his hand sliding into her hair, and slanting her head for the deepest kiss of her life. His breath, staggered and sharp, rushed into her throat. She cradled his unshaven jaw in her palms and hung on for the ride, his body tense as a spring beneath her. The air choked with their ragged sighs and the sound of rippling water. Grasping the edge of the tub, she wiggled atop him, searching for relief, her thighs burning, blood racing through her veins.

Dear heaven, where was bliss hiding? She ground against him, searching.

Catching her under her bottom, he rose in a burst, scattering droplets. "I'm sorry, but I'm done with lessons, lass. I want the test. Wrap your wee legs about my waist."

She would have laughed had he let her. But with a fearsome glance, he reclaimed her mouth, reclaimed *her*. Carrying her to the bed, he dropped her to the mattress, and crawled atop her, the sheets clinging to her damp skin.

Both naked for the first time, they gazed at each other, recording the moment. His eyes flooded, pupils expanding into blue as he stared. Whatever he felt, whatever he was thinking, was taking him from her. Clasping him by the nape of the neck, she brought him back, brought him *in*. Wanting his weight, his passion, his fury.

Wanting him.

Sighing, he acquiesced, enfolding her in his arms.

Kissing, petting, stroking. Leisurely to fevered. A skirmish, an onslaught, twisting the bedding into a jumble as they made proper use of the space. There was too much sensation for her to highlight one element. A thousand shards of paradise laid out before her. His hands were everywhere, pressing, smoothing, stroking, pinching. She mirrored his enthusiasm, her teeth nipping his jaw, his shoulder. Nails digging into his back, his biceps. Circling his nipple with her tongue, watching it harden as he growled. Urging him to go faster, do *more*, begging with her bowed body, whispered moans in his ear, harsh promises traced on his skin. It was mindless, feral, and quite the closest she'd ever felt to the animals she'd read about in her biology texts.

With a tattered moan ringing in his throat, Dash left her, moving down her body, slick skin making it an easy journey. Branding each part of her he touched. Roughly capturing her breasts, he ringed her nipples with his lips, his teeth grazing the aroused nubs until she whimpered, her delight echoing off archaic stone. She caught his head in her hands, fingers twisting in his hair, guiding him lower.

He laughed, his wonder washing across her belly. "*Leannan*, I didnae ken this about you. Your appetite for this, for me. Had I known"—he bit her hip, then soothed the spot with his tongue, his fingers drawing delicious designs on her inner thigh—"I would have taken you during the writing of me book. Every damned day in your brother's study. On his fancy desk, in that chair that creaked until I thought I would tumble out of it. He would've had to club me to keep me away from you. Climb up that tree into your bedchamber, *aye*, I would have. Any night you asked it of me if I'd known."

She started to tell him she'd not known, either. If she had, she would've knocked down doors to get to *him* despite her brother's wrath. But her husband was occupied, having moved lower, settling between her legs, spreading the folds of her sex, doing as she'd asked—even as she had no inkling what she'd asked for.

Her emotions were a perplexing jumble.

Discomfiture that Dash was seeing her, *really* seeing her. Intense yearning combined with a dangerous longing for knowledge, her Achilles heel. Despite her concern about what she looked like from such an intimate vantage point, she wanted his lips moving over the center of her, his fingers parting her, fondling, stroking. His tongue following, licking into her. Sucking the sensitive nub at the top of her sex into his mouth.

It became a heady mix of sensation too volatile to track. Moist heat, his fingers thrusting, his arm underneath her, lifting her to his mouth. His whiskers abrading her tender skin. Their sounds of pleasure swirling about the chamber. This act excited him as much as it enthralled her. A windy whisper from the window trailing across their bodies. Silver pinpoints exploded behind her lids as her body arched, bumping him.

"That's it, lass, let go."

"I want..." She gasped, fingers clenching in the sheet, nearly yanking it from the bed. "I want this with you."

"Ah, Theo darling," he whispered in such a fond tone she opened her eyes to find him with his chin propped in the curve of her thigh, his eyes as blue as she'd ever seen them. The color of midnight skies and mystery. He stroked his fingers inside her, his thumb sweeping over her aroused knot of skin. "You can come again, *leannan*, with me buried inside you. Three times even. It's men who require time to recover."

She closed her eyes rather than say, *please, then, finish*. When he knew. She was exposed in a way she'd never been. Familiarity she would worry about tomorrow.

For now, she was his.

She cried out as he bent his head, returning to his task. Diving back in. He made up for the pause, bringing her to a mindless existence in seconds. His hands full, a bounty. The edgy sensation started at her toes and swept her body, taking everything with it. Reason, rationale, breath. Her legs locked around his shoulders, clutching, keeping the piercing buzz within, struggling to contain it. Yet, he wouldn't let her hide from herself or him. The suggestions he whispered into her skin, into *her*, erotic and decadent. Lewd notions she secretly yearned to hear and never thought she would. Fantasies published to the night as clearly as the learnings in his book.

There was no stopping him and no denying her. Together, they forged ahead, finding each unexpected similarity, each shared longing.

Her body bowed, coming off the mattress as she shattered, pulsing around his fingers, his tongue. Her release wrecking her, perhaps ruinous when she found the strength to pick up the pieces. The swells surged and rolled, rippling madness. There wasn't enough oxygen in the room, in England, for her lungs in that second.

"Hell's teeth, lass, you'll bring the house down with your cries," he said and crawled up her body. Before he dropped his weight atop her, he made a sweeping gaze to her toes and back, his throat clicking as he swallowed. "*Aye*, you bring me to my knees you're such a wonder."

Then he kissed her as the last remains of her orgasm pulsed. Used her moment of reckoning, softening, to work his shaft inside her. Deliberate, a measured glide as her body opened, admitting him. His tenderness extended to the bedchamber. A pinch of pain, his lips at her ear murmuring assurances she didn't need. His hand cupped her breast, swept low to cradle her waist. Inviting her to join him in an age-old rhythm.

Sexual congress felt extraordinary. Strange. Glorious. She was dazed by the discovery. Dazed by the woman she became, the wife. Dash filled her, his body *filled* her. Words on the page had prepared her when nothing could prepare her.

No libidinous drawing could compare to *this*.

When he could go no farther, touching hip to hip, he rested his brow on hers with a winded puff. The muscles beneath her fingertips quivered as he shuddered. "I'm not going to last long, *leannan*. I'll try, but I want you so bloody—"

To halt his words, Theo whispered what she wanted him to do, let it roll into the dawning morning. A raw phrase she'd heard on the docks on one of the few occasions Helena had let her visit the shipping warehouse.

It was the right thing to say if she wanted her husband to fragment like a vase around her. Become a raging storm atop her, their bodies slapping, the chamber ringing with their efforts. An erotic symphony of gratification. His hand reaching to grasp the headrail, shaking the bed with their fury.

It was the wrong thing to say if she wanted him to last the morning.

But he was a competitive lover, a man who liked to win, she couldn't forget. His hand traveled between her legs, his fingers doing brilliant things his cock couldn't.

She couldn't outlast both.

They arrived together, or close to it. The kisses to contain their shouts of ecstasy frenzied, questing hands exploring each other as tremors raced along muscle and slick skin. She lost herself and marveled that he seemed the same. When Theo had never imagined she had the wiles to tempt any man in this manner, much less one as experienced and skillful as Dash Campbell.

Gasping, he braced his forearms on the mattress, holding himself off her enough to let a whisper of air slide between them. His head dropped to the curve between her neck and shoulder. "Where did you... learn that term, lass?"

She wove her fingers into the damp strands at his temple. "The docks. Limehouse."

"*Christ*," he whispered, the pronouncement streaking into her ear.

They lay like dazed survivors from the scene of an accident for long minutes until she wondered if he'd fallen asleep and feared she was about to do the same.

Exhaling raggedly, he traced his fingertip down her arm.

"Remember when I told you I'd make you forget what day it was? Ah, *leannan*, my mind is blown to this very fact."

"Saturday," she murmured with a smile.

He lifted his head to catch her gaze, dashed a bead of sweat trailing down his jaw away with his shoulder. He'd never looked more beautiful, his skin glowing, his eyes alight. "I dinnae think they held school on Saturdays."

She rose to brush her lips over his. "This teacher does."

Chapter Thirteen

Fear is not a capable companion for a career gambler.
Dashiell M. Campbell, *Proper Etiquette for Deception*

Dash crept along the darkened corridor, his arms loaded with enough food and drink to carry them through the night, praying he wouldn't run into any of his guests. Only Xander Macauley, Pippa, and their children were still in residence at Southgate, he believed. The rest of the Leighton Cluster had returned to London to manage business affairs and busy lives. Something he must soon do as well. He had a literary discussion at a baron of ill repute's Regent Square terrace in two weeks. Furthermore, the gaming hell couldn't run forever without him.

Or maybe it could now that they'd hired a new factotum. Maybe it could.

He and Theo had spied from the bedchamber window as Tobias Streeter, Hildy, and their brood departed in the early afternoon. Dash would have gone down to wish him a safe trip, but his wife had been standing behind him, her arms around his waist, her hand stroking a governing part of his body.

Suffice it to say, he'd not said a damn thing to anyone except her all day.

He crossed to the east wing of the second floor, closing in on the bedchamber they'd torn apart in their pursuits. Mr. Darcy wound in and out of his legs, nearly tripping him. He drew a narrow breath, preparing to see Theo in some guileless pose that shook his heart. That crooked smile and tooth melting his resistance like sunlight to frost. This day had been wrapped up in things he hadn't known he wanted. Add to that, his house was beginning to smell like *home*. Lived in. Fragrances of linseed oil and beeswax, the faint aroma of Theo's soap lingering beneath. Or perhaps her scent was merely adhering to his clothing. He couldn't take a breath without her reaching in to tap areas he'd closed off long ago. The niche he'd carved out for her one she wasn't going to stay neatly tucked in like a good little wife.

Despite her stubbornness or because of it, he wanted her frantically.

Mind, body, and soul.

It was the first time desire and fondness had waged a battle inside him. Always before, he'd been able to separate need from anything resembling affection. Theo, with a deceptively clever touch, was leading him down a path he'd not traveled. He didn't think she was even trying. He'd whispered something shocking in Gaelic as he thrust inside her the second time, a forbidden sentiment never uttered in *any* bed in Scotland, England, or Wales.

He glowered and shifted the bundle in his arms. However, he'd never come inside a woman, risking a wee bairn, either. Maybe three times in that intimate a manner in a short period of time was enough to jumble a man's brain. His back was stinging even now from her nails.

His cheeks fired as he halted at the door to her bedchamber. *Fookin' hell*, was he blushing?

He bumped his forehead to oak, hoping to restore his sanity. Wondering where he'd put his dice before this foolhardiness began.

This was not a love match—and the woman in question, the bloody *wife*, agreed. The Gambling God was deceiving no one. No thievery, no cons. Hearts on silver platters like the rest of his idiot family was not part of the settlement.

Nevertheless, Theo cared. A novel experience for him. She asked questions. She wanted to *talk*. He'd escaped for provisions not only because her stomach had been growling but because he could see the queries lingering in her mind. Not since his mother or Nanna had anyone wanted to know what he was *thinking*. Why, why, why—when he didn't *know* why. Not about any of it. She'd be disappointed as hell by his answers.

He understood her, though. She'd examine him like a piece in a grand puzzle if he let her, reworking the arrangement into a tidy whole. Even as this scared the life from him, her concern warmed his soul.

Unfortunately, there were enduring issues. She didn't trust him. The doubt in those lake-blue eyes wasn't well hidden. No practiced gambler, his wee wife. If he was smart about this wager, he'd let her distrust rule. Let it push her away enough for them to breathe.

As it was, he wanted to heal it like the paper cut on her thumb. Banish any uncertainty until—

He stumbled back as the door opened, and Theo peeked outside. Her flaxen hair was flowing over her shoulders—he'd brushed the curling locks into submission a mere hour ago—her skin radiant from lovemaking. She was wearing his shirt, unbuttoned past her breasts, the hemmed edge topping out mid-thigh. He'd been left with a dressing gown he didn't even particularly like.

There he was, his heart dropping at the sight of her. What was *wrong* with him?

She grinned, an expression that had grown more perceptive with each encounter. "I could hear you out here, ruminating."

Mr. Darcy darted between his legs and into the room.

Dash followed the feline, recorded his wife's plump bottom shifting beneath rumpled cotton as he closed the door, and leaned against it. "Ruminating."

She glanced over her shoulder, her delight expanding until it nearly filled his chest. What did she know that he hadn't told her? God, he hoped it wasn't everything. "Musing. Pondering."

He nodded, adding the word to his list. "*Aye*, I see."

She did, too, which spelled doom.

Theo strolled to a makeshift sitting area she'd created before the hearth. The counterpane from the bed spread in a neat square, two glasses from the sideboard in his bedchamber's miniature parlor sitting on a silver tray he'd never seen in his life. A set of tasseled pillows resting against the settee leg for no reason he could discern. Southgate had treasure upon treasure he'd yet to discover, another family's heirlooms now his. It was sad, but a fact of life. He hadn't rolled the baron's dice or wagered away his birthright. The man had ruined his legacy quite effortlessly on his own.

Theo went to her knee, then her bum, flashing all kinds of superb bits, easy as you please before him. Chewing on a strand of hair, she grabbed a quill lying atop a pad of paper and scribbled a note. "I'm planning lessons for my students." Then she glanced at him with the loveliest smile, making everything he'd promised that foul vicar worth it. He'd build the man a new *church* if it meant making his wife this happy.

She tilted her head, nodding to his supplies. "Are you coming in? I'm starving."

He coughed beneath his breath, shaking himself free of his reverie. "*Aye*, that I am."

He settled on the coverlet, observing with amusement as she fussed with the foodstuff he'd pilfered from his pantry as if they sat in a royal box. Rye bread, a local Suffolk cheddar, ham from his own stock, a bottle of Bordeaux he'd opened downstairs. She doled out the items on two mismatched plates he'd found in the servant's quarters as he had no notion where the quality dishware resided. For a lass raised in Shoreditch, a rookery district not unlike the putrid Glasgow township where he'd grown up, she was polished as a teapot. She'd taken to the Duchess Society's society lessons like a natural. More a lady than a scruffy scoundrel like him deserved.

She handed him his plate, her gaze sly. She had a mark on her neck from his teeth, he realized with giddy pleasure. "What are you smirking about, Dash Campbell?"

He dropped to his side and perched his cheek on his fist, putting the plate before him. He gestured with a slice of cheese to the room. "Can't a lad be happy with what's occurred here today? Thrilled, in fact. Overjoyed. Exhausted."

"Three times," she whispered, her cheeks firing a rosy, adorable hue. "I can hardly believe it. *Three*."

His heart stuttered. Had he forgotten himself in his enchantment? "Was it too much?" The last time, he'd bent her over the settee, rough play, indeed. Although it had been *her* idea. *Dash, I saw an interesting picture in a book at the emporium...*

"Lass, you must tell me these things, else how will I know?"

She shook her head, her attention fixed on her food. Her lips tipped at the edges. "It was perfect."

Perfect. Hmm... he'd never heard that word used in this context. Perfect worked fine for him.

The hearth fire was warm at his back, his belly being tended to, his body subsisting in a glorious state of gratification. As he lay there thinking how magnificent life was, his wife went to her tummy, stretching her slender legs out behind her, and wiggling her feet. A pose he'd not seen a female perform since he was a child. Munching on a slice of bread, her gaze sliced over him like droplets of summer rain.

"Deliveries will be arriving from Hatchards next week. Textbooks for my students. Many of them don't own even one. I made a list of titles to review with the vicar. Even if I'm not instructing the younger children, they should have access to a modest library."

Dash chewed, washing down the slightly stale bread with wine. "He'll be elated, I have no doubt. Name it after the Campbells, this archive of manuscripts. Make sure you discuss women getting the vote. Don't forget to review that critical topic."

She hung her chin on her palm, her smile edging into wonder. "You don't like him."

Reaching, he took a golden strand and wound it around his finger. "He's what we Scots call a criticaster. A meek judge of life."

She mouthed the unfamiliar word.

"Ah, ha!" He smirked and gave her hair a tug. "One I'm able to share this time."

Her smile dimmed, a fierce light coming into her eyes. "Did the vicar insult you? I won't have it if he did. Schooling or no. I don't care what he thinks of me as long as he allows me to educate his students. I'm used to the affronts. Women live amongst them like tigers in a jungle. But I won't allow him to talk poorly about you."

Dash let her hair drift from his fingers, his gaze smacking the ceiling, the floor, anywhere but her radiant face. It had been years since anyone, aside from Xander Macauley, had sought to protect him. His wee slip of a wife offering comfort was almost more than he could bear. "He thinks what the rest of London thinks, *leannan*. There's nothing special about the man, even with the gods on his side. Never you fear, I'll kick his arse from here to Glasgow should he say one unkind word about you."

Theo made it worse, adding touch to her ferocious expression. Placing her hand directly over the open V of his dressing gown, directly atop his heart. Branding him from the inside out. "There is something special about this one."

He was up on his feet, crossing to the window, before another breath passed between them. Panic weakening his knees, his heart drumming in his ears. The sky was dark velvet punctured by a wealth of stars rarely displayed in the city. He raised the window, letting the chill dance across his fevered skin.

She stepped behind him, his courageous lass, arms circling his waist. Unlike the earlier erotic embrace, this one carried far more dangerous intent. "You can't run every time I get close, Dash. That isn't the friendship we'd hoped to build. My life is open to you, wide open, though you know much of it already. I know my past isn't as frightening as yours." She trailed her fingers over the scar on his back without asking, when it was clear she wanted to know *everything*.

Shoulders slumping, he gripped the window ledge to keep his hands off her. "You can read what I've written, I won't hold you from it. There are folios, twenty or so. Easier than speaking. I have to return to London in two weeks for a reading at Lord Raines. I'll bring them back. I've been considering gathering them into something... whole. A book, a different one this time. Like you've been nagging me about for months now. Southgate is a fine place to work, innit?"

"London," she said, the word slipping through silk to scorch his skin. "Raines."

He turned in the circle of her arms, recognizing her uncertainty. The baron was a degenerate of the worst caliber, but Dash had no intention of conversing with the man outside the reading in his salon. "You'll go with me. Right by my side." If she thought he was reverting to his old ways, the mad races at dawn, the grasping women, the tomfoolery, he'd have to earn her trust with his sincere efforts to be a better man. He knew he could do it with her waiting for him each night, her smile gliding across the sheets each morning. He wasn't letting Theo Campbell slip through his grasp, not in this lifetime.

She snuggled against him, cheek finding the spot on his chest that still burned from her teeth, her nails. "I can't. Not if I'm teaching. My students will need consistent instruction to make progress. Once they're following a stable lesson plan, I can leave for short visits and find ways to check in." Her fingers tensed, digging into his hip. "You see, Bury is where I'd like to live. I don't enjoy the city. I'm realizing how the air reeks now that I've had the chance to be relieved of it. The scent of coal smoke not clinging to my hair and layered upon my skin is glorious. And... I'm odd, Dash, not welcome as you are, despite my brother's influence. Nothing I can do, beyond hiding myself completely, is going to please them. I no longer have the desire to try."

"You've made that worse, lass, by marrying me. Pushed yourself further afield."

She lifted her head, capturing his gaze, her expression wondrous. "Oh, no, darling Dash, you've given me *freedom*. I'm going to discover who I am in a fascinating home I'm coming to love. I won't be a duke's sister or a rookery urchin. I'll be your wife, with the means to challenge society for the first time. If I want to write about women's rights, I'm going to do it. In addition to finding a tutor somewhere in England who will work with a woman on advanced maths. Economics. Latin. I'll attack the barriers until I break down at least one of them. The Gambling God's wife will know no bounds. I plan to give the *ton* exactly what they expect. Scandalous inattention."

He leaned against the window ledge, stunned, *darling* ringing in his ears. Her clever expression was what he should write about in his next book, *The Feminine Art of Swindling*. She had grander plans than even he'd envisioned. "You've been thinking about this."

"I have. For days, while you slumbered like a babe next to me."

Yawning the instant sleep was mentioned, Dash dipped his lips into her hair, breathing in her bonnie fragrance. "As much as I'd love to talk until dawn, lass, I'm about to drop. You've worn me to the studs with your wifely pursuits."

Giggling, she took his hand and drew him toward the bed. He followed blindly, unable to recall a time when he'd held someone's hand. Never? Helplessly, his fingers tightened around hers. It was surprisingly intimate for such a trifling thing.

"No more lessons today, Mr. Campbell, is that what you're saying?"

He tumbled to the mattress when they reached it, face-down, a spill. "Nae more until morning unless you want to bury your new husband," he murmured into the pillow.

Climbing in beside him, she tucked the sheet around his waist and shoulders. With a drowsy sigh, he looped his arm over her waist and pulled her in as close as he could get her. He didn't understand society's inclination to sleep in separate chambers. That was not occurring in this union.

"Ride with me... in the morning," he whispered as fatigue claimed him.

She gave a little wiggle he would have liked to exploit if he'd had an ounce of strength left. "Dash, I don't know how. I'll slow you down."

"Teach you. I don't mind slow. My mum loved to ride."

Then Dashiell Malcom Campbell fell asleep, having shared a memory of his mother for the first time in twenty years.

Chapter Fourteen

Even the experienced wagerer tends to ignore his strategy in a familiar gaming den.

    Dashiell M. Campbell, *Proper Etiquette for Deception*

The pungent odor of despair lingered in the dank halls of the workhouse. Sunlight struggled to pierce the grimy glass panes, damp sliding through the cracks. The chill was unrelenting. There was no comfort, no sense of home, nothing to keep a soul going.

With Dash's words sounding in her mind, Theo grasped her mare's reins, following the path he led through the frost-encrusted meadow. His descriptions of a dismal childhood and his struggle to survive were a needle prick to her heart. The morning after his promise to share his past, he'd presented her with two folios.

She'd been a captive reader since.

Captive to many things in the two weeks marking the most joyous of her life. And the most troubling.

By day, he wrote and she taught. Her group of students in the village, and one young man with high hopes of attending Cambridge she tutored in the estate's vacant coach house, where she was creating a library of sorts. She'd accepted her role as mistress of Southgate, supervising the staff while Dash coordinated necessary repairs and directed restoration of the church's roof. The arrival of new pews—which Theo suspected was a condition of her employment—marking a small celebration in Bury.

By night, they played.

Explored their bodies and their desires. A French text with extremely descriptive sketches had arrived by post last week. They had a game, a roll of the dice determining the page—the position—they tried. Some were silly, ending with them tumbling from a chair or the bed, while others were... incredible. She'd never expected lovemaking to be fun, for Dash to gaze down at her with mirth and a fierce expression of ardor on his face. Experiments in pleasure, her theories about herself proven or refuted. Last night—

Theo groaned and tilted her head into the wind to cool her skin. The scent from burning hearths reached out to sting her senses.

Last night, he'd tucked his shaft between her cupped breasts and stimulated himself in a manner she'd never envisaged. Arousing her to weak-kneed delight in the process. She giggled into her gloved fist, embarrassed and elated. What a strange creature intimacy was. Forcing the revelation of oneself in decidedly shocking ways. They'd been in his study, a chamber she'd finally convinced Dash was his to work in, a right he'd more than earned to own, when she'd started teasing him. A tender kiss leading to a rougher one, wandering hands, whispered suggestions, their passion igniting like dry tinder. The door had a lock and a plush rug she suspected was Aubusson. They'd utilized both.

Their staff had learned a lesson about newlyweds. Knock first.

Theo studied her husband as he directed his sleek bay through a shallow puddle on the bridle path, his back straight, broad body rising from the saddle with a knight's command. Long fingers tangled in the leads, the other hand steadied on his thigh, at ease. She'd seen no rider with such elegance, even at the Derby. And his intellect was as impressive as his talent on horseback. His wit hidden to most, displayed when he needed it, and never when he didn't. Unlike most men, he didn't possess the loudest voice in a parlor. Dash was secure to sit back and watch while charming them all.

Of course, he *was* the finest looking scoundrel she or any other woman drawing breath had ever seen. She didn't discount how his handsomeness helped, although beauty was also a burden. Often, it was the only thing people noticed about him.

She plodded along, having found comfort in the saddle in the days he'd been teaching her. Rides at dawn across land that was *hers*. So many realizations swamping her of late.

Sighing, she bumped her fist to her chest, trying to dislodge the sensation.

This was love. Fundamental, splendid, unstoppable *love*.

Despite her stupid plans, she'd fallen and fallen hard.

Something she'd promised she wouldn't do. Promised herself, promised Dash. She'd been reckless to share with not only Pippa, but poor Helena, her silly proposal. Now she understood why they'd both stared at her with subdued expressions of amusement. *Foolish girl.*

Of course, she was going to tumble for Dashiell Campbell, he of talented hands and sharp mind. Beautiful smile and generous heart. If she were honest with herself, which she hadn't been before this second, she'd likely fallen when they'd worked on his blasted book. Now, *Proper Etiquette for Deception* was taking him away from her. Tomorrow morning, he returned to the temptations of Town. A literary reading at Lord Raines' home, a man lugging around an even fouler reputation than her husband.

She could go with him; Dash had asked her to. Protect him from the avaricious society chits, an endeavor in direct opposition to her dreams. The village teaching position wasn't much, but it was a start.

It came down to trust.

She could trust him, couldn't she? Twisting the reins in her hand, she shifted, unsettling her mount. She wanted to trust him. She wanted to tell him she loved him, but the words were sealed in her heart under lock and key. Someday. Someday soon. He might be angry, displeased that she'd broken the agreement. Or...

His gaze frequently sparked with a remnant of emotion buried deep. The way he whispered *leannan* in her ear before he claimed her body. In the darkness of their bedchamber, he woke from nightmares and pulled her near. Unconscious gestures of faith and affection as he sought comfort. Even if he went back to his shocking ways, he'd never have this connection with another woman.

This may have to be enough.

As if he heard her musings, Dash twisted in the saddle. He mistook her expression, whatever it revealed, or maybe he didn't. Grinning, he tapped the horse's flank and sent the beast into a gallop, racing around a majestic elm in the western field, tossing up bits of mud and grass before leaping a hedge on his return. Leaning over his bay's neck as he reined in beside her, the horse prancing when the man would have liked to, Dash sent her a devastating smile.

She shook her head, secretly pleased by his display. As if they were in a ballroom, and he'd made a gallant gesture before leading her into a waltz. She was unused to anyone seeking to impress her. "You're a braggart, Dash Campbell."

He scrubbed his fist across his jaw, his smile growing. "*Aye*, a wee show for my lady wife. Seeing as I am the finest horseman in Suffolk, I have no qualms admitting."

"I'll be leaping hedges soon myself." She said this to incite.

He yanked on the reins hard enough to have his horse side-stepping. "Nae, you won't, lass."

She angled her mare next to him. "Whyever not?"

He sighed, shooting her a surly side-glance. "We've discussed this, Theodosia."

Her horse whinnied, and she released her death grip on the rein. Dash only used her full name when he was vexed, so she returned the gesture. "I'm getting better every day, Dashiell."

"You've bonnie form for a chit new to the saddle. You'll be a grand rider soon enough. But riding astride *and* jumping hedges? Over my deceased body."

As a surprise, he'd had a seamstress in the village create a habit that allowed her to ride astride, since he believed that was the safest method. He'd also managed to miraculously acquire a pair of Hoby boots in her size. Theo swept her hand down the fitted crimson jacket, the covertly divided skirt. The ensemble was outrageous, and she loved it. "How will you know what I do while you're gone? I'm going to keep riding."

When they entered the stable yard, he reined in his mount with a jerking motion. Unhooking his boot from the stirrup, he dropped to the dirt. Cursing, he stroked the horse's neck, his gaze furious when it hit her. "Are you trying to make me angry, *leannan*? On my last day home?"

Home. They were both coming to think of Southgate as such.

Petulant, she was hoping to make him angry. Force a discussion about what they could and could not do while separated. She wanted his pledge, but she couldn't find the mettle to ask for it.

When she moved to slide from the saddle, he threw up his hand. *Wait.* Then he was there, at her side, foot tapping impatiently but his manner caring as always. He caught her in his arms on the way down, his mouth seizing hers. *Oh,* could the man kiss. She loved the temperamental ones, his fury rolling through her to land at her feet. Slowing, he grazed his tongue over her tooth, something he did so often she'd finally asked him about it.

He liked that crook, liked *her*, damn him.

While she *loved* him—not part of their deal. When did life follow the plan you set, anyway? She must have been insane to imagine it would.

Shoving him away, she dusted her hands down her jacket, willing away this feeling of anguish. She could be happy without him. She could.

He shifted from boot to boot, patted his pocket, seeking the security of his dice. Yanked his hand through his hair, knocking his hat off in the process. "I'm going to miss you, too," he said, reaching down to snatch his hat from the ground. Grumbled, in fact, clearly not comfortable admitting it.

"What does missing each other have to do with my riding while you're cavorting around London?"

"Insolent baggage. Stubborn chit." Murmuring things it was better she didn't hear, he grasped the reins, leading his horse into the stable's main building and expecting her to follow blindly with hers. Dawn was breaking, and the stable master hadn't arrived, so they were set to rub down their mounts on their own.

They worked in silence, she in one stall, he in the next. Brush, rub, pat. The repetitive motions calming her ire as she formulated an apology. Theo wasn't skilled at them, and her husband was even worse. Why did women always have to go first? The only sounds in the small space were the horse's panting snorts and the crackle of straw beneath their boots.

Until another noise broke the morning quiet. A ragged moan, a shift from the storage garret. Theo caught Dash's gaze over the stall's dividing wall. Then they looked up at the same time.

Another moan, a bump, a shift. Straw drifting from the cracks above like snowflakes.

Her lips parted, breath leaking out. Was it? Could it be?

Dash was in her enclosure in seconds, his arm coming around her from behind to cover her mouth. "Shh," he whispered in her ear.

The sounds were unmistakable, especially with her newfound knowledge.

Coupling sounded like coupling, no matter the pair instigating it.

She and Dash stilled, frozen, listening. Frenzied groans and ardent murmurs, creaking wood. Bumping bodies. Theo knew it was improper, but was it wrong? Did it make her an immoral person if hearing another couple having sexual congress was heating her up like her husband had touched his wick to her tinder? He was similarly affected, his rigid shaft jammed against her lower back.

We should go, she thought, but she didn't move. *Leave them to it.* It was likely servants, maybe the handsome groom Dash had hired last week. She'd noticed the scullery maids eyeing him with ravenous stares. He was a sight.

This deduction did nothing to shake her from her reverie.

Dash made the decision for her, locating a delicate spot on her neck, his teeth sinking in. He knew she *loved* this. In truth, he'd placed so many marks there at her direction that she'd started wearing higher collars. Leaving his hand over her mouth, his restraint exciting her, he walked her forward, into the stable wall. They'd be sheltered if anyone should come upon them in the dim corner. Or sheltered enough.

He whispered two words in her ear. "Quiet. Fast."

Complying, her hands went to the rough wood to brace her body as his tunneled beneath her divided skirt. A design that not only made riding astride easier. He gathered the material at her waist, silently destroyed the slit in her drawers, and dipped his finger inside, stroking, finding her wet and ready. Embarrassingly so, as she was unable to hide her reaction to what was happening above them.

Their difference in height was ideal for this endeavor, a theory they'd proven multiple times. Working his close, he shifted to the balls of his feet, and angled her body into position. She could see his wide-legged stance in her mind, the spellbound expression on his face.

His entrance was fast, hard, and exactly what she needed. What she wanted.

She bit the fingers pressed to her lips, the heels of her hands scraping the wall, the coarse grain abrading her skin. Hips tilted, she steadied for his thrusts, his weight pressing into her. A slow glide increasing with their excitement, as rapid a pace as they could quietly manage.

It was the ultimate challenge, the effort to remain silent provoking her to a point of delirium, another couple's cries of pleasure taking over where theirs could not. Again, Dash lifted on his toes, sinking into her, hitting the *exact* spot essential to shoving her over the edge. He thrust as bright flashes exploded behind her lids, the power of her orgasm catching her by surprise. Sensing her release, he trailed his hand from her hip to her breast, pinching her nipple through layers, sparking another round of tremors that rocked her so violently she had to prop her brow on the wall.

The hand over her mouth tightened as her moan shot out, moistening his skin. "Shh," he repeated, his voice shattered.

She'd never experienced pleasure without sound. Been held transfixed long enough to record the stages Dash went through on his way to release. Not in this detailed a study. The muscles in his arms stiffening, his hips straining, his shaft twitching at the base. A flood of heat, dampness, and shudders as he lost control. Two bodies in motion, working to arrive at the same place at the same time. Their scent overpowered the aroma of horses, hay, earth. Frantic, he slanted her head toward him, their lips meeting in a rough half kiss as redeeming as a benediction.

When it was over, he held himself inside her, not moving, his breath scalding her cheek, her neck. For a tense moment, Theo wondered if they were going to be found out by a couple stumbling from a stable loft, also hoping not to be discovered. Swearing beneath his breath, Dash grabbed her hand, yanked her down the aisle, and into the dawning morning. They rounded the stable, entering a lean-to structure on the yard's boundary in a burst.

"Did I hurt ye?" he asked, his brogue twisting his words in a way she found utterly endearing. A tell that happened often. *After*. Charmingly undone, his chest heaving in a frenzied cadence, his hair a catastrophe. He'd lost his hat in the stable.

Knees giving way, Theo slid to the ground. Instead of answering him, she began to laugh, stunned, shaky, gasping snorts. A chilled rush of air raced between her legs and into her gaping drawers, cooling her fevered skin. *Brilliant*. She would have ripped her jacket and chemise off, exposing her aching breasts to the morning cool if she could have.

"Dammit, Theo," he whispered and hung his head, releasing the groan he'd been holding inside to save them from being detected. "I'm sorry. I lost control. Those carnal noises coming from the loft and your eyes burning through me when you heard them." Back to the wall, he went down, legs sprawling out before him. He'd not buttoned his trouser close. She thought to tell him but didn't have the heart. "I long for you. Madly, desperately. One twitch of your pinkie, and I'm consumed. Every secret I have right there for you to see, a gambler's disgrace. I dinnae have another way to phrase it more skillfully for you if I could. I mislaid my meaning somewhere." Dazed, he glanced around. "I think I lost my hat."

She stretched out her leg, knocking his boot with hers. "I crave your madness, your desperation. Your blind need. This was..." She licked her lips, struggling to put her feelings into words when words weren't enough. When her body was melting, rolling across the ground toward him even now. "I never dreamed anyone could desire me this much. Or that I could experience such yearning for another human being. We're well matched, Dashiell Malcom Campbell. This salient truth you should never question. Apologies for our shared obsessions aren't required. I'm your wife, *take me*. As often as we'd like. As forcefully as we'd like."

She left off the list that she'd never dreamed she would love anyone this much.

Although she knew, she *knew*.

He glanced up, her world reflected in his eyes. "I'll be back in a fortnight, no more. Maybe ten days if I can reschedule a few appointments at the distillery. Keep the bed warm for me, *leannan*."

"I'll be here, waiting for you," she said, having no idea their reunion wouldn't come that easily.

Chapter Fifteen

Admitting you know the rules of the game means you must follow them.

    Dashiell M. Campbell, *Proper Etiquette for Deception*

Sullen, Dash yanked his watch from his waistcoat pocket, tilting it into a thin slice of moonlight to catch the time. He'd been without Theo for somewhere in the region of four days, five hours, and eleven minutes. Missing her was similar to phantom pain. He'd read about the phenomenon in an article in the *Gazette* on soldiers who returned from war with a lost limb but still felt its presence. An aching wound. Ceaseless torment.

He'd suspected from the start that love, if this was the malady he was suffering from, was going to drive him to his knees. If he gave in to his feelings, he would join the ranks of the vulnerable lovesick. He grinned despite his angst.

They should change the name. The Leighton Lovesicks. Damned if it didn't fit.

The orchestra was playing a waltz when he didn't know how to waltz. The clamor of voices, shouts, and the occasional crash of a flute shattering upon marble drifted to him through the veranda's open doors. The merriment in the ballroom wasn't interesting to him in the least. He wondered if it ever would be again. He'd discussed *Proper Etiquette for Deception*, done the dance required by the baron to entertain his guests, sold two boxes of books, talked up the new distillery and the gaming hell, but now he wanted *out*. He'd escaped to the terrace when he felt his temper brewing after a dowager duchess made a veiled comment about audacious wives. His new status—wed to the willful, bookish sister of a duke—was the most fascinating thing about the party.

More the pity, them.

He wanted to go home. To his audacious wife. To his *fookin'* cat and his *fookin'* dog. He wanted to sleep on sheets smelling of lavender, of Theo.

He wanted happiness and lovemaking and acceptance.

An image of taking Theo in the stable roared through him. Pelvis pressed to her buttocks, cock buried deep inside her tight channel. Her hands palming the wall and rocking with enough force to shake it. Another couple's aroused cries drilling into him while he struggled to contain his own. His fingers over her mouth—*aye*, he'd almost exploded when she'd bitten him—keeping her whimpers locked inside her throat. His lips at her neck, her nipple budding beneath his fingertips.

That messy partial kiss as he came harder than he'd come in his life.

His cock hard as stone from the memory, Dash calmed his body with a glass of brandy and his mind with a pair of dice. Theo was right about a great many concerns. The air in London was overpowering with the stench of coal smoke, and the days were too prescribed. Wrapped in a standard little box, tight confines. He'd lain in bed the previous night, unable to sleep, listening to the midnight carousers stumbling down Bruton Street. Men with a title and a future, each and every one of them. A phaeton resting at the curb waiting to be over-turned on the next block. Posh nobs with a thousand burdens they were running from.

While Dash believed he was running toward the complications. His whispered endearment in Gaelic at a key moment was a clue. At first, those initial days after the wedding, he'd wanted to hold on to the past while holding on to *her*. Not fair to Theo, that wager, but he was a born con. An effort to protect his freedom, a blessed state that made a man feel absurdly formidable despite his shortcomings.

In control, when one wasn't truly in control.

Dash rolled the dice on the low brick wall. Four and three, a combination that could be very fortunate indeed. Maybe his luck, his *personal*, hidden-in-his-heart luck, was changing. For all his success, this area of his life had been ill-fated from the start. Family and love. Pieces he was coming to see mattered more than any other.

The supple footfall behind him was too light a tread to be one of his friends. He exhaled wearily before turning. Some chit he didn't want to deal with had tracked him down. It was his disgrace that there were a hundred it could be.

Julia Demarest, the widowed Countess Graves, stepped into the hushed space, her sly smile betraying a knowledge of him he wished he hadn't given her. Her gown, stunningly unremarkable, shimmered in the moonlight. "Mr. Campbell," she said in a breathless tone he imag-ined she'd practiced until it sliced through a man's reservations like a saber. "Fancy meeting you on a terrace on such a glorious evening."

He bowed his head the Scottish fraction, by his countrymen's design not as respectful a gesture as an Englishman's. "Lady Graves."

She motioned to the glistening lawn stretching a full city block. Lush, lavish wealth surrounding them. Comfort he no longer coveted. He had what he needed. "You've returned from the wilds of Suffolk, is that correct? I have a distant cousin there I've been meaning to visit. A charming village near the coast. Picturesque, I'm sure, and perhaps close to your estate. I've missed your colorful waistcoats, among other things."

Leaning his bum on the wall, Dash pocketed his dice. This conver-sation would begin his campaign to cut himself loose from the dock he'd anchored at for years. He'd realized it was coming. How long could it be before one of his former paramours, bloodthirsty chits the lot of them, knocked on his door in the wee hours, crawled up the domestics' stairs, and slipped beneath the covers of the bed he planned to share with Theo. He was ashamed to admit it had happened. More than once.

Laying the groundwork, this morning Dash had a brief conversation with his mortified butler about this no longer being acceptable. The resolution to station footmen at the back entrance and ground-floor windows because women sometimes chose those, too. Danvers, who was sixty if he was a day and had only taken the job with a dissolute gaming hell owner to secure his pension, had been surprised that his employer planned to honor his marriage vows. And equally surprised that he was being allowed to hire more footmen.

"I could find a reason to be in the vicinity of your estate next week, as a matter of fact. We had fun together, didn't we?"

Sipping slowly, Dash made no effort to touch the lady. The kindest rejection he could offer.

She was cunning, Countess Graves. Protective of her role. "So that's the way of it," she murmured. Taking his glass from his hand, she drained the contents. "The men in your group, the faction led by that temperamental duke, seem to fall impressively in love. I wonder why that is when it's not society's way? Frowned upon, actually. Roland, my husband, may he rest in peace, certainly never claimed to love me, nor I him."

Dash experienced a pinch of sympathy for her, but felt a larger measure of certainty for himself.

Taking his glass from her hand, he placed it atop the wall, signaling their time was concluded. "My friends seem to fall harder than most, that's true. I dinnae ken why that is. The sad bastards enjoy being in love, I guess." He wasn't giving this woman one word more on a topic he'd yet to discuss with his *wife*.

The countess leaned in to dust a departing kiss across his cheek. "Love? I never saw the point myself."

"Neither did I," he whispered when Lady Graves had moved out of earshot.

The sound of clapping arrived from a shadowy corner of the veranda. Dash swore soundly as the Earl of Stanford and his half-brother, Xander Macauley, strolled into view. They wore matching smiles of delight, their eyes the color of the blade jammed in his boot, the most unique hue in England. Their fraternal relationship had never been confirmed, since the deceased earl hadn't thought to acknowledge Macauley, but the twin gazes clearly tagged them as brothers.

Macauley passed him a tumbler when he reached him, and Dash gladly accepted. *Aye*, Streeter, Macauley, and Campbell whiskey was welcome upon his tongue. He couldn't wait to open the distillery in Shoreditch, only hoped he'd be able to do much of the work from Southgate. Theo might have ideas about ways to better market their goods. Signage and such. He'd discuss the project with her upon his return.

Macauley winked, his merriment evident. Why was he so bloody happy all the time? "You didn't sell many books tonight, mate. Not with that stern expression. Only two boxes when five or six is your normal dump."

The Earl of Stanford, who everyone in the family called Ollie, crossed to the wall and peered into the darkness, his gaze on the stars. A returning soldier once addicted to opium, he only partook of celestial temptations now. Indeed, Dash was shocked Macauley was drinking around his brother. He usually abstained in his presence. "Raines doesn't have a telescope. I asked during your recitation, I'm sorry to say. Too stupid to manage a scientific piece of equipment. Moronic nob."

Macauley settled in beside Dash. He'd only come to the event to keep tabs on the lads he'd taken under his wing. "Why didn't Theo come to London with you? Don't tell me there's trouble already. Pippa will have your hide if there is." Grimacing, he took a sip. "Please don't place that burden on my shoulders."

Dash shrugged, folding in on himself. "I secured her a position teaching in Bury. She has to stay with her students."

Ollie turned, significant news able to separate him from the night sky.

"Well, well," Macauley murmured into his closed fist. "You've gone and done it. I did the same, set Pippa up with an entire charitable enterprise. A gift when I was courting her, and I was blinded by emotion. It's taken on a life of its own, laddie. Teas twice a week with stale biddies seeking lost souls to place in their households. Grown beyond our visions, it has. Situated near fifty orphans so far. Madness, innit?"

Ollie turned back to the sky, the scar on his cheek he'd gotten protecting his brother from an attack emphasized in the moonlight. "Nessie works. Her enterprise is more successful than any I've entertained. Just this week, she received a note from a gardener at Carlton House requesting a visit regarding a disease plaguing elm trees." His wife, Necessity, the legendary female landscape architect, was more noteworthy than the entire Leighton Cluster combined. "Why not have Theo teach? It's what she's always wanted. If you marry a capable woman, you can't expect to hold her down. Or back. Plus, it gives her something to *do*. Women are less trouble if they have an occupation."

Macauley toasted his brother with his glass. "How wisely progressive of you, Ollie."

"Nothing's been the same since I married her," Dash found himself admitting, much to his seconds-later chagrin. The whiskey he tossed back in response to his blunder burned his throat.

"Isn't change the point, mate? What did you expect? Theo's a disrupter, always has been. Mouse-like about it, the quiet kind you can't turn your back on, but a radical. Gads, she'd have women in the House of Commons if it were up to her. I had to sit through a lecture about it over breakfast at Southgate. My eggs and toast tasted like ash going down."

Dash grunted, having no notion how to address such concerns or tame the woman.

Ollie turned, crossing his arms over his chest, playing earl of the manor. Dash assumed brotherly advice was coming. "The way to put this train back on the tracks, like those steam engines we're considering investing in, is simple. Have you told her?"

Dash shook his head. Not in English, he hadn't.

Ollie sighed, his gaze returning to the stars.

"Why do I have to go first?" Dash huffed out a tense breath, sounding a bit like a wee lass. "I *always* apologize before she does. Let her be the one to say it, then I'll cheerfully follow."

"Maybe she doesn't, mate. Nothing to say, that is. Gotta be lovable to be loved." Macauley swayed, and it was then that Dash realized his partner was foxed. "Have you *been* lovable? I can help you if you haven't. You don't *seem* lovable. Not this evening, anyway."

"I can handle my own charm offensive, thank ye. Ask the countess who trotted out here after me if I'm lovable."

"Charm offensive," Macauley repeated, his voice tinged with rapture. "You're a writer, lad, you are. Only risk to your sojourn is the countess's kiss journeying beyond this terrace and on to Suffolk."

The suggestion swept Dash like a fever.

Ollie snapped his fingers, bringing their attention to him. "Take his whisky, will you, Dash? He's only traveled down this rabbit hole because he had a quarrel with Pippa, and he finally understands I'm not going to take another drink in this lifetime."

Dash reached, attempting to grab Macauley's glass before the stubborn fool could sidestep the intervention.

Macauley laughed, dancing away, liquor splashing on the flagstones and his sleeve. "You're going to tell her first, I can picture it. You're going to *grovel*. After years of your taunting, chits parading in and out of the Devil's Lair, join the club, mate. Like a warm pond once you've plunged in. The Serpentine. It'll feel fine."

Dash bared his teeth. "Like you're going to grovel, guv. After you lose your dinner to the rubbish bin."

"Indeed, I might. Both are a man's prerogatives." He bowed, bumping into the wall before straightening himself. "As is my decision to stop for flowers for my vexed wife on my way home. An extravagant bouquet has been known to tame my female beast. She's grown particularly fond of lilies."

Lilies? Dash scoffed. How tiresome, how trite. He'd have thought Macauley would do better. Theo's birthday was coming up, and he'd purchased a veritable bounty of books to stock Southgate's coach house, her would-be library for the village. Theodosia Campbell had no use for blasted flowers.

But he'd secure her heart, if he wanted it, with books.

"Let yourself fall, Dash. That's my advice." Ollie tilted his head, squinting at the clouds. "It's really not painful. The anticipation was much worse than the tumble."

Dash patted the dice in his pocket, checking to make sure he had them. Talking about love made him anxious as hell. "My situation isn't the effortless view from a telescope, my lord. It's complicated. I wed the chit the *ton* is calling the Runaway Bride, remember? She stole a carriage and ended up with the scoundrel who owns it for a husband."

"You're no worse a bounder than the rest of us, excluding the dukes." Macauley snorted, his eyes glowing above the rim of his glass. "You think Ollie's wife is *easy*? Laddie, where have you been? Nessie Aspinwall isn't afraid to tell anyone what she thinks, prince to pauper. My brother had to charm, and I do mean charm, to get her to say yes. Yours said yes on the first attempt, pretty as you please."

Ollie smiled, adoration flowing over his face. "I don't want easy. I never have. I only want her. And this family. And the stars."

"Good, because you didn't get easy."

Ollie punched Macauley in the shoulder, bouncing him back two steps. "Neither did you."

Dash made a grab for Macauley's drink and got it this time. "Theo and I have a *rèiteach*. An agreement. We were clear from the start. She doesna want to own or be owned. And neither do I. This wasn't a love match if you recall."

"Agreement?" Macauley and Ollie asked in unison.

Although the agreement seemed ridiculous when he recalled them tangled up like fatigued cats in their massive medieval bed. And all the other places they'd not been able to keep their hands off each other. The unforgettable stable incident. The linen closet when it was raining too hard to ride that morning. The study that night they couldn't sleep. The back staircase after attending Pippa's impromptu game night, a bit of risk as they still had guests wandering about. The breakfast table the evening before because they'd made a bet on how sturdy a piece it was. The scullery. Who could forget the scullery and Theo on her gorgeous knees before him? *Aye*, and the coach house that balmy afternoon simply because they could.

He smiled a private smile. His plan to tup Theo in each of South-gate's rooms was proceeding nicely.

"We're friends," he murmured and peered into Macauley's glass. "We agreed. Absorption, and that's Theo's word, not mine, dinnae have to be a part of this union. Never is with society alliances. Countess Graves told me her husband didnae love her, and they were content. I suppose. Maybe. Although he died three years ago, and she continues to speak poorly of him." Dash shot a gust of frustration through his teeth and yanked his dice from his pocket. His cheeks were firing, and if Macauley said one word about it, he was taking him down right here on the baron's veranda. "Can't passion—insane, reck-less passion, the grandest of me life—be enough for you two? Must every damned moment be about *love?*"

Ollie braced his shoulder on a brick pillar, his expression absurdly solemn. "You didn't. Tell me you didn't agree to this friends insanity with your wife?"

Macauley sputtered, hilarity exploding across his face. He was even drunker than Dash had guessed. "*Ah*, mate, he did. Painted himself into the tightest corner of his bleeding life! He'll have to buy out London's supply of lilies. Amusing, innit?"

Ollie recrossed his arms over his chest, contemplating the dilemma like the scientist he thought himself to be beneath the earl business. "Books. For Theo, it's books, you coxcomb. Unless Dash can get her accepted into Cambridge. She'd tell a goat she loved him if that was the case."

Dash let the last drop of Macauley's whisky slide down his throat. "*Nae*, books are out for the grand deed. I have a veritable archive arriving for her birthday in two weeks."

"How about a tiara?" Macauley offered. "I have that jeweler I used to use down on..." His words trailed off, a tender smile etching his face. "You know, I can't recall where he was located. It's been so long. My darling Pippa doesn't care much for jewelry." He rested back against the wall, looking drowsy and content. "Love is a strange bird, innit?"

Dash settled beside him, cradling the glass against his chest. He tossed Macaulay's wallet that he'd filched for fun at his feet. "Back off. I'll tell her when I'm duin."

Macauley grinned and shrugged, having no idea what *duin* meant.

"Ready," he snapped. "When I'm bloody well and ready." *Aye*, hell, if he was slipping into Scots speech, his heart might truly be involved. They didn't know he'd let her read his most private thoughts. Those folios were treasures to him. Talk about serving up a man's heart on a platter.

Ollie and Macauley glanced at each other over his head, their doubt evident.

Except, Theo wasn't Pippa. She wasn't Nessie. She was her own lass, unique as they made them. His wife had a bonnie grasp on her emotions, a nearly masculine sense of rationality about her. Wise. Prudent. Sensible. The smartest soul in the parlor, any day of the week. Not a chit to cry over spilled tea, she wouldn't race in without thinking an issue through—and wouldn't respect him for doing that, either.

If feelings became a problem, he and Theo would discuss the problem.

Convinced, aside from the forlorn ache in his chest, Dash planned to work on getting his heart in line with his head.

The ping echoed through his bedchamber. Twice more before Dash shook himself from sleep. He shoved to his elbows, his heart sinking. Hadn't Danvers gotten the message? *No women.* His townhouse was off-limits. His shop closed. He would speak to Leighton about employing a squadron of his footmen, former soldiers set to pound a man into the bricks, but then he'd have to explain *why* he needed bruisers when the normal blokes should have sufficed.

That was a conversation with a brother about a sister that the husband wasn't having. Ever.

The noise rang out again. Dash glanced to the window, identifying the sound. A pebble hitting the glass pane. He hung his head, beaten. She was not the most inventive lass, this one. Theo would never resort to tossing stones at his window. Sucking his cock until he passed out, *aye*, begging him by means such as this, *nae*.

Growling, he yanked a rumpled shirt from the floor and shoved his arms in the sleeves. He wasn't sure where his trousers had landed. He needed a valet, according to Danvers. A proper gent to organize his rig and shaving utensils and such. It might be time as he had the blunt for a bevy of keepers, but his bedchamber was his only point of privacy in London. Because he had wealth, he was to allow another man in his space, to dress him and comb his hair? He already had a wife changing up his routine, scenting his sheets, and jamming flowers in odd containers all about the house. It appeared he was doomed and may as well throw in the towel on the rest.

Crossing to the window, he swore when he stepped on one of his dice. Tossing aside the drapery, he peered into the night. It was not even dawn, dammit. Squinting, he leaned in, knocking his forehead on the pane. What was Jasper Noble doing stalking about his garden, fog swirling around his ankles like he was a wee ghost?

Alarm bolted through him. Was someone in the Leighton Cluster in trouble?

Perhaps Macauley had encountered a spot of misfortune on his way home. The streets of London could be vicious, especially for a bloke with enemies and blunt. Or the Earl of Stanford, who wasn't much of a brawler even if he'd killed men in battle and looked like, with that wicked scar marring his face, he wasn't a laddie to mess with.

Dash didn't particularly like Jasper Noble, but he respected him. Which counted for a lot to a Scot. The scoundrel wouldn't have paid a visit for nothing.

Dash took the servant's stairs two at a time. Seconds later, he was traversing the twisting gravel path, in tender bare feet, no less, rounding the corner of a garden Necessity Aspinwall had gotten her hands on last year, sprucing it up until it looked better than most. Truthfully, better than he cared for it to look.

Jasper turned at the sound of his footfalls, thrusting a sheet of newsprint into Dash's hand before he could utter a word. The paper was slightly damp from being yanked off the press and ink smeared his palm. Dash grimaced and dropped the page to the ground. "What is this?"

"You could have taken the time to attire yourself properly, Campbell. One of those horrid tartan waistcoats you insist on wearing."

Reaching into his greatcoat, Jasper retrieved an etched silver flask. He had a scar to rival Ollie's that Dash hadn't noticed before trailing into his shirt collar. Yanking the cork from the decanter with his teeth, he pointed it at Dash rather like he would a weapon. "This is a favor, friend. Noble gestures, despite my name, I rarely make. Ask anyone. I wasn't able to keep the story out of print, too late for that, but it hasn't hit the mail carriages lining Fleet Street, either. Waiting to transport news out of the city on the postal routes. You'll have time to beat the telling of your misdeeds to Suffolk if you leave now." Repocketing his flask, his lips tilted in a loose smile befitting a notorious reprobate. "Maybe."

Startled, Dash went to his knee, smoothing the crumpled page over his thigh. Fog obscured the moon, their feet, their legs, making it too dark to read. "I canna see a word, Noble."

Jasper reached into his coat and came out with a small metal tin. He grinned and flipped the top open with his thumb. "Friction matches. Though these are technically Lucifers that I get in the states. South Carolina, specifically. The original design by that Walker fellow flamed out, if I may jest, as I was an early investor. Lost two hundred pounds on that venture." He flicked a wooden stick against a narrow length of sandpaper, producing a shimmering glow. "Read quickly, before this blisters my finger. Antimony sulfide and potassium chlorate only burn for about thirty seconds."

"Who *are* you, guv?" Dash asked, the stench of burnt sulfur filling his nostrils.

Jasper cupped his hand around the flickering blaze without comment.

Unbelievably, the light produced was enough to see the type. Jasper tapped his index finger to the correct column to speed Dash along.

There's an answer to the question regarding the ton's *sudden interest in gambling. Female interest to state it plainly. If one were to ask a certain countess about her brief rendezvous with a certain gaming hell owner following his literary reading at Lord Raine's, the reply might be shocking. Perhaps they were merely discussing his popular book but looks can be deceiving.*

Dash crumpled the newspaper in his fist and rocked back on his heels. "If Theo sees this—"

"She'll have you in front of an addlepated judge, citing this slip of gossip in her appeal for a divorce. Knowing her as I do, insolent chit, I imagine she'd enjoy becoming one of the first women in England to determine the course of her marriage." Jasper blew out the flame with a succinct puff. "It's one step closer to Cambridge in a manner of thinking, isn't it? Maybe the girl will get what she wants in some roundabout way."

Dash shoved to his feet, his mind spinning. That *fookin'* countess and her *fookin'* kisses. He stalked down the path, headed to his bedchamber, his coat, his blunt, his weapons, and his boots, calculating how swiftly he could flee the city. "How do ye have access to this information, Noble? Macauley and I have tried to infiltrate *The Times* without a shadow of success."

Jasper followed, feasibly enjoying the show. "If I tell you that, I'll have to kill you."

Dash eyed Jasper as he used blunt force to open the domestics' door. The wood swelled after a rainfall, the repair a task he'd been meaning to look into. He was handy, but Danvers would faint if Dash fixed it himself. Not something the elegant chap he was pretending to be should attempt. "Why do I suspect you're not jesting?"

"Let's settle on the theory that I have contacts who alert me when the Leighton Clan's names are going into print. Now that I'm an honorary member, mustn't I protect my tribe? Also, I'm inside *The Morning Post, The Morning Herald,* the *Chronicle.* Frankly, between us, every newspaper in town and many outside it. Fourteen in London alone at last count. That charming ditty about you and the actress last year, the brawl at the opera. I did enjoy that one. I could have stopped it, of course. But why should I redeem my precious markers for a man as busy as you, overturning carriages and tupping unsuitable women? Even with my resources, calling off the hounds twice a week was more than I could accomplish." With a sigh, he dropped the match to the ground, and stamped his boot over it. "Now that your book is selling in France better than baguettes, I'll have to access my contacts there. Only so long before they want a piece of you. They're still vexed about the Revolution."

"It's Cluster, Leighton Cluster. Why help me now?" Dash asked, climbing the stairs in the same mad rush in which he'd descended.

Jasper trailed along, his weary groan echoing down the corridor. "Because I saw the way you and Theo looked at each other the day of your wedding. If I had someone I felt that way about, I'd do anything in my power to protect her. If I was allowed to. Sometimes one is simply not allowed to."

"This recitation makes me think you have someone in that black past of yours, though I canna imagine it."

Jasper's gaze shuttered, letting in no light, letting out no light.

Dash glanced wildly about his bedchamber as he entered it, seeing one boot and a crumpled stocking beneath the settee. Where had he left his coat? His hat? "How many secrets do you have, guv? My God, I wonder. At least my deficiencies are there for everyone to see. In ink, blast it."

"Too many for me to keep up with." Jasper strolled into the room, taking inventory, his gaze keener than Dash was comfortable with. He circled the perimeter with the same vigilance as a police inspector Dash had tangled with in Glasgow. "My carriage is at the ready, Campbell. Horses fresh. I'm guessing you need to borrow it versus waiting an hour for your German impracticality to be prepared."

Dash located his trousers beneath the bed and did an awkward dance to pull them over his hips. "You're turning out to be a bonnie chum, Noble. When a man canna have too many able friends in this world."

Jasper chuckled, revealing naught in expression or word. "My heart is warmed to hear it."

"Do you employ a valet?" Dash yanked his hand through his hair, scrubbing his hand over his whiskered jaw. Arriving at Southgate disheveled but sincere was better than arriving late and sorry. If he didn't make it to Bury in time, nip this calamity in the bud, Theo was going to leave him. Simple as that. Move to the village, teach her classes, and adopt more cats. Another mutt to keep Wordsworth company. She read the morning newspapers religiously, including the absurd gossip columns, and she wasn't a lass to take his supposed betrayal lying down. Jasper was right. Divorce and the scandal attached, a happening she might like to experience. No one would be surprised by any of it.

He took a calming breath. It was one tiny newspaper to filch. How hard could that be for a man born to steal?

"Leighton will be next in line to murder me," he reminded Noble. "Someone needs to get to him as I'm headed for his sister."

"Xander Macauley is on the case. He was a witness to your lack of a scandal, or so he says. As for you, let's move before morning traffic starts invading the streets. Your unkemptness reduces the splendor, actually, when you possess more than any chap requires."

Dash wrestled into his boots, grabbed a pair of dice, and the wad of cash lying on his escritoire. "I have to tell her, even if I manage to sneak the story from beneath her nose. Word travels through servants quicker than by post."

Jasper snatched Dash's hat from the floor and slammed the door behind them as they took the stairs at a run. "One step at a time, Campbell. You're a husband in training, learning as you go. When you involve love in a contest, even for natural gamesters such as us, makes it tricky business."

Snatching his hat out of Jasper's hands, Dash jammed it on his head. "Who said anything about love?"

Why did every man in his godforsaken band of brothers speak about nothing else?

Jasper laughed uproariously and shoved him into the London night.

Chapter Sixteen

Don't judge your hand until every card has been dealt.
Dashiell M. Campbell, *Proper Etiquette for Deception*

Theo bit into her marmalade toast while checking the mantel clock, counting back time. She'd been without Dash for five days, two hours, and seven minutes. His promise to return in ten days, if he was able to rearrange meetings, seemed like the longest wait in eternity. His side of the bed was cold to the touch, and for the first time since moving to Bury, she'd had trouble sleeping. Waking during the night with a sudden remembrance that she had a husband.

And that her husband was gone.

Annoyed, she pushed a piece of sausage around on her plate. She had many activities to occupy her time. The instructor in the village, Mr. Crumkins, was delighted to have assistance, giving her another subject, geometry, to prepare lesson plans for. Additionally, Adam, the student headed to Cambridge if they were very lucky, was proving to be a joy. A motivated young man, respectful of her position and hungry for knowledge. Not only knowledge from textbooks, but about such topics as appropriate conversation and how to survive a tea party, conventions he'd not taken part in as a bricklayer's son. The Duchess Society had prepared her well enough to teach the basics.

She knew the rules, she simply didn't believe a girl always had to follow.

Theo flipped a page in Dash's folio and gave Wordsworth a scratch with her toe. The hound loved hiding beneath the breakfast table and possibly getting a slice of bacon for his effort. Theo giggled, the memory rushing through her.

The table was a piece she could attest was stronger than it looked. It had held two writhing bodies without a hint of complaint.

Returning to her reading with desire swirling through her belly, she traced her finger over his precise lines of script. *1811*, making Dash around thirteen years of age. The chapter described in candid detail the daily beatings, the lack of food, heat, basic necessities. The stink of unwashed bodies, the illness, and despair. The offers he'd received from older men, an undeniable fact of life for 'bonnie' boys. He'd turned them down, he'd written, resulting in more whippings. His desperation finally led him to befriend a gambler of some renown in Paisley and learn the trade. A trade he'd proven extremely adept at. So much so that his mentor had run him out of town two years later.

As promised, Dash had shipped a box of folios to her. She understood, or thought she did, that it was easier to let her read them when he wasn't in the room. Even better if he wasn't on the estate. Questions as they huddled under the counterpane would have been unavoidable. She wasn't sure he was ready for that level of interrogation.

Although his words, his memories, the grim accounts, the way his prose brought her into his world, astounded her. A gentle, kind-hearted man coming from such anguish was a miracle.

Theo sat back, resting her hand on her belly. It was early, only five weeks into her marriage, but she suspected she was pregnant. There'd been nausea some mornings and a near fainting spell yesterday in the coach house. One of the chambermaids proficient in these matters made mention of the possibility.

Her menses had not arrived, true, but it was only two weeks late.

Was it rare for a woman to get pregnant so quickly? With Pippa and Helena, it had taken more time than this. Hildy and Nessie, too. Perhaps they hadn't tried as often. Theo covered her mouth, her delight rolling between her fingers. Or as diligently.

Because she was delighted. She *wanted* this baby.

Dashiell Campbell's baby. With bluestocking Theodosia Astley.

She nibbled on toast and took a gulp of chamomile tea, running through his responses in her mind. What would Dash think when he found out? She rather imagined he'd be pleased. They'd discussed children, but without an expectation for such a prompt arrival. He was wonderful with the Leighton Cluster's brood. Patient, amused, generous, much as he was with her. He'd be an excellent father, giving everything he'd not been given.

Theo smiled and gave her teacup a tap against the saucer. A family. She might be starting her own family.

Mr. Darcy sidled into the room, shooting Wordsworth a derisive glance. Making his way to the window seat, he stretched out, issuing a purring sigh of satisfaction. The feline had settled into his new home with decided contentment. *Home.*

Theo released an edgy breath, trying to locate the source of her unease.

The issue was her inability to fully trust the man she'd married. She'd tried not to read the outrageous stories about him over the years, especially when they were working together, and she had to gaze across a desk at a veritable god in living form, imagining the women described in the latest on-dit stretched across his lap. Lying beneath him, doing the fantastic things he was now doing to her.

Love assaulted her from all sides. Jealousy. Greed. Dreadful, ordinary, expected, *acceptable* emotions.

How could she *not* worry? Was she enough to keep him? Her belly clenched as she imagined the trouble he could get into with more beautiful playthings, more interesting playthings. Skilled, sly, vapid creatures who'd snickered at her since the day she'd arrived in London.

What chance did a bookish scholar have to capture such a man's interest and *keep* it? Dash had unexpected depths when one looked closely, making him the most fascinating man of her acquaintance.

She hated—*no*, she shook her head, not hate—she disliked this weakness in herself. To be possessive of another human being, to need them to need you, and you alone, spelled disaster. Because Theo didn't think men generally had that brand of loyalty in them, not like women did. Xander Macauley, Tobias Streeter, her brother, the Duke of Leighton, of course, but they'd married for love. That Theo would demand it of a husband who'd never offered more than friendship, who'd been kind and decent and giving, seemed greedy on her part.

She was absolutely greedy where Dashiell Campbell was concerned.

And more than a little senseless.

However, she thought as she debated with herself, her budding love was her problem. Her distrust and the jealousy associated with it was her problem. He'd said he was leaving his wild ways behind, and she had to believe him. What choice did she have?

She'd about worked it out in her mind, in her meticulous way, when the morning edition of *The Times* was delivered to the breakfast table. Seven pence of entertainment. Crisp sheets, a new edition, not days old as was often the case. She'd made sure the arrivals would always be current when they were in residence. The scent of ink, an odor she loved, swirling about the room.

The gossip column wasn't her first choice. Theo took politics and crime over infidelity and slander any day. Despite the detailed reporting surrounding Scottish explorer Alexander Gordon Laing's travels across the Sahara, she made it to *About Town* in the middle of her second cup of tea. Startled, she jostled her drink, staining the tablecloth, and the cuff of her sleeve.

Perhaps they were merely discussing his popular book but looks can be deceiving.

Theo scrubbed her eyes as if this would wipe away the text flashing before them. She reread the veiled accusation, three sentences set to prove what a fool she'd been to believe him. Consider trusting him. Letting herself fall in bloody *love* with him, which she would, babe or no babe, make herself fall *out* of right... this... minute.

Theo shoved back her chair, where it rocked, nearly tumbling to the floor. Wordsworth howled, crawling into a dark corner while Mr. Darcy blinked and continued washing his belly. Unlike most wives who'd been given news in this manner, there were no tears, no wringing hands, only blind anger. She was going to smother Dash Campbell with his feather pillow. Pull that knife out of his over-polished boot and jab it in his gut. Twist one of his foul plaid waistcoats about his neck and squeeze the life from him.

Of all the—

After she had—

And he thought that she would, that he could—

Swearing like a sailor, Theo stalked from the breakfast parlor, a woman on a mission.

The staff scattered when they saw her coming, maids upstairs, footmen out the front door, scullery to the kitchen, leaving the trenchant Mrs. Irving, who thought little of her employer and was just now thinking less.

How could Theo forget? They all knew. Gossip traveled faster by mouth than print.

"Can the carriage be made ready for London? Now? This hour?"

Mrs. Irving sighed, her exceptionally ample bosom drooping with her weariness. Theo had overheard her say the day they'd arrived that she could not wait to take her pension and be gone from the rabble arriving daily in the once-charming Suffolk. "The coach house is habitable, Mrs. Campbell. Aside from the volumes taking up most of the main parlor now that you're turning it into a library of some kind, the bedchamber is quite comfortable. Quite delightful. We've kept the space in excellent condition, cleaned twice a week, the mattress beaten last month. Fully serviced for tea and light refreshment, as you already know from the, uh, *lessons* you've held there. The baron, my last employer, had a penchant for turmoil, not unlike your husband. His wives, all three of them, choosing to reside there at points in their marriage. I'll make sure a footman is close during the night for security."

Theo stilled, strategizing, listing the options in her mind.

She didn't want to return to London.

She was coming to love Bury and Southgate.

She had students.

She might be pregnant.

Finally, taking a note from the Bard, revenge would be best served if she stayed, not ran. Let Dash come to *her*. Then she'd sock him in the nose so hard, she'd knock him back to 1820. She'd not grown up in the stews without being taught how to throw a blasted punch. A knee to the groin wasn't out of the question, either. Not if he truly had kissed a countess!

"If I may be so bold, Mrs. Campbell, while you stand there looking like you're planning to commit murder, the baron never stared at anyone the way Mr. Campbell stares at you. From the moment you walk into the room, his gaze near pinning you to the floor. Besotted, if I were writing the tale. When I'm no wordsmith." She gave her apron a forceful yank, the chatelaine at her waist jangling. She had every key to every door on the estate tucked close. "Such an occurrence hasn't been seen around here in years, as not a one of the baron's wives mattered a whit to him, nor his staff, or his tenants. I wasn't sorry to see him go, only regretful it took so long for him to lose his inheritances. He tried for years, you see, to shake off all his family had taken two centuries to gain. Not your young buck's fault the baron wasted his promise. Finders keepers, am I right? The clever man wins the race."

Theo wheezed, reaching for her words. "But..." She gestured to the breakfast room and that damnable newspaper.

Mrs. Irving's lips tilted in what could possibly, if one were charitable, be considered a smile. "Not everything in print is the genuine article."

Theo swayed, stunned to her toes. "You *like* him. That persuasive oaf has charmed the most intractable housekeeper in England. Another woman falling into line. How does he do it?"

Mrs. Irving's mouth tipped full tilt, a smile, definitely a smile, gracing her wizened face. "Mr. Campbell reminds me of my grandson, Nigel, he does. Such keen wit wrapped in a dazzling package. Likewise, I've always been taken with a regal Scots accent, not one from the stews, mind you. His only slips into the gutter when you've vexed him, that I can see. Why, your young man helped me prepare blackberry preserves one morning while you were sleeping in. Said his dear, departed mum used to make the best apple butter in Scotland and claimed the making calmed him. A man with a kind heart deserves the chance to explain his misdeeds."

Theo's jaw worked, her throat dry as toast. "But..."

"Near to blinding a woman, he's so fetching. An obvious truth you knew going in. Mayhap he can't be held completely accountable. Can you imagine the unsuitable arrangements that come his weak way?"

Theo's temper moved through her body like the force of a wave crashing off the sea. She realized she wasn't enough to keep a man as *fetching* as her husband enthralled, but she didn't need her housekeeper highlighting this fact. "Mr. Campbell can't be held accountable for his transgressions because he's so handsome? Is that what you're telling me?"

Mrs. Irving lifted a fleshy shoulder in a truncated shrug. "Men will be men, dear. And most men don't look like him."

Theo exhaled, swallowed, smoothed her hand down her bodice. Counted to ten and back. Translated that filthy gossip sheet into Latin before she spoke. "I'll be moving into the coach house immediately. Get that footman, the strapping, surly one—"

"Evans, Mrs. Campbell. A former soldier, and a most dedicated domestic. He can shoot a jar off a fence at one hundred yards should you require it."

"Brilliant. Have Evans guard the dwelling. Mr. Campbell stays out, do you understand? Or in his charming language, do you *ken*? No breaking down the door, no crawling in my window. That scoundrel has climbed in a hundred over the course of his notorious career. He did the day of our wedding, in the chapel. Sins he's too beautiful to be held responsible for. I'm mistress of Southgate, and for the time being" —she pointed furiously toward the coach house, rage taking over— "I'm *king* of that castle. A castle filled with books!"

Mrs. Irving exhaled, her bosom ultimately settling below her ribs. "I did hear tell that you were a harridan. Temperamental in your own right, like that reckless duke brother of yours. Unyielding, even. I hadn't believed it until now, as you're quiet as a mouse most days, kind to the staff and genuinely a lovely presence, face buried in the pages.

But now..." She clicked her tongue against her teeth, studying Theo with fearful appreciation. "Makes me worry for poor Mr. Campbell, what he's coming home to. I'm not sure what he might think of this plan. I hope I'm not sorry for my part in it. You know, in the end, women don't have rights, don't you, gel?"

Theo growled and spun on her heel, preparing to do battle with anyone who got in her way. Especially her gorgeous, larcenous husband.

~

"Your carriage, Noble, is not worth a good goddamn. You have some nerve ridiculing mine when yours lost a wheel and nearly killed us. This is what we'd call a *boorach* back home. A fine, fitting calamity. I lost my best set of dice, too, buried somewhere in this muck."

Jasper glanced up from his review of the fractured undercarriage. The force of the impact had cracked the transport's axle nearly in two when it landed in the ditch running alongside the toll road. Thankfully, the team of horses had survived and were calmly munching on grass yards away. "You act as if you haven't been tossed from a carriage before. Wipe your face and gather your mettle, man. I sent the coachman off to the next village. He'll be back soon enough with a vehicle to get us to Southgate. We offered top blunt, and money always provides solutions." He winced, flexing his hand. "I think my finger is dislocated, and you don't see me crying about it."

Dash rolled his shoulder, which throbbed like the devil. He had a cut on his cheek, and blood was streaked over his shirt collar and across the lapel of his coat. Though it was clearly vanity, he didn't want a scar to match the one on his chin. He liked his bonnie countenance, and it was a gift he employed to great effect when necessary.

"Quit scowling, it's a nick. Your face will heal as will this tangle with Theo. Breathe through your angst. Your brogue is so pronounced, I can barely understand you. I've never heard a bloke's speech go from refined ballroom to Glasgow rookery in seconds flat."

Dash groused, wiping grime on his trousers. He was covered in mud from head to toe, as was Noble. Muck mixed with dung from the stink of it. They weren't far from Bury but not close to civilization, either. Stuck in the middle of a field, miles of naught laid out before them. He was a city lad, uneducated about farming, and he wasn't even sure what crop it was surrounding them. Dusk had fallen, darkness and a decided chilly evening arriving shortly, with the only promise waiting at the end of the journey a livid wife. "The mail post passed us at the Rooster & Kettle when we stopped to refresh the horses. I ken the plan was to overtake them, which we easily could with a lighter load and faster team, but now, she'll get the news before we hit the outskirts of Suffolk proper."

Jasper Noble didn't understand. Mild-mannered, bookish Theo in a rage was a frightening sight. Everyone thought she was a sweet lass until they witnessed her temper. More like the Duke of Leighton than Pippa, his sister by blood, he'd be happy to tell them.

Dash sank to the ground, massaging his shoulder. He was tired of talking, tired of *words* when they were usually his solace. "I'm doomed. Blundered my first wager with this marriage gamble."

Jasper dusted straw and dirt from his trousers, indifferent about being discarded in the country and covered in shite. "Start composing your apology. You're a bloody writer, aren't you? 'I didn't kiss the countess, the reporting was shoddy, darling,' that sort of thing. It happens, libel in print, although not often to you. Your tales tend to be accurate."

Dash dabbed his sore cheek, damp seeping through buckskin to chill his arse. The wind was picking up with the setting sun. Soon, he and Noble would be hugging each other to keep warm. "I didn't kiss her. She kissed *me*."

Jasper exhaled vigorously and settled next to him. "Please don't say that." Straightening his crooked finger as best he could, he yanked it into place with a foul curse.

Dash's belly clamped as a wave of queasiness hit him. He made a choking noise and wiped his hand across his lips. "Noble, you are truly an odd case."

Jasper grimaced, wiggling the swollen digit. His ministrations hadn't worked. "I don't believe that helped. It still hurts like hell. Sorry, I should have warned you. Dislocations only get worse if you let them go, but this may be a break. My father was a doctor. I worked alongside him in his surgery from the time I was a boy. Doesn't bother me a bit, blood, gore, you name it."

"Is that true, guv?"

Jasper chuckled, dying sunlight highlighting blue-black glimmers in his jet hair. "Gads, no, the man was as far from a healer as one can get. The stories I could tell are worse than the sight of me mending a broken bone in my finger. Actually, I don't relish the sight of blood. But the fabrication could serve as a reasonable explanation for my unique abilities. I'll keep it tucked away for future use."

"I dinnae even ken my father. Maybe a bonnie thing. A horrid one is worse than none."

Jasper was silent, the conversation having gone in a somber direction neither man wished to pursue. "Make sure you tell Theo that the countess was never your mistress. A vital statement that should be made early in the argument. Take the wind right out of her sails and enter the debate from a position of strength."

Looking across the field, Dash kicked at the mound of dirt before him.

"Ah, so she was connected to you at one time. Well, you can't win them all," Jasper murmured and rested back on his elbows, tilting his head to the sky. "With your reputation, Theo wouldn't have believed you, anyway. You're better off doing your finest performance of groveling."

"Your standing is no better, Noble."

"Quite right, but I don't have a wife to answer to, and I never will."

Dash fidgeted, yearning for a pair of dice. He'd mentioned his father, for God's sake. This man made him want to spill secrets, a talent that crept up on a person. "It isn't like you haven't considered marriage. You asked Necessity before Ollie slipped in and stole her from you."

Jasper shook his head, his smile wistful. "A man can't lose what he never had, friend."

Dash started to agree that the Countess of Stanford had eyes only for her husband and always had when the rattle of a cart sounded down the lane.

In a flash, Jasper straightened from his slouch and reached, sliding a knife from his boot beneath his sleeve. The blade glittered against his skin, open and ready for use. It was a practiced move from a bloke who closely guarded his back, and it highlighted the vast difference between them. Dash was a cardsharp, not a killer. An author, not an assassin. He didn't know what the man sitting next to him was, but a rogue swindler from the stews wasn't it.

Dash exhaled in relief as a beaten horse cart rolled into view with Noble's coachman perched on the seat, leads in his muddy hands. The rest of the journey wouldn't be comfortable, but it would suffice. There'd be no showdowns on this lonely stretch of road. His friend could tuck away his lies and his knife.

Unfortunately, Dash's confrontation was coming when he returned to Southgate.

And a woman's tongue could slice deeper than any blade.

Chapter Seventeen

A gambler's reputation predicts who joins the game.
Dashiell M. Campbell, *Proper Etiquette for Deception*

T heo only opened the door because her husband was covered in blood.

And excrement, she realized as he stumbled past into the coach house's main chamber, his gait decidedly unsteady. Lifting her hand to her nose, she coughed into it. He positively reeked. What had happened to him, and why had he not bathed before coming to inform her about it?

When Dash turned to face her, as unkempt as she'd ever seen him, and the familiar hunger sought to claw its way out of her, her alarm turned to relief—then anger. How could he look this good when he looked this bad? The sheer nerve of the man! Attractive while covered in shite. Making her want him when he was a lousy, double-crossing, smelly rat.

"Get out," she snarled and pointed to the door. "*Out!*"

Dash tunneled his hand through his hair, the cut on his cheek oozing blood down his whiskered jaw in a tight bead. Shadowy slashes sat beneath his eyes, grooves alongside his lush mouth. Exhaustion riding him hard.

Don't comfort him, Theo, don't you dare.

"I already went through this routine with Evans, *leannan*. I'm not going through it again with you. I canna and remain standing. If you hadn't let me in, I was going to brawl with the gigantic laddie in the courtyard. He's loyal. I'll give him that much. I plan to hire ten just like him to guard this estate."

"Fine, I'll go then."

Before she reached the door, Dash was there, arm braced on the jamb, blocking her way. He groaned, favoring his right shoulder, his body trembling. "*Nae*, lass. I'm not leaving until we talk about this. Why do you suppose I raced here the minute I saw that rubbish in the newspaper? I knew you were going to be crabbit, mad as the devil to translate, but I didnae fathom you'd have moved out of the house. My ring off your finger, a statement I'm not taking lightly. Your fury is truly lightning speed."

"What is there to talk about? This is exactly what I expected. London was more temptation than you could handle. Women stalking you like felines a round of Stilton. The solution to this problem being that I guard you like Evans is guarding me, or you'll be off gadding about. Well, I won't do it." Heart breaking, she wilted inside but thankfully, *thankfully*, concealed it. "I'm the fool, Dashiell Campbell, not you. Friends who wed can have countesses on the side. Fair play in this game."

His lids slipped low, fatigue and pain twisting his features. "You have it backwards, as lasses often do. Even with the sharpest mind I've encountered in this life, you leap first, think later. I dinnae see reason in this resolution of yours, and if you looked harder, you'd not, either."

Theo's temper exploded. Shrieking, she punched him in his injured shoulder, wishing she could lay him out flat. "You supercilious bounder!"

Rubbing his chest, his lips tilted in an act of contrition she was not accepting. "Super-what?"

She drilled her finger in his chest. "I'm not teaching you another word as long as I breathe, you arrogant goat! I hope your vocabulary dries up like a prune in the sun. That your accent comes back so thick no one can understand a thing you say ever again."

"I want to battle with you, lass, I do. Get this misunderstanding tied up nice like a wee present. Take you to bed and have you scratch my back up in your fury. Swallow your cries of pleasure, then make you cry more." He swayed, his cheeks blanching. Tipping his head back, he slid down the door, coming to rest with his brow on his knees. "Except, I hit my head when Noble's carriage took that twister, and the dots floating before my eyes are as big as snowflakes. If I pass out, get that burly laddie out there patrolling to help me into bed. Too, a visit from the village doctor might not be a terrible idea. I think I cracked a rib as well."

Brilliant, Theo raged and stalked to the linen closet. He was hurt. How could she argue with an idiot man on the verge of collapse? Oh, she could imagine the advice Jasper Noble, that puffed-up, smuggling peacock, had given him. 'Tell her you didn't do it, that it's all a mistake. Careless reporting, it happens every day.' Swearing, she grabbed a rag, and on the return, a bottle of brandy and a tumbler from the sideboard.

Halting by her husband, she shot an exasperated breath through her nose. He looked pathetic, shaky, and helpless. Bloodied clothing, his boots covered in mud past the ankle. His head on his knees, shoulder held at an odd angle, his hair a tragedy. She would have liked to coddle him, bring him against her bosom, and hold him close. *Love* him.

But he was making love hard. When she'd not made trusting easy.

She went to her knee beside him, her touch gentle when her mood was not. "You're the curse of my existence, Campbell." The greatest love of her life, too, damn him!

He groaned and slanted his head, giving her access to the cut on his cheek. His lashes fluttered as she dabbed at the wound, inky smudges against his skin. They were burnished a golden hue at the tips, a detail she'd not noted before. The freckles on the bridge of his nose stood out from another day in the sun. His hair was getting longer, curling over his ears and jaw. The little boy aura swirled about him, the facade that made her crumble.

"I told her no," he whispered, his voice raw. "I had no intentions in Town. Only coming back to you, lass."

So, the countess had kissed him. The gossip rags had it right. Maybe more than kissed him. No newspaper would go too far in describing a lapse in judgment. The struggle to keep him for herself would never end, and eventually, her soul would be dashed like a ship's hull upon the rocks. Swallowing hard, Theo poured a measure of brandy in the glass and bumped it against his elbow. "Drink."

Reaching blindly, he downed the liquor, his wheeze puffing out his cheeks. "The problem here isn't me, *leannan*. Truly, it's not."

Grabbing the tumbler from him, she rocked back on her heels. "How do you figure that?"

Squinting one eye open, he sighed when he got a glance at her fierce expression, and let it shut again. "Because you dinnae trust me. When I'm only beginning to trust meself. I'm as imperfect a man as there can be. Flat out. Not smart enough for you, good enough, kind enough. But I want to be. I said I'd try my hardest. I've not fibbed to ye about my shortcomings. This is who you married, right here in a clutter on the stones."

He was wearing her down, breaking her heart. His Scottish charisma overwhelming her. His sensitivity genuine, a rare thing in a man. "The women, the kisses. The rumors that are going to follow us until the dawn of time. How do I accept them, accept that?"

He shrugged with a groan, his hair knotting on his knee. "You believe me."

She brought the cotton rag to her nose and inhaled the scent of his skin. The muck, yes, but beneath this, the splendor. At her back, a hearth fire crackled, the wood popping and hissing on the grate. Night had fallen, persistent gusts tapping the windowpanes. Love surrounded her, opposing forces. Pulling her in as it pushed her away. Accept or deny?

The validity of Dash's statement slammed into her with such force she nearly lost her breath. Their marriage couldn't work, not as they'd planned. Not when she loved him but didn't trust him. Not when she needed his love in return, his faithfulness secured. Vows they'd not uttered in truth. Not when indecision sketched his face every time he looked at her. If she was correct in her assessment, his decision about her, his future, was hanging in the balance.

"I think I'm pregnant," she whispered, laying her hand over her belly. "Which, unexpectedly, changes everything. We were foolish to imagine it wouldn't."

He lifted his head, color draining from his cheeks until they were chalk white. "Repeat that, Theo, if ye please. I canna hear for the sudden ringing in my ears."

Shaking her head, she was up and out of the coach house before he'd be able, in his condition, to even think to gain his feet.

Evans tipped his chin at her approach, his face showing none of the curiosity she suspected was racing through him. He was, indeed, an able servant. And one of the tallest men she'd ever stumbled upon. Craning her head, she caught his gaze. "Can you summon the village doctor? I'll alert Mrs. Irving to Mr. Campbell's condition."

Evans hummed, hooking his thumb toward the main house. "His friend, Mr. Noble, isn't in much better shape. Bruised ribs, busted lip, broken finger he tried to mend himself. Quite a sight. His fancy carriage smashed to bits on the main route between here and Westley. Arrived clinging to the side of a farm cart that doesn't look much better than they do."

This is who you married, right here in a clutter on the stones.

"Ma'am," Evans murmured when it appeared she'd gotten lost in thought, "are you well?"

"I'm well. I'm merely trying to figure out what to do about the adorable halfwit I married."

Evans broke character, his mouth curving in amusement. "If I may be so bold, ma'am, my pap had a saying I think would apply agreeably here. Action brings the verdict. It's the doing over the words with men, to my knowing. From what I read in the scandal sheets"—he coughed, tugging his cap off and twisting it in his hands—"begging pardon, apologies for my candor, but the Gambling God and his admired book haven't had to work for a woman's favor. Not once. A man who can crook his finger and be given such selection gets lazy if you take my meaning. I speak to you as I would my sister iffin' I had one."

Hmm... She and Dash had gotten married without an ounce of courting on his part. Although she'd necessitated the speedy nuptials with her carriage theft and runaway bride ploy, relief and a side-helping of resentment were the emotions coursing through her at the time. She couldn't discount what Dash had done for her, certainly saving her from a worse outcome than ending up a gambler's wife. Nevertheless, perhaps she would learn to trust him if he worked to win her, instead of her feeling like he'd done her a favor.

Didn't every woman deserve such gallantry once in her life?

"You might be onto something, Evans. I didn't have the courage to make Mr. Campbell work for anything. I didn't think he would."

"Then this will be his test, won't it?"

Theo smiled. She loved tests.

Once upon a time, Dash had been an excellent student.

Evans winked and gave her a jaunty salute, heading toward the village to retrieve the doctor. While she remained in the scattered moonlight, a night chill rushing through her, wondering if her husband had it in him to love her.

If she had the courage to let him.

"The boy's clearly smitten. Look at the way he's lingering in the doorway when his lesson is good and well finished. Headed to Cambridge, my arse. I could have made it there myself with a wee bit more schooling."

"*Any* schooling," Jasper murmured at his side.

Dash scooted forward in his chair, in the midst of an impromptu afternoon tea Mrs. Irving had organized for the convalescents in the gardens off the kitchen. She believed sunlight and fresh air had the power to heal. It was also a wonderful spot to spy on Theo at her new home, although she'd yet to glance at him even once. "Did the laddie touch her hand? There's to be no flirting with my wife, I'll bloody remind him. She'll help with geometry and such drivel, but that's where the relationship ends."

He was the only man Theo would teach the facts of life.

Jasper yawned from his sprawl on the chair opposite Dash, patted a belly full of rum cake. He'd taken to Mrs. Irving's coddling like a kitten to cream. "Give the brooding a rest, friend, will you? I'm trying to allow these curative sunbeams to restore me. There's currently a pulse beating out an erratic tune in the tip of my splinted finger. Let the boy flirt. It's harmless. He's practicing. What is he, seventeen?"

Dash grunted and slumped back, balancing his teacup on his knee. "Do you remember what you were doing at that age, Noble? How harmless yer wee flirting was? Mine was deadly, nothing harmless about it."

Jasper stilled, a slice of cake halfway to his lips. "Excellent point, Campbell. And every man, no matter how young, understands a cross woman is easier to seduce. Time to break it up. Trot over and ask her a question about, oh, that slaphappy hound of yours, the regrettable Wordsworth. Say he's got a bum noggin, similar to his papa." Shoving the last bite of cake in his mouth, he glanced dubiously at the pup slumbering at their feet. "She'll come running. Or better yet, tell her you've lost the cat. Maybe then, this dream will come true. That creature slept on my bed last night. Fur was everywhere!"

Dash watched his radiant wife and her cheery student gab until his temper started to get the better of him. Closing his eyes to the sulk, he leaned his head back, the sun striking his face just so. Since his return two days ago, most of the time spent in a medically provoked haze, Theo hadn't spoken a word to him. Scant messages conveyed through Evans or Mrs. Irving if at all, the rest of the staff scared to death to approach her. She'd shown them her true colors, a fearsome hellion in hiding. He felt slightly redeemed if little else.

Although he recalled, or thought he did, his wife's hand on his brow that first night, her bonnie voice blending with the doctor's as they discussed his condition. He'd taken a hard knock to the head (not the first and likely not the last), had a cracked rib, and a slice on his cheek requiring three stitches. The scar he'd not wanted making a home on his skin right this second.

Scars and love... and babies. Items not on his list even a short month ago.

Dash's heart more than skipped, it leaped in his chest, breathless.

Theo was pregnant. A Campbell bairn on the way. Maybe. There'd been hesitancy in her voice, uncertainty threaded with wonder. She wasn't unhappy about the development, thank the heavens, only unhappy with *him*. As for him, he was thrilled. Overjoyed. Terrified. He wanted tots, a passel of them if life worked out that way. Children with golden hair and eyes the color of Scottish lochs. He'd do it right, the earnest lessons from his mother and Nanna resonating, the awful everything else a path he would not take.

He groaned and sank lower in the armchair. Theo's delight about the development could be considered half the skirmish won, couldn't it? Only, she wasn't wearing his ring. Which was a tell, a big, fat, jumble of a tell.

Jasper stretched his legs out, fiddling with the splint on his middle finger. "With a once-in-a-lifetime face and a crudely appealing accent to go with it, I can't believe I have to help you win over your wife. A month into your marriage, and she's living in other quarters. I'm saddened to see this is where you ended up. Some romantic you turned out to be. The Leighton Cluster's first failure."

"Six weeks married, guv," Dash corrected. "Almost seven."

"Gads, Campbell, if you're counting, the deed is done. She has you tied up and laid out. Poor chap." Jasper crossed his legs at the ankle, his thoughtful gaze straying to the clouds. "Mrs. Irving, that hulking footman and I were discussing your setback and—"

Dash straightened, his boots hitting the ground, sending a jolt of pain along his ribs. "Dinnae tell me you went and discussed me with my staff, you rotting mongrel."

"They have the most knowledge, Campbell. Household dynamics, dramas, affairs. Always include the servants in your consultations. I've gotten in many a back door that way." Jasper flashed a lazy smile, his lids at half-mast. He'd taken another dose of laudanum; Dash had best gather the wisdom being doled out while he could. It might not be the worst time to ask the man who he actually was, too. "We came up with the picture-perfect solution, minus a sliver of your pride being cut away in the process."

Dash hung his head, crooked his fingers. *Come on, give it up.*

"Go back to the beginning. Pretend you have to win her."

"She's not speaking to me, guv. I *do* have to win her."

Jasper stretched, sighed, on the slender cusp of sleep. The man made himself at home in any space afforded him, proving he'd seen many a space. "Not a husband's campaign. Consider yourself the young chap flirting from the doorway without a lick of confidence she'll say yes. Which I realize is not the typical narrative in your amorous ventures. Consider the situation as one where she isn't yours, the menacing possessiveness swirling about you like London's fog uncalled for. A challenge, the biggest of your life. Win your wife."

Dash rubbed his temple, the headache bouncing around his head for two days manageable but present. "Handfasting, you mean?"

"Indeed, if that's the Scots eloquent description of courting." Jasper patted his chest with a lengthy yawn. "Woo her. Make it worth her while to trust you. Change her mind. Take the lead, man. If she's running around thinking you married her to save her from society's dismissal, you know what you have to do. Tell her you actually *want* this. Except don't tell, friend, show. We'll come up with ideas. I'm an idea bloke, don't you know?"

"I have notions, Noble, dinnae you worry." Dash slipped his dice from his waistcoat pocket and spun them in his hand. *Woo her.* Truthfully, he didn't have ideas. He'd never had to work for a single kiss in his miserable life. Most days, he spent rejecting offers, not facilitating them. This ease had put him in a position of inexperience for the other, far from what he was used to as a lad who laid down a card and usually won.

But this was Theo. Kind, brilliant, beautiful Theo. Worthy of the generous piles of angst she caused him. The only lass to make his heart trip, make him want above any want he'd suffered before. He was covetous—*aye*, this particular word fit perfectly—of not only her body but her mind. The expression on her face when she came wasn't far off from the look she got when reading a boring science text. Concentrated passion. He'd given her his folios, his most personal possessions,

184

and memories in an existence lacking solidity of any kind. This was his vow, bigger than any he could make in a church, if she'd only realize it.

She made him want and wonder.

She made him laugh. Dash adored his days spent with her, and his nights. She made him feel exceptional about his writing, a bloke with a gift in a world of talentless people. She saw beyond his handsomeness. He knew she did. Sometimes disregarding this aspect too much for his taste. His future was an exciting premise with her in it. He longed to grow old with her; fancies he'd never entertained.

And now, a wee bairn had entered the picture.

A family. Dash Campbell, Papa.

He burned to show Theo how much she meant to him, to gain the trust she'd withheld. He decided he didn't even mind having to do it first.

"About these ideas, Noble..." But the only response from his injured companion was a gentle snore from his spot in the Suffolk sun. Leaving Dash to stare at his wife and her smitten student, the ache in his chest not wholly from his carriage accident.

It appeared as if he'd have to figure this courting business out for himself.

Chapter Eighteen

The game shifts unexpectedly with each card slapped to the table.
Dashiell M. Campbell, *Proper Etiquette for Deception*

T heo lay in bed, staring at the ceiling. Tracing a slender crack with her gaze she'd need to tell Dash about once they were speaking.

His gifts had started arriving the previous morning, tucked in a rattan basket that had made its way to the coach house's portico. There were no notes attached, but the swath of blue and green plaid lining the interior made the message clear. Campbell property. Theo hated to admit her heart raced every time she opened the door, a twinge of disappointment if the hamper was empty.

When the offerings were ordinary at first glance.

A cluster of buttercups gathered with a hair ribbon Theo had been missing for weeks. A volume of Keats' poetry with a calling card from the chapel where they'd been married tucked between the pages. A note she'd passed to Dash during her year of tutoring encased in a magnificent medieval frame. *Stay the course in this chapter*, she'd advised. Which he seemed to be doing but, this time, not in a book. A journal with her new initials—*TAC*—burned into the leather corner. A beautiful writing set, the inkstand and blotter decorated with detailed watercolor scenes of Suffolk. The pen knife was especially charming, featuring hounds that looked exactly like Wordsworth dancing across the barrel.

Today's offering? A desk plate that simply said, *teacher*. This one tugged at her heart so fiercely it brought a fresh bout of tears, partly a condition of her condition. She'd cried a veritable river in the two lonesome days Dash had been back.

The presents arrived at odd intervals, keeping her guessing. Like the man. Thinking about him, wondering if she ought to jam his ring back on her finger, march to the main house, climb into his bed, and accept she was married to the handsomest man in the world. The ring sat on her bedside table, never far from reach or view. She was certain of her pregnancy, her menses absent, the morning nausea having lessened as the days passed. She'd even begun to imagine her waist was expanding in small measure. Joy filled her at the thought of a baby. Their baby.

Life was perfect—except for the missing husband.

The escritoire was covered with his writings but not the man. Her lonely bed, her lonely nights, a fire between her thighs igniting when she recalled his hands on her. She replayed their lovemaking until she thought she'd go mad with longing. Until she debated giving up the fight when she'd lost sight of what she was fighting for. Seeking relief, she pleasured herself as they'd done together, Dash stroking his cock while she watched, then she falling into play alongside him. She'd never imagined so intimate an act, although it had seemed natural with him.

His name was scrawled in the margins of her lesson plans. His touch imprinted on her skin, her senses brimming with his scent, spice and leather. She underlined words in books to share with him at least twice a day. She'd made a list of baby names. She had a shirt of his tucked beneath her pillow.

Obviously, her heart knew this separation wasn't permanent even if her head was a little behind.

She'd give Dash satisfactory marks. He'd played this game of courtship with finesse, treating her as if she were a spooked filly he'd recently purchased from Tattersalls, instead of striding in and tossing her over his shoulder as she imagined he'd like to do. As she feared she would *like* him to do. He'd stayed away while remaining close, returning from his morning rides or recuperating in the garden, his gaze glued to her, the distance between them snapping with heat. His expression decipherable because he'd finally let her in. He no longer made any effort to hide his longing. Or his loneliness.

The cut on his cheek was healing and possibly so was her heart.

Because Theo didn't believe he'd done anything but be foolish enough to assume women would stay away from him because he was married. Evans had learned from a chambermaid who had heard it from her brother, a second footman in a household in Piccadilly, who had heard it from a scullery maid, that the kiss had been nothing but a dusting of the countess's dry lips across Dash's cheek. That for once where women were involved, her husband had seemed completely indifferent.

Theo sat up in bed, Keats falling by her side. '*Made sweet moan,*' the poet's most famous line chiming in her ears. She glanced at the mantel clock; it was past midnight.

Today was her birthday, and she wasn't spending it alone. Her test had gone on long enough.

Her husband needed a sign that she loved him, and she was ready to give it.

Clouds obscured the moon, giving no quarter as Theo crept across the lawn, and down the graveled path leading to the servant's entrance. She didn't want to alert the staff to her change of heart as they were placing bets on who would give in first. Evans had his money on Dash, Mrs. Irving's wager on her, of course, since the woman was half-besotted.

Theo was going to ask, *after* she pleasured him breathless, if Dash would take the hit and say he'd given in first. Her pride demanded it, and if he was delirious enough, he might agree. She had learned how to arouse him in seconds, and for long minutes after his release, he was pliable as putty.

In any case, most of the scullery staff were on her side, the grooms, the coachman, and the vicar on Dash's. He claimed it was against the bounds of marriage to live in separate dwellings and repeated the universal consensus that a man with Dash's immense magnetism must be given greater leeway with regard to his transgressions. Theo grumbled, wishing people would stop telling her how lucky she was.

She *knew* how lucky she was.

However, brash chit that she was, she thought Dash was lucky, too.

Southgate was shrouded in solitude. The gentle rustling of the branches above her head and the call of an owl in the distance the only sounds. Shivering, Theo tugged her wrapper around her shoulders, and sprinted along the path. Dash's signet ring was weighty and full of promise on her finger. Wordsworth trailed behind, panting lightly. If she left him in the coach house, he'd whine and scratch the door, doing damage. Mr. Darcy, in a blatant act of betrayal, had remained in the main house throughout her campaign, likely sleeping with her husband. Reprehensible feline.

Not that Theo was any better, sneaking in like one of his doxies, half-dressed, her hair a spill down her back, clothing in disarray, her thoughts...

Theo tilted her face to the sky, her smile sinful, the knowing rumble in her throat surprising her. She was going to make her husband forget what month it was, never mind the *day*.

Frowning, she halted, slipping behind a thicket of rosemary, the scrap of metal against metal reverberating through the calm. Peering around the shrub, she took a startled breath. A hulking man stood before the service entrance's portico, a tension wrench in his hand that he was fitting in the door's lock. His cap sat high on his head, a tangle of ginger hair bursting from beneath it. The rounded handle of a knife jammed in his waistband had worked its way outside his rough woolen coat, its placement created for ease of use. She wouldn't be surprised to see a pistol in his pocket or his scuffed leather boot.

Unlike her usual methods, she didn't take time to strategize. She merely pictured Dash asleep in his bedchamber, his slumber deep, his body healing from his injuries, and this knave sneaking in to assault him. He'd said at one time there were men in Scotland who wanted the last of the Campbells gone. Curling her hands into fists, she glanced around the garden, protective rage unlike any she'd experienced claiming her. The father of her child, the adorable scoundrel she loved, wasn't getting caught up in this.

A pair of pruning shears and a rusty spade sat on a marble bench by the copse of untamed roses bushes she'd asked Welles, the assistant gardener, to thin. Theo slipped the shears into her dressing gown's pocket and marched forward, not taking care to keep her step silent. She wanted the burglar to know she'd found him.

The man spun around at her approach, ripped his knife free from his waistband, and brandished it in a way that said he'd had to protect himself in this manner before. His tension wrench clattered to the flagstones, the ping reverberating through the night. Giving her a sweeping glance, his arm lowered a fraction, his lips lifting from his teeth in a feral smile. "What do we 'av 'ere? Are you lost, luv?"

The accent wasn't Scottish but rather pure London rookery. This man wasn't here to kill a Campbell over an age-old rivalry. Theo pressed her lips together in vexation. It probably had something to do with *Proper Etiquette for Deception*. Or a squabble over a misplaced bet at the Devil's Lair. Or a woman Dash had entertained before he married her. This could be the enraged husband seeking justice. It would not be the first such incident, she'd bet.

Thinking swiftly, she came up with an identity. A senseless chit, Delilah, perhaps. Or Rosabell. A maid returning from a hasty assignation. Half-dazed from being tupped to within an inch of her life, a part Theo could play with skilled precision. She'd dressed the part, too. Rumpled clothing, tangled hair, flushed cheeks, bare feet. A character she could have written had she had Dash's talent. Somehow, letting this brute know she was the wife of the man he sought didn't seem the best plan.

Strolling forward as if she hadn't a care in the world, Theo whistled through her teeth. "I'm returning from an outing. Covert like." She placed her index finger before her lips and gave it a twist. *A secret.* Nodding in the direction of the coach house, her smile was one she employed when she wanted Dash to toss her on the bed and have his way with her. She hoped the cur was confused about her standing in the murky moonlight and discussing anything with him.

The bandit snickered, his mind instantly going in the direction she'd intimated. Taking another glance, this one blistering a sluggish path from her breasts to her toes, his smile kicked two notches higher. His eyes were a hot, horrible green. "I'd enjoy taking me time with ye', darlin' girl, that I would. All those strands of spun gold wrapped around me fist. But for now, you'd best be away. Back to your honey nest until morn unless you want trouble the likes of which this corner of the country has never seen. The man who sent me is high up the ladder, you understand. Topping high. I'm known about the docks at getting the job done. Any job, no matter how filthy." He gestured with his knife, the blade glinting. "Get on now, get off with ya'. You seem like a sensible chit. A ready and willing gel, my favorite kind, but alas, now is not the time."

"I can't go back, put my job in the scullery in peril. Not when I worked two years to get out of laundry service. I'm on duty in less than an hour. Just let me by, I'll go to my chamber, and hide. My gentleman caller, he'll be locking up anyway, slipping back into his bed in the main house." She glanced up, gauging the time by the sky. "Only tidying up before he returns as we tend to wreck our—what did you call it?— honey nest in our enthusiasm. The guv likes his play rough." Then she laughed, her breath hitching enough to make it believable. Her only thought, her only plan: *get this beast away from the house.* Away from Dash, away from Mrs. Irving, Mr. Darcy, away from the staff. Away from Wordsworth, who was cowering beneath a copse of azaleas, the clever hound. Perhaps if she let this bounder ramble on long enough, someone on the staff would hear him.

He smirked, his brandy-scented breath washing over her. She couldn't decide if it was better, or worse, that he was legless from liquor. "I'm needing a partner, darlin', and 'ere you appear. My brother was supposed to ride with me, the horse's arse, but he got scared and stayed behind. When he's the knack lock-picker. I'da been inside already with him working the tumblers, my knife at my target's throat." Chuckling, he flexed his arm, his bicep popping beneath tattered cotton. "I'm the muscle, ya' see. Spilling blood, which can't be avoided in my line of commerce, disturbs his slumber. Whilst I sleep like a babe."

Theo twisted her hands in her gown, trying another angle. "The men inside are armed. These aren't society nobs you're thinking of taking on. You know they're rookery blokes. Maybe you'd best come back when you have your brother with you."

"I was born and raised in Seven Dials, darlin' girl, nothing here a surprise. Campbell and his band, dukes and earls and such, have a fearsome reputation, the genuine article. Beat each other senseless at that famous pugilist's outfit on the regular. One of 'em tossed out of a gent's club every week. I seen it once myself, down St James." He tapped his temple, his defiant smile sending a shiver down her spine. "Only, I've been watching Town surroundings, those posh districts a delight even from the shadows. They're in London, the lot of 'em. Leighton and his merry men, so I'm *here*."

Theo's heart hammered, her throat going dry. She was running out of options, the shears, her only weapon, heating against her thigh. "If Campbell is who you're after, for a reasonable bit of pocket change, I'll take you right to him. I hold no loyalty to any man. He's in a distant bedchamber, not easily located. Down a series of winding hallways such to confuse a caller."

"A caller, am I?" The brute threw his head back, drunken laughter rolling out. "You imagine I'd risk me arse for that writer? What is this, a tiff over a misplaced snatch of advice on rolling weighted dice in chapter three? What do I care if he teaches nobs how to count cards from here to Wales and back? Why come to bleeding Suffolk? I could find Campbell any day of the week at his gaming hell. Roams the streets without reluctance. Or St Anne's in Soho. Frequents there often enough the story goes." He popped his chest for emphasis, three firm whacks. "Gel, I'm here for Jasper Noble. I'd not chance me life for a bleeding *writer*."

Tossing her a boozy wink, he squatted to pick up his tension wrench, taking his gaze off her. Putting himself in perhaps the only vulnerable position he would all night.

Adrenaline, and no short measure of wrath at hearing her husband had frequented a notorious bawdy house, pulsed through her like blood. The shears were in her hand, the metal cool against her palm, before she took another breath. Closing her eyes, she plunged them into the offender's shoulder.

She would have gone for the neck, but she didn't quite, *quite* have the nerve.

The sound was horrific, a dull snap as the shear's tips encountered bone. The assailant gurgled, screamed, bumping her, then falling to his knees. He reached, grasping the hem of her gown and yanking. Silk split down Theo's back, letting in the chill. She danced away, her breath ripping from her lungs. Turning, she raced through the garden and along the crushed stone footpath leading to the front of the estate. Up the marble stairs, her feet sliding on edges buffed smooth from centuries of wear. The door was locked but her shouts were enough to rouse London's West End. She beat on the door, looking over her shoulder. What if he caught her? She hadn't delivered a killing blow, merely one to slow down a monster intent on mayhem.

It happened swiftly, so quickly her mind could not take everything in. Dash flinging the door open, his cheeks robbed of color. Mrs. Irving behind him in a heavy dressing gown that had once been crimson and was now was a pale, putrid pink. Evans and Jasper Noble pushing past her, down the stairs, and around the back of the house. A swarm of maids she was still learning the names and duties of speaking at once. Millie. Katherine. Beatrice. Wordsworth at her feet, dancing, yipping. The call of an owl in the distance. The sound of a scuffle, men shouting. Lights from the sconces diving into the blue of her husband's eyes as he lifted her into his arms and strode into the house, slamming the door behind him.

She blinked when he deposited her on a settee, stunned to find a tumbler shoved in her hand, a scratchy woolen blanket tossed over her shoulders. The scent of whisky rose to sting her nose. Dash had taken her to the yellow parlor, a room that received a flood of morning sunlight. The scenes of Italy on the paper lining the walls looked dreamy in the hazy light. Closing her eyes, she sipped, the liquor blazing a path to her belly. "I killed him," she whispered, the dull thunk of the shears driving into bone echoing in her ears. "Although I tried not to."

Dash sank to his knees before her, his breath as unsteady as hers. His quivering hands raced over her, checking for injury. "Theo, there's blood. My God, there's blood all over you."

She shook her head, and in a move she'd seen the men in her family do a thousand times, tossed back the whisky. It rolled down her throat, liquid courage. "It's his, that drunken sot, not mine. The gardening shears." She made a stabbing motion with the glass. "In his shoulder. Not his neck, though I wanted to. I had to keep him out of this house. I had to. Keep him out of this house." She dropped her head to her hand, her pulse throbbing in her temples. "Away from you."

"What happened, *leannan*? Why were you outside? Where? When? I dinnae understand. Help me understand why you were alone out there."

After letting her heart settle, she opened her eyes. Dash looked crazed, his hair in shambles, his shirt open to his belly, cotton flowing past his hips. Blood from that cur lying by the back door smeared across his chin. His eyes were wide, black prisms when they met hers. "I came to you. To give in, to give up. Tell you I know you were just a silly fool with all this mess with the countess. He was there, trying to pick the lock. I couldn't let him in. I had to stop him from getting in. Talk him out of it, get him away."

Dash's cheeks shifted from the color of a spring lily to the crimson fire of a ruby. His hands grasped her shoulders, shaking her. "You mean to tell me your wee self decided to take a criminal on? One breaking into this manor? Reason with him? Disarm him? Tell me that's not what you're saying, what I'm hearing. *Please*."

She started to argue, then frowned. Who was she to argue with the bald truth?

Dash rocked back, his lips parting, closing, parting. With a foul set of directives aimed at her, he rocketed to his feet. She was insensible to imagine he made a pretty picture at that moment, parading from one end of the parlor to the other, shirttail flying, dark hair whipping about his head, hands fisting into hard knots at his hip. Gaelic, *oh*, she liked the sound of the ancient language pouring in a mad stream from his lips. Reckless being the only word he presented in English. Every time he seemed to calm himself, he glanced at her, swore, then started his assault on the Aubusson carpet again.

It would enrage him if he knew how beautiful he was to her, how seeing him like this was twisting her heart, placing it at his feet when he was ready to accept it.

Purposefully staying across the chamber, he halted by the sofa, leaning his long body against the curved cherry wood back. He looked in turn as if he wanted to weep or rip something apart with his bare hands. "*Tha gaol agam ort.* Do you recall me saying that to you, lass? I canna recall the exact instance, my mind is lost when I'm inside you." His voice was raw, cracked, full of emotion he'd kept from her for weeks.

She gripped the tumbler to keep from going to him. It wasn't the right time. She feared they would both shatter upon contact. "You say a lot of things in Gaelic"—she swallowed, her face heating, her body warming to his closeness even now—"during. I like it, it makes me wild for you, but I don't know what any of it means. Maybe I shall add this study to my language collection."

Laughing but not amused, he buffed his fist across his chin, coming away with blood. He stared at his hand as if he didn't recognize it. "*Leannan* isn't what I told you it was in Scots. It's beloved. A sweetheart. A lover. An endearment. *Tha gaol agam ort* means quite simply, I love you. A rather ragged turn of a phrase, innit, for words meant to give someone your heart?"

Theo slid the glass to the table, starting to rise, clutching the blanket at her throat. "*Dash.*"

He swiped his knuckles beneath his eyes, his throat pulling. "Dinnae come closer, Theo. I can't. Not yet. Not now. I'll go up like tinder to wood if you touch me and burn us both to the studs. You dinnae appreciate my situation. You have a family, you have *love*. Even if you lost it for a wee time, Helena swooped in, and took you under her wing. Brought you in, where you thrived. I lived among strangers in the workhouse, foes even, not one night of solid sleep until I crawled out of a scullery window at fifteen and made my way to London. Nanna tried, despite the setting. But the things I saw there, the things I *heard* changed me." He tunneled his hand through his hair, leaving his head cradled in his palm for a long moment. "Then you imagine to give me the world, love and family and *life*, and in one foolish second, take it away. In the name of protecting me. I should have known better. I should have seen this coming. That being connected to the brutality I employ would be the ruin of you."

She rose, crossing to him. He flinched when she touched his shoulder, stumbling back. "Dash, listen to me. Stop it. I love you, too, you know I do. Maybe I did, maybe it started when we were writing your book." Cupping his jaw, she brought his tormented gaze to hers. "I want you. I want Southgate. Our baby. Our life. That's what I was coming to tell you. I've been foolish, thinking to make you work for me when you've been there all along. My insecurities the thing driving us apart."

His eyes roved the length of her and back, his chest rising with sharp inhalations. When his gaze met hers, shock swirling in indigo, she began to see that reasoning with him might be harder than she'd like. This night had taken him to a horrendous place in his mind. "I saw you covered in blood, *leannan*, and I thought you were dying. The bairn dying. My future gushing away in a crimson flood at my feet. The old haunts coming to get me, payback for every horrible thing I've done. You're connected to me because I couldn't let you go. Because I had to jump in and save you that day in the chapel. When I'm no hero, lass. We should have known better. For certain, I should have. My family canna be exposed to this. I won't allow it. My hunger for you isn't going to consume you."

They stared, lost in each other. Her body swayed toward his, her fingers trembling on his jaw, the blanket sliding from her shoulders. His lids fluttered, the ragged groan streaking from his throat. She'd never missed anyone with her entire soul, yearning until she had no dreams left that weren't his. She'd not imagined love this earth-shattering was possible.

Kiss me. Show me what I am to you. Prove it to me, Dashiell Campbell.

"*Leannan*," he whispered and stepped in, crowding her against the sofa. His lips dusted hers, parted, settling in to turn her world upside-down.

A heavy step in the corridor had them stumbling back.

Jasper stalked into the parlor, his expression frightening. "You are a tempestuous couple, Campbells. Even in the midst of a catastrophe, you're near to climbing all over each other." Gone was the amused dandy, the corrupt scoundrel. In his place stood a dangerous man intent on homicide himself. Blood streaked the coat he'd hastily thrown over his shirt and trousers, staining his hands, his jaw. Her heart sank to see a knife clutched in his fist. A weapon she recognized.

If Dash had been angry before, he was about to get angrier.

"Is he dead?" she asked before anything else could be said, gathering the blanket about her shoulders. She wanted to know if she was a murderess before her husband tore into her.

Jasper jammed the knife in the wall, yanked a brandy bottle off the sideboard, and lifted it to his lips. Wiping his hand across his mouth, he released a frayed breath. "He is not. To his sound fortune, you struck him in the fleshy part of the shoulder. Although, exhibiting the business end of the stick, you made sure to drive those damned gardening shears deep. Your hulking footman and I had to wiggle the tip out of his collarbone." He took another gulp and stared unseeing at the knife still quivering from the force of being imbedded in plaster. "The copious amount of blood exiting his body made it quite easy to wrestle his weapon from his hand, however. Thanks for that."

"He'll live," Theo whispered, unsure if this was the information she wanted to hear.

Jasper shrugged and took another drink. "Perhaps. Infection is usually the culprit, anyway. Evans is loading him, bound and gagged, into our revered horse cart for transport to the surgeon. I only need the ruffian to make it long enough to tell me who sent him. He's fairly incoherent at the moment. I'm sorry, more than you know, Campbell, but it's me he was after. I brought this to your door, but I'll make good on it or die trying. I'll interrogate him in a manner that will make him wish those gardening shears had ended up in his eye, then it's off to actual Hades for all I care. I hope the fever fries his brain. The village constable can handle the trouble." He slapped the bottle to the side-board. "And the body."

Dash caught her around the wrist. "He had a dagger, Theo? You kent this, and you still engaged the fiend in conflict?"

She stalled, not understanding how to defuse this situation. When Dash's accent turned toward the bonnie Isles of Scotland, silence was best. Actually, both men appeared close to exploding like pyrotechnics and spraying their ire about the room. Saying she'd known the drunken sot breaking into the house had a knife crammed in his trousers before she approached him was undoubtedly a poor defense for her actions.

Dash dropped her hand like her touch burned. "Get her out of here, Noble. Back to London, back to Leighton's Mayfair fortress. Before I do something I regret. Somehow, with your secrets and your skills, I ken you can keep her safe until you hand her over to her brother. You owe me that much after this farce."

"It's my birthday," she whispered for her husband's ears alone. As if this fact would abate the fury radiating off him in waves. "You can't make me leave, not today."

"I ken it's your bloody birthday." Taking her arm none too gently, he hauled her down the passageway to a little-used parlor. It was filled, floor to ceiling, with books. Stacks and stacks of them. The room smelled of leather spines and moldy pages, her favorite scents in the world. "Today was the day I set to take my courting to another level, after giving your stormy temper time to calm. No more mooning from afar like a tormented hero in a shilling novel."

Theo stumbled into the parlor and turned a stunned circle. There were scientific texts, literature, poetry. Volumes on art, nature, history. Children's books, a hundred at least, a scarcity in Bury. She went to her knee beside a pile she recognized as rare treasures at first sight.

Expensive editions she wouldn't place in a lending area. These should be stored behind glass.

Dash stalked to the window and stood staring into the darkness. "They're for your library. I didnae ken what you needed, so I bought most everything I could get my hands on. I only wanted to make you happy with this, with all of it. This life with me, what I've asked of you, I dinnae..." He gave the glass panes two hard knocks, his shoulders falling. "This time it was Noble they were after but what about the next? A mad bloke who loses at the tables. Someone I angered in a past lifetime. I've never had anyone to protect except myself. I canna breathe with the weight."

A tear edged from her eye, and she brushed it away with a shallow breath. She placed her palm on her belly, reminding him of the future, using what she could if he'd only look at her. "I won't go, Dashiell."

"*Aye*, Theodosia, you will. This way I'm feeling, you have to."

"When will you come to me, then? Bring me home?"

His chest fell with a prolonged sigh. His jaw muscles flexed as the silence drew out like her question had no answer.

"I won't do it unless I have your word. That you're coming for me. I have you, Southgate. I have my classes."

"We can find needy students in the city, lass." Finally, his gaze strayed to her, dropping to the hand she held over her belly. She heard his words as if he'd spoken them. *Without me is best for you and the babe, leannan.*

She started to go to him, shoving to her feet, letting the blanket flutter to the floor. Her face glowed with affection. She could feel it. Her heart expanding in her chest until the pressure hit her ribs. *Love, love, love.* Surely, he could see it.

When he did, he bolted like a feral dog, crossing the room, and sprinting into the hallway.

Jasper strolled into the parlor before she could follow Dash, holding up his hand in a universal gesture. "Give him a flash to breathe, sweetheart. You're both upset. Or he is. You'd be the able assassin of the two of you, that's certain." He snatched the blanket off the floor and held it out to her, his gaze sweeping the room. "Makes a grand gesture, doesn't he? Macauley, Streeter, and I have spent the past week locating books. Criminy, librarians drive a harder bargain than shipping tycoons. Campbell's literary gains are lining quite a few pockets around Town, I'll tell you."

Theo flopped to a sit atop a stack of atlases that shifted slightly with her weight. Her cloak stunk of hound, and it was then she realized Dash had covered her with Wordsworth's bed blanket. "I wanted to protect him. I didn't think overly much about the risk, which is unlike me. He doesn't have to get so angry when it wasn't my fault. It was *yours*."

"He wanted to do the protecting. It's a pathetic masculine tendency." Jasper trailed his finger down the spine of a medieval history book, his smile benevolent. "Love changes you. Ridiculous decisions abound when emotion's got you by the throat. He isn't sending you away for long, sweetheart. Not if he's keeping Mr. Darcy and Wordsworth in Suffolk. If it was permanent, he'd ship you off with the hound at least. I think he's become attached to that damn cat. As I said, give him a moment to breathe."

She huffed and clasped the scratchy woolen cloak at her throat. "You sound experienced about love *and* assassins. Poorly trained ones, I might add. Overpowered by a fragile female with a gardening spade."

"You're the least fragile chit I know, Theo Campbell. I can't believe I'm confessing this, but I wish I'd met you first." Grinning, he glanced at her, his expression giving away only what he wanted her to see, which was little. His gaze was as shuttered as Dash's heart. "As the final word, a birthday gift we'll call it, I'll admit it's not my first time with either, hence my wisdom and ability to maintain calm control. Your calm control, however, is a *talent*. Trust me, I know."

Theo glanced around the room, his unexpected praise strangely pleasing. She wondered if Shakespeare was in this pile somewhere, although his tales had nothing on her turbulent love affair with Dash. "What do I do now?"

Jasper picked up a medical text, flipped to a page, and grimaced. "This is horrid. Why would anyone want to read this?" He snapped the book shut and let it drop to the desk with a thump. "I have a plan. You return to London with me after I complete my interview with my careless killer in Bury. You can even participate if you're feeling terribly ferocious. Meanwhile, let your husband stew like a pot of broth on slow simmer." He tilted his head, squinting at the ceiling, thoughtful. His eyes weren't completely blue as she'd thought but dappled with hazel and green. They were changeable, like the man. "I give it three days before the lovesick whelp is knocking on Leighton's door. If he hands you over to your brother, he'll have to go through the steps of asking for you all over again. Distasteful spot of dignity amputation I pray I'm there to see. Never know when an instance of temperamental entertainment is coming with your brother leading the way."

Theo swallowed back tears at the thought of Dash brawling with Leighton over her. Although crying in front of this ruffian wouldn't help her case one whit. "What if he doesn't come for me?"

Jasper crouched to buff a scratch from the toe of his boot. "I'll make sure of it. This debacle is my fault, and I never leave a debt unpaid. Ask Necessity Byrne, now Aspinwall, the Countess of Stanford. She's married to the earl because of our friendship and a telescope I purloined from a museum I'd rather not name. The Metropolitan Police are still searching for it, which brings me a slender ray of delight most days, I admit."

Theo smiled, aware of the part he'd played in Nessie and Ollie's engagement. The Earl of Stanford was a renowned star-gazer, and Nessie the best giver of gifts. "Jasper Noble, are you saying I can trust you? Even without need of a telescope?"

He hesitated, as if the question was one he hadn't heard in years. "I am."

With a rogue's declaration of friendship on the table, Theo made plans to leave her husband for the second time.

Chapter Nineteen

Fear makes for unpredictable play.
  Dashiell M. Campbell, *Proper Etiquette for Deception*

Dash waited two days before following Theo to London.

Chasing her was the better way to phrase it, and a writer always desired the best. When all he'd done with his ridiculous outburst was put himself in the position of having to beg a cranky duke for his sister's hand. Again.

Seeking permission to see his wife. The soon-to-be mother of his bairn. The love of his misbegotten life. Cursing, Dash pitched the dice across the hazard table. Double twos. A lucky outcome for a man out of luck.

"You don't have to pitch them so hard, mate. We had that table recovered last week. You'll leave dents in the baize with your temper."

Dash glanced over as Macauley sauntered across the deserted gaming floor. His children must have been sleeping through the night because, for the first time in months, he looked well-rested. "Advice from a man known for leaving dents in baize? Thanks, guv, but nae."

Macauley laughed, in a superb mood. "Ah, boy-o, you've arrived at the ideal moment. Word from the Leighton household is that young Theodosia is threatening to return to Suffolk if you don't show. His Grace is praying the sight of your pretty face calms her down. If he doesn't change his mind and decide to bruise it first."

Dash braced his hip on the table, spinning the dice in his hand. This was glorious news. Theo wanted to see him, and he was fairly expiring to see her. Evidently, she hadn't given up on him yet, even with his piss-poor admission of love. *Tha gaol agam ort* circled his heart once a minute it seemed.

If he could erase the vision of her covered in blood from his mind, he might recover.

Stalling a conversation he needed to have, he tracked Macauley's loop of the room, his partner verifying chip amounts and placing unopened decks of cards at each station, tasks usually done by the croupier when they signed in for their shift. His friend, his mentor, his brother, in truth, was waiting for him to make the first move. No one in this country or any other had the fortitude of Xander Macauley when the situation involved someone he loved.

Dash was honored to be included in the group. More than honored. He loved in return.

Tossing the dice, he circled the table to retrieve them. "Theo is expecting."

Macauley froze, the deck of cards he held tumbling to the floor. Dash experienced a moment's joy at the surprise attack. Then Macauley smiled, his eyes warming to molten silver. "Your reaction makes sense now. White with fear, the expectant papa. It's only been a few weeks since your marriage, or I would have considered this possibility. Scots magic to work so quickly, innit? I'm impressed. Enjoy your slumber now, mate. It'll be gone soon. But the living gets wonderful."

Dash dragged the die across a ripple in the baize they'd need to smooth out before tonight's gaming session. "How do I live with the fear that something will happen to her, Mac? The trouble at Southgate, nearly killing a man, is nothing you've had to deal with. When I found her on the doorstep covered in blood, I canna describe my panic. My world stopped, then it began spinning, mixed with such rage as I've never encountered. She foolishly thought to protect me without regard for herself. Now a wee bairn added to the mix? I canna sleep for fretting about them. Hell's fire, I want to defend, not be defended."

Macauley stooped to grab the deck of cards. "Pippa isn't an easy jaunt through Hyde Park, so don't put yourself in my boots. The women we adore are complicated, but this exceptionality is the reason we adore them. My darling Pip has never come close to what Theo faced, that's true. Knife at her throat? I can't imagine it, nor do I want to, because I'd lose my mind if anything happened to her."

"Only Theo," Dash muttered, wondering why his wife had to be the rowdiest chit in the Leighton Cluster.

"Oh no, she's not. Hildy was kidnapped before she married Streeter. You know about that, don't you? He was frantic, out of mind with worry, and here she comes prancing into the room like nothing untold had occurred. He put security stronger than Buckingham House's in place for a year after at the warehouse, their terrace, Derbyshire. Until he understood that life wasn't going to take her from him. Any man who has such grand luck worries about losing it. It's normal."

Dash sighed, nodded. Slipped the dice through his fingers. Everyone knew about the kidnapping because, like his wife, Hildegard Streeter had saved her own skin, no man required. In fact, the idiot who'd snatched her over his despair at having to marry off five sisters was now a model employee of the Duchess Society. Of course, his sisters had made excellent matches with the Society's assistance.

"Increase your security. Watch her like a hawk. The worry will lessen, I promise you."

"It's done. I've got guards posted at the estate and here in town. Footmen-cum-soldiers, former colleagues of Ollie's from the wars in India who'd kill a man without giving it more thought than they would a sneeze. I've placed a loaded pistol in the bedside table. I've slept with a blade beneath the mattress for years."

Macauley shoved to his feet with a snort. "Old habits, mate. How rookery lad of you."

"*Aye*, but the wife is a new habit. The bairn more so."

"You'll adjust. Trust me. A babe will help. I recommend three. Four, even." He crossed to the other side of the hazard table, bracing his hands on the ledge and leaning in. "If you repeat this, I'll swear on my life I never said it, but children quiet the soul. A mother's even more than a father's. You understand?"

Dash gave the dice a roll across baize. "You mean Pippa has calmed down?" Macauley's spirited wife was not what Dash would call *calm*.

"A little," Macauley whispered and glanced over his shoulder. As if the wee lass was set to pounce on him.

Dash flicked a card to the table that had been housed beneath his sleeve. It landed face-up, queen of hearts. "How little? Theo is a smidgen like Wordsworth with a cut of steak in his jaws. I need more than a little."

Macauley frowned. "The poet?"

"Nae, laddie, the *dog*."

"She named that scrappy hound she rescued Wordsworth?" Throwing his head back, he released his mirth into the gaming den. "Southgate is going to be overflowing with creatures with uncommon labels, I'd wager. You should ask Streeter to borrow Nick Bottom for a few days. Felines with Shakespearean names will fit right in with your crew."

Dash lifted his fist to his lips and smiled behind it. *Aye*, he hoped for loving madness, their estate overflowing with animals and tots. He missed Theo. Missed his scrappy hound and his lazy feline. Missed home. Missed sexual congress, to use Theo's dainty phrase. *Christ*, did he miss sliding inside her welcoming body while she cried out and scratched his back to ribbons. His dreams had been wickedly vivid of late, his shaft hard, followed by a sudden slice of disappointment upon realizing he was waking without her.

"Go on, mate, the sorrowful expression on your face is making me want to trot home to Pippa, snatch her up from our babies, and dive beneath the covers. Go get your tenacious chit. Lovesickness such as yours must be divvied up between the willing parties, not wasted on the rest of us. Welcome to the pining husbands club, by the by. We're a surprisingly contented lot."

Dash rubbed his chin with the die. "How is Leighton's mood these days? I dinnae need to take me boxing gloves, do I? I only want to retrieve my lass, not come away battered."

With a sputtering laugh, Macauley pushed off the hazard table. "I'd start with the baby news. That'll soften him up for the rest. There isn't a duke alive who likes children more than Leighton. Make sure Helena is close by, just in case. She holds the power to tame the beast."

Dash stopped Macauley on his way past. "Thanks." He swallowed hard, emotion stinging the back of his eyes. All this talk of love and family was making him maudlin. "For everything. You've changed me life in more ways than I can ever repay."

Macauley pulled him in for a one-armed hug, a firm slap on the back cutting the sentimentality. Making it a reasonable gesture between brothers. "Go get your lass, mate."

~

Theo braced her forehead on the window and peered into the night. A gust of wind rattled the panes and whispered down her spine, an icy caress matching her mood. She opened and closed the book in her hand, realizing she'd not read a line this evening that she could recall.

Where was he?

Dash's preposterous but incredibly recognizable German carriage had been parked in the drive of her brother's Mayfair terrace for a solid hour as daylight gave way to a hazy, classically foggy London twilight. She'd worn a groove in the Axminster rug with her pacing, the words she wanted to say to him stacking atop each other until her mind was littered with notes and scribbles, a visual picture looking remarkably similar to one of her lesson plans.

I'm sorry, I love you, being the foremost message she wanted to convey.

Maybe the last three words would be enough.

She turned to circle the room, her gown, the most flattering she had in residence and chosen for a potential reunion, whipping about her ankles. It was a deep shade of cerulean, close to the hue Dash's eyes shifted to when they made love. A color she could tumble into and never climb out. If she'd left her undergarments in the wardrobe for easier access should the situation arise, no one needed to know.

She'd never cared about clothing before. Or her coiffure. Reaching, she smoothed her hand across a chignon so tight it was giving her the megrims. If she was honest, she'd never worried about making anyone happy aside from herself. She'd tripped along, Dash was right, love in her pocket. Helena, Pippa, Roan. Their friends and their families. Mr. Darcy. While her husband had had no one. He'd come to London a boy still and had to figure out how to survive. Which he'd successfully done using his shrewd wit and generous, though cunning, heart.

What did it matter if there'd never be a day when he'd walk across a ballroom and not have a hundred hungry gazes follow him? Every man of her close acquaintance had a rather questionable past. Dash's certainly not the worst. Didn't rakes make the best husbands? Too, he'd given her the world. A home, a family, a teaching position he'd bargained to secure. There wasn't another man in England who'd have thought to do the same. What did the actresses and opera singers and lightskirts matter if he'd chosen her?

Theo halted, her gaze dropping to the signet ring on her finger.

If she'd chosen him.

She shifted her text, *A Complete History of Medieval Medical Practices*, from hand to hand, the realization a bright flame lighting the room. She could have retired to Roan's antiquated castle, Leighton House, or his estate in Hertfordshire, and become a cheerful spinster never again forced to attend a horrid musicale, the power of a duke firmly at her back. Her days of propping up walls and being an oddity concluded after the appearance of an expectant mistress at her engagement ball. She could have adopted a hundred cats, a thousand hounds. Written her own books, though her prose was nothing compared to Dash's. Learned to cook or garden or cross-stitch. Some tedious society-approved hobby.

Yet, she'd chosen *him*. Knowing in her gut, she could admit this now, he was the man she'd wanted all along but been afraid to get in there and try for. In the end, she'd chosen to roll the dice and take the man. Theo smiled and clutched the book to her heart.

What a perfect way to snare Dashiell Campbell.

He wasn't anything like Edward. Dash loved deeply when he pushed through his fear. Although the reasons varied, he was as scared of loving her as she was of loving him.

Through the window Theo had left open came the clatter of a carriage pulling into motion. The bellow of horses and the slap of wheels against cobblestones. She rushed over in time to see Dash's Wourch journey to the end of the drive and take a hard right on Curzon Street. Theo wilted, hugging the drape to remain standing. Was he leaving without her?

With tears swimming in her eyes, she saw a man prowl—there was no other word for it—across the lawn and begin his accent up the elm flanking her bedchamber. She squinted, glancing around for the spectacles she hadn't worn in weeks but obviously needed. It didn't take long to recognize Dash's lean form as he moved up the tree trunk like he'd been born to the sport of breaking and entering. Which he had.

She cranked the pane wide, allowing space for him to climb inside. Hung out the window with laughter rolling from her lips. "Get in here, you fool," she whispered when he got close. Her pulse beat a swift, mad rhythm in her ears. She was excited to see him, more excited than she'd been in her life.

He halted, his head tilting up. His smile was equally delighted, his eyes brimming with so many emotions that she couldn't read them all. Glancing down to ensure they weren't being seen by anyone, he gestured furiously to her. *Get inside.*

Tossing the book aside, she stepped back. But when he clamored over the window ledge, she pounced.

Laughing, they spun to the floor in a tangle of arms and legs. Cradling her face in his hands, Dash fit her body beneath him and plundered. The kiss was brutal, ravenous, a grasping effort to erase the loneliness of the past days from their hearts.

His glorious weight atop her pushed every doubt aside. This, this, *this.*

They made use of their shared knowledge and the quickest way to gain pleasure, to *give* pleasure. A swift rhythm, a grinding exchange that had them groaning within seconds, releasing greedy breaths and tormented sighs. Lust rending the air that entered their lungs.

Breaking free of the kiss, she nipped the spot beneath his ear that drove him wild. Caught his hair in her fingers and tugged. Her hand slid down his body, over his cock, tracing the rigid shape as his hips rounded into her touch. Catching her around the nape of her neck, he brought her back, kissing her crazily as he palmed her breast, his thumb finding the aroused bud. Then his lips were there, moistening silk over her nipple, biting gently, tugging until she moaned into the night.

"*Leannan*, darling," he whispered when he realized nothing stood between them but the flimsy layer of her gown. "You think to make me lose my mind, lass, with such ease? To have you spread before me when I've missed you so? I willna last long, not with this."

"I do. I mean to make it very, very easy, Mr. Campbell." Grasping her skirt, she tugged it to her waist, letting his hips settle between her spread legs, his shaft wedged against her molten folds. A ragged murmur caught in her throat when he began to move, his mouth returning to hers, his hand going to his close, and slipping buttons free in impatient movements.

The earth's rotation ceased. Night, day, she couldn't have said. Day, month, year gone. His tongue swirling against hers, his hand cocking her leg high on his hip, his rigid shaft held at her entrance. He rubbed his swollen crown over the aroused bundle of nerves topping her sex until she gasped, cried out, urging him closer, sounds she wouldn't have claimed as her own at any time prior ripping from her throat.

Yet, even with her deprivation on rampant display, he played. Toyed, feasted, an unselfish lover. She was first, *always* first with him. With this. Nudging his length aside, he glided a finger deep and came close to bringing her to climax with a series of powerful thrusts. A curl, a twist, his skill in finding her bliss immense. Ensuring she was ready, at a moist pitch, her body primed to welcome his. Tunneling his arm beneath her, he tilted her hips, and executed a languid glide inside her while flashes of ecstasy lit behind her eyes. When he could go no further, their hips bumping, he shifted from side to side, grazing her core in a sublime way.

"Dash," she whispered into the curve of his neck, "don't stop. Don't... stop."

He stroked in lengthy, glorious lashes, refusing her plea to increase the pace. Controlling her in the one place she'd let him.

"I have no intention of stopping, *leannan*." Cradling her jaw, he wrenched her gaze to his while he thrust. "But this time, I'll ask that you beg. Dinnae think I won't. Do you recall the devious trick you played while you were on your knees before me, a chair jammed under the linen closet doorknob to keep everyone out?" Reaching between them, he touched her, his fingers merciless. Thumb circling the aroused nub of her sex, tracing the folds surrounding his cock, sending her pulse kicking. "I mean to pay you back, three times over."

Three? She thought to question his methods, dare him, goad him into a furious tempo when her orgasm started and swept high, centered on the aroused button of skin he continued to caress, the sensation tightening every muscle it claimed before rolling back through her, head to toe. Spilling her to the floor in a tumble of spent pleasure.

"That's one," he whispered in her ear while she clung to him, gasping. Her vision dotted, her breath tangling with her cries. Sitting back, he disengaged, crouching between her legs. She shook her head, unable to speak for the fever seizing her. Hooking his arm over his shoulder, he dragged his shirt over his head, exposing his sculpted body for her view. Wiping his sweaty brow with the rumpled cotton, he tossed it aside. He looked ferocious, intent on destroying her. His hair damp and sticking to his jaw, the muscles in his biceps quivering, his chest heaving. His eyes, the blue-black of a Suffolk night, waiting for her.

She shook her head again. *I can't.*

Chuckling mischievously, he rolled her to her stomach, and resumed his campaign. His teeth nipping her shoulder, her back. The gentle rise above her bottom. His fingers finding her, spreading her slick dew across her folds. Teasing, allowing her time to recover. From somewhere he located a pillow, placed it under her hips—*oh*, the glory —and slipped tenderly, sweetly, fully into her.

This position made her body accessible in an extremely titillating fashion. Cupping her breasts, thumbing her nipples all part of his clever plan. Winding a strand of her hair around his fist and giving it a delicate tug. He guided her hips into a steady rhythm until the chamber echoed with the sound of their joining. Curving his broad body over hers, slick skin to slick skin, he groaned into the nape of her neck, his breath scalding her. It was less of an invasion and more a melding into one being, one mind. Palms pressed to the floor, she angled her hips, seeking more. Seeking *all*. Again and again as the tremors hit the base of her spine and unfurled.

"That's two," he rasped, voice breaking, body shaking.

She shrieked, and his hand was there, covering her lips. She nipped his palm, heard him grunt as he trembled, pulsed, shivering, his release flowing into her. Long moments of suspended bliss. Gaelic tripped through his words—endearments, curses, she didn't know.

The moment was as ancient as the language and seemed as meant to be.

They continued to move together past the point of pleasure, wringing the last seconds of delight from the act. Bracing his arms on either side of her, he cradled her chin, and seized her mouth in a messy side-kiss, depleting the last of her reserves. Gasping, she hung her head. He agreed to quit, rolling to his side with a tattered groan, and taking her with him.

They were a puddle of limbs, bones dissolved, bodies as malleable as clay. Air from the window a chilling rush over damp skin. She wanted to bathe in it, cool her blistered skin.

"Marry me, *leannan*," he whispered into her hair, his hand going to the curve of her belly and the baby there. "Without any reason except the only reason, because you want me. Want *us*."

She opened her eyes to find his head turned to her, his gaze solemn despite the intimacy they'd shared, ripples of satisfaction still swimming over them. She trailed her hand over his jaw and guided his lips to hers. The kiss was delicate but a clear statement. "I already have. I will. Ask me every day if you'd like and the answer, until the time I pass, will never change. *Yes*. I love you Dashiell Malcom Campbell, author, entrepreneur, oft-gambler. The kindest man I know, the most generous. The man of my heart."

He took her hand, traced the signet ring's emerald facets. "I'll buy you anything you'd like if this isn't—"

"This is the only ring I need. Want."

The hand cradled over her belly trembled. "I'm terrified, lass, I have to tell you. The arrival of this wee bairn has me up at night, staring at the blasted ceiling, counting cracks. I dinnae have siblings, no one but me. I barely ken how to hold a babe, much less care for one. What if—"

She slipped her hand over his mouth as he'd done to capture her cry of pleasure. "You love children, and they love you. They can see your generous heart from a mile away. I can't erase your fear, only say I'll be here every day to walk us through it."

He swallowed, his lids fluttering, a fierce exhalation rattling from his lungs. "Macauley recommends three tots for calming wives down. I'm nae sure you're calm-able. I'm damned sure Pippa isn't."

Theo freed a shout of laughter, her body shaking with it. "Oh, he does now. Wait until I tell my darling sister about this brilliant deduction."

Dash rolled to face her, alarm in his eyes. "Dinnae dare, lass. He'll strip me of my skin, he will. It's cracked for a man once feared like no other, from Shoreditch to Limehouse and else between, but Macauley's scared of his wee wife."

"Speaking of frightening men, does Leighton even know you're here? Your climbing in to get to me leads me to believe he does not."

Dash snorted, a scowl curling his lips. "He reckoned to make me wait 'til tomorrow. *Fookin' hell*, I wasn't waiting another second to see you. I had Meekins drive the team away, leaving me to scale that hulking tree, practically a staircase to your window."

Theo's toes curled at his brutal tone. No one had desired her badly enough to break into a duke's house to get her. No one but Dash. She pressed her brow to his, her heart overflowing. For their baby, for their future. "Tell me."

His jubilant sigh washed over her cheek. "I'm going to pen a new novel. My story this time. With your help, of course. No unethical tips and tricks in this one."

Theo craned her head back. "Dashiell Malcom Campbell, if your stinking books are the only topic you can consider discussing at a momentous time like—"

He caught her lips in a laughing kiss, his amusement traveling down her throat. "*Tha gaol agam ort.* I ken what you're asking, lass. I love you, Theodosia Astley Campbell, with me every breath. On this day and every other. My friend first, then my lover, my wife, my passion. I dinnae have more to want, to need, to give. I'll tangle with ya until the end of time."

"*Comes animae,*" she whispered in return.

He mouthed the words, his gaze searching, a groove appearing between his brows.

She smoothed her fingertip over the pleat, loving it, loving him. "It means 'companion of the soul' in Latin. That's what I feel."

He laid his head upon his bent arm, drawing her into the sheltered cove of his body. She felt him swallow, his breath hissing through his teeth. For a charged moment, only the crackle of the hearth fire and the gentle flutter of the velvet curtains roamed between them.

"*Comes animae, leannan,*" he said, his accent giving the Latin idiom an uncommonly sensual twist. "Two languages into one. Two lives into one." He kissed the crown of her head and pulled her closer. "And here you claimed you'd never teach me another word as long as you lived. Darling lass, a spot of sexual congress, and she can't keep her word."

"Perhaps we can negotiate an exchange. My editing expertise for information you might be more skilled at providing. I propose we resume our lessons when we return to Suffolk." She dusted her lips across the hollow beneath his collarbone and drew his sweet scent into her soul. "What say you, Mr. Campbell?"

"*Aye,* Mrs. Campbell, I think this exchange can be arranged. And gladly."

They giggled and cuddled and whispered until dawn, making plans, sharing promises and pasts. The world was theirs in that moment, as beautiful and crisp as the dawning morning.

Somehow, Theo realized as she dropped to sleep in her husband's arms, she and Dash had gambled on love and won.

Epilogue

If one waits patiently, life inevitably provides a favorable roll of the dice.

Dashiell M. Campbell, *The Forgotten Life of Swindling*

Bury St Edmunds, Suffolk, 1831

Theo halted in the arched entryway of the stables, a delicate afternoon breeze sending dust motes drifting through the air like snowflakes. A dappled splash of sunlight pierced the splits in the plank and tumbled over her husband in shades of tawny gold. She drew a shallow breath so as not to disturb him or the babe in her arms.

She wanted a quiet moment to thank the heavens for the life she'd been given. The man, the child. Her gratitude was unending, ceaseless, an everyday pulse in her heart.

Dash was crouched before a perambulator of his design, essentially a wicker basket on wheels he'd been tinkering with for months in preparation for their daughter's first visit to London. It was as stunning as its creator, the length of Campbell tartan lining the hamper and flowing over the sides an elegant flourish. The handles were covered in the finest leather her sister, Helena, had been able to secure through her shipping contacts. The sleek top adjustable, able to cover a napping tot on a rainy day. On his most recent visit to Southgate, Tobias Streeter had ordered one for himself, then suggested they try their hand at producing them. He'd promptly secured capital from Leighton, the Duke of Markham, the Earl of Stanford, Macauley, Viscount Remington, and Jasper Noble. Hence, the Leighton Cluster had entered into a new business venture, Campbell Prams. They were convinced orders would pour in once the *ton* got a look at Dash, Theo, and Hannah traversing Bond Street in such elegant equipage. Chance's wife, Franny, had begun sketches for the company's logo as well as gorgeous illustrations of the product.

Dash turned at her step, rising to cross to her, his smile magical in the hushed light. She'd never known a man to cherish home or family more. He'd begun talking about another child, a son possibly, when their daughter, Hannah, was only four months old. Theo was overjoyed —and exhausted—at the thought.

"Give her over, greedy mama," he whispered and took his slumbering daughter into his arms. He pressed his lips to Hannah's brow as she released a drowsy sigh and nestled against his chest, her fist gripping his coat lapel. Their daughter had bonded with her, certainly, but it was apparent she was her father's darling girl, right down to the jet-black hair topping her head.

Theo walked to the pram, running her fingers over the spooled handle. "How is the project coming along? It's beautiful, Dash, it really is. I bet you and the Cluster sell twenty in the first month. When they see the most scandalous couple in England prancing down the street, society will decide they, too, must have a Campbell pram. I've never seen the like myself."

Dash ambled toward her, although his gaze was fixed on Hannah. He told Theo once a day that he couldn't believe how bonnie she was, each tiny toe, each slim finger. The delicate curve of her ears an endless source of delight. Of course, Theo agreed. Actually, she found her husband almost as perfect, though he didn't need to hear this statement again in any lifetime.

Halting by the pram, he shifted Hannah in his arms with a tender smile. "For safety's sake, three wheels instead of four, a keen improvement over Kent's design. Thankfully no beast hauling your tot down a crowded boulevard. When we test this one, it's Wordsworth going in the basket. The weight will be about right. Mr. Darcy would work but that blasted feline won't do a thing I tell him to. I'm not risking my wee lass in an unbalanced contraption." In 1732, the Duke of Devonshire had paid the architect William Kent to design the first pram, the vehicle pulled by a goat or a small pony.

Delaying, Theo made a deliberate review around the stable's main chamber, noting the changes Dash had put in place. New thatch on the roof, rotted boards on the stalls repaired, each and every tool in its place. The straw beneath her feet fresh, the space spotless. He'd done the same with their tenant's cottages and the church in the village, which she now knew to be part of the agreement to offer her a teaching position. She'd taken on two more classes for the younger children, literature and grammar. Additionally, her student, Adam, had gotten accepted into Cambridge, much to his parent's surprise and delight.

She braced her hip on a worktable and turned to face her husband. The news needed to be delivered carefully. "A box arrived a bit ago by messenger. It's from your publisher in Islington."

Dash glanced up from a rapt inspection of his daughter's toes. His jaw flexed, his throat working in a tense swallow. "*Aye*, I suppose it did. Expecting them any day now."

Theo couldn't stand there doing nothing as his face etched with apprehension. Crossing the room, she put her arm around him, and tucked them against her chest. Dash wasn't anything like society thought he was. He was vulnerable and, at times, questioned his unique talent and the desperate choices he'd made. Things he shared, as she shared her hopes and unreasonable dreams with him. They were partners in a way few men allowed a woman to be in their world. Their marriage was, as they'd recklessly planned, a friendship first.

With a blazing passion mere steps behind.

She breathed in the sweet scent of leather and man, pressing her lips to her daughter's downy cheek. *"The Forgotten Life of Swindling* is lovely, Dash. Such a thoughtful series of essays. The prose beautiful, honest, gripping."

"Real," he whispered into her crown of curls.

She nodded and stepped back enough to see his eyes. They were the blue of summer skies this morning, clear of much of the trauma of years past. "Yes, it's real."

He gave his daughter to her and wandered the small space, straw snapping beneath his boots. When he yanked the dice from his pocket and began spinning them in his hand, she realized how unnerved he was by the prospect of releasing the story of his life to the masses. "I dinnae understand how..." Shaking his head, he halted by the worktable, giving the dice a toss across it. "I dinnae ken how valuable telling someone..." He glanced at her, his gaze intent. "Telling *you* about all that would be for me. How nightmares burnt away like the city's fog in bright sunlight with each horror you let me describe in the darkness. Your gaze like that loch I dived into as a child, as bloody cleansing as a bath. You didnae push or wheedle, you waited. Patient as any lass I've ever known. I adore you more than you know for this alone, among the thousand others."

He covered his heart with his hand and dipped his head. "And this healed me."

Theo hugged Hannah close, her eyes stinging. *"Dash."*

He laughed, making an awkward swipe beneath each eye. "Dammit, *leannan*, you know this subject makes me sentimental. I'm compelled to put me memories down on paper, then I'm scared as a starving rabbit in the wood to share them."

She went to him then. And he let her. *"We're* sharing them, darling. They're your remembrances, but it's our life how we handle them. You have nothing to be ashamed of, nothing to fear. We're already a scandal, your first book a literary miracle despite itself. What can they do to diminish our happiness? Nothing, unless you let them. You're meant to write, so write. Tell your story with me standing by your side."

"What would I do without *you*, Mrs. Campbell?"

"You'll never have to figure that out, Mr. Campbell."

He yanked her in, unsettling Hannah, who gave a whispery cry. "*Aye*, now I've gone and done it. The lassie willna go back down for hours."

Theo giggled. "She's yours until her next feeding, darling husband. You know our wager, the one who wakes takes all."

Dash stepped back, his grin absolutely buoyant. "I have a surprise for you, then I'll filch the wee lass until it's time for my favorite activity and hers." Dash loved to watch her feed their daughter in the tranquil splendor of their nursery. Their family, their lovely, secure little family.

He strode to a satchel hanging from a nail by the door. Reached inside and pulled out a rumpled letter. Returning to her, he held it up, not offering to let her read it. More a dangling tease. "Have you heard of Thierry Welles?"

Theo's heart stilled, then raced to a speeding rhythm in her chest. "The professor of mathematics at Cambridge? I have his volume on spherical trigonometry though it was too complicated to comprehend."

Dash shivered as if she'd drawn a chip of ice down his arm. "That'd be the lad. Maths holds little interest for me but knowledge is your nirvana." His teeth flashed. "Nirvana. Did you see how I used that in a sentence?"

Theo laughed and made a grab for the letter, Hannah giving an indignant murmur at the rocking motion. "Tell me already, you Scottish scoundrel."

"He's offering to tutor you. On the sly, in secret, due to you being a female. But he'll use the same texts, the same notes, the same *testing*, as he does with his students in the area you two decide upon. He may travel here from Cambridge next summer. We have things to discuss." Incredible declaration complete, Dash pocketed the letter, making her wonder what else the esteemed professor had stated. Even with his begrudging assistance, the man likely expected her to fail and fail big.

Thierry Welles. He was a celebrated scholar with a life somewhat shrouded in mystery. There were claims he was the distant son of a marquis who'd fled France during the Revolution. At current, he was the youngest Fellow in Cambridge's history with reports he would be named the next Lucasian Chair of Mathematics, the most prestigious academic post in the country. Why would he... with *her*? Theo frowned, Hannah's wispy complaint striking her neck. "How did you coerce Welles into this?"

"Coerce is a rather brutal way of describing my negotiation, lass." He pocketed his dice with a shrug, his smile beatific. He used his persuasive charm all the time with her—and it often worked. "I wanted to guarantee you didn't give up your dreams in service of someone else's. Mine, in particular. That's how the idea started, not how it finished. This arrangement will work well for both of us."

Her lungs squeezed so hard she feared they would burst. *Oh*, her husband was the kindest man. The most generous, the most wonderful.

Dash fidgeted, tossing his dice from hand to hand, her evident adoration making him cagey. "Dinnae go showing that bonnie smile, lass. You know what seeing your crooked tooth does to me. Welles needed a favor, and I gave it. Jasper Noble connected me to him. I helped secure investment for an enterprise of his. Has heaps of ideas but scant blunt and no manpower. Steam locomotives are the future, *leannan*, and we're going to jump onboard with this genius and ride it to sickening wealth." He shifted from boot to boot, endearingly discomforted. "Anyway, it's the closest I can get you to Cambridge."

The tear tracked down her face, and she scrubbed it away with the velvet trim of Hannah's blanket. Another followed, and another.

Dash was there in seconds, pulling them into his arms. "Dinnae weep, lass. It's *mathematics*, for God's sake."

"They're happy tears," Theo mumbled against his shoulder. "Very, very happy."

Hannah bellowed, her sniffles not of the cheerful variety.

Dash steered them toward the door and into the sunlight. The wind rippled over her skin, drying her tears but doing nothing to ease the fluttering of her heart. The scent of Suffolk whispered through her, solace in its path. "How about we journey to the nursery, feed our tot, then you and I conduct a different sort of negotiation altogether while Hannah naps?"

Theo snuggled into his side as they crossed the lawn, the hidden nook between her thighs coming alive at the suggestion. "I saw a sketch in the French text that arrived last week that, um, looks promising. It could involve the library ladder, I think, if you remember to lock the wheels this time."

Dash's stride increased, his arm tensing around her. "Do tell. This is my favorite kind of story."

Leaning, she whispered in graphic detail what she wanted him to do to her.

He tripped over a loose flagstone, his exhalation ripping through the air. "Theodosia Campbell, you are a cheeky lass. Getting a lad worked up in the middle of the day."

Handing Hannah to him, she lifted her skirts and raced down the stone footpath, turning back only when she reached the marble staircase. Striding behind her, Dash was caressing his daughter's cheek, the joy on his face no longer an emotion he cared to hide.

He held out his hand as he climbed the steps, their fingers linking. And holding. "My girls."

"Forever your girls."

He shot her a side glance, his expression as serious as she'd ever seen it. "Dinnae place a wager against it, *leannan*. I'm not a man to lose what's his."

"And I'm not a woman to lose what's hers."

He laughed as they entered the house, the welcoming scent of lemon and beeswax settling around them. *Home*, it smelled like home. Her family made it home. "I'd never bet against you, lass, not once. I ken the best gamble of my life when I see it."

The End

Thank you for reading *Two Scandals and a Scot*!

Next in line in *The Duchess Society series* is Jasper Noble's story, *Three Sins and a Scoundrel,* coming early 2024.

In the meantime, have you read all of the Duchess Society books including the prequel and the newly released Christmas novella *The Governess Gamble*?

THE DUCHESS SOCIETY SERIES

To save her reputation, American heiress Franny Shaw has fled to London in search of a desperate nobleman with a title for sale. An impulsive decision places her in the path of lonely libertine, Chance Allerton. Can a make-believe governess teach a wicked viscount a sizzling lesson in love?

Thank you!

FROM TRACY SUMNER

Thank you for reading Dash and Theo's extraordinary love story! Dash really stepped onto the page with his introduction in *The Wicked Wall-flower*. Xander Macauley to the rescue again, am I right? Crazy, innit? 🌀 Aside from Ollie (The Earl of Stanford/*One Wedding and an Earl*), Dash is his other little brother.

Next in line in The Duchess Society series is Jasper Noble's story, *Three Sins and a Scoundrel,* coming early 2024. I can promise second chance, second chance, second chance! My favorite trope, as many of you know. Jasper has a lot of secrets—and a lovely heart underneath the bluster. I'm beginning to know him well.

This is early news for my devoted readers, and merely a kernel of an idea at this point, but I'm intrigued by Thierry Welles, our brilliant Cambridge mathematician set to tutor Theo—and make Dash even wealthier with his steam engines! (Which were fast becoming the rage in the 1830s.) I have a holiday novella in a WOLF Publishing anthology in November 2023 (title TBD) that will introduce Thierry. Let's have fun with a sexy, Regency scholar!

AND... surprise, a new series with WOLF Publishing will be mentioned in the novella. The Mayfair Misfits, a companion series to *The Duchess Society*, set for 2024 release.

I repeat this because it's so true: Stephen King says in *On Writing* that we reuse themes as authors. I love writing stories about brothers and male bonding. *The Duchess Society* is actually a series about the men in the Leighton Cluster. My series, *The Garrett Brothers*, is full of back-slapping and brawling. In fact, if I think about it, the *League of Lords* follows this theme as well. All I can say is, men and their complex relationships are my joy to write!

Check in with me at www.tracy-sumner.com to receive a free book (the award-winning novella, *Chasing the Duke*) with my newsletter. I know series get confusing when they grow so big. The Duchess Society is holding at six now—four books and two novellas—with seven coming with *Three Sins and a Scoundrel*. The Books page on my website lays it out nicely for readers. Look out for the VIP section with bonus scenes of your favorite couples! A Duchess series companion of sorts is coming to my website soon as well!

Little nuggets from *Two Scandals and a Scot*:

1. The perambulator wasn't used often until the Victorian era. However, the mention here about the first being designed by William Kent for the Duke of Devonshire in the 1730s is accurate. I truly can see Dash and Theo striding down Bond Street with Hannah in a pram of Dash's design. And Tobias Streeter and Xander Macauley making a mint selling them!
2. I based Dash's gambling book, *Proper Etiquette for Deception*, on an actual book, *Sharps and Flats*, published in 1894 by John Nevil Maskelyne. It was an instant success and one of the first books to detail the secrets of cardsharps. Is that Dash or what? It is STILL considered a classic! So, I guarantee that *Proper Etiquette for Deception* had holding power well into Dash and Theo's grandchildren's lives.

Happy reading, as always! Historical romance is the best.
xoxo
Tracy

THE DUCHESS SOCIETY
SERIES SUMMARY

THE MEN AND WOMEN OF THE LEIGHTON CLUSTER

(or as Dash calls them in our story, The Leighton Lovesicks)
Much love to Mya Wall for her assistance!

THE ICE DUCHESS

Series Starter Novella
Dexter Reed Munro/Duke of Markham
Georgiana Whitcomb/The Ice Countess; co-owner of the
Duchess Society
Cat: Merlin
Tropes: Second chance, best friend's little sister, widow, first love
Best Historical Romance 2021 – One Book More
Reviews

THE BRAZEN BLUESTOCKING

Tobias Fitzhugh Streeter/Rogue King of Limehouse Basin, by-
blow of Viscount Craven

Hildegard Templeton/Daughter, Earl of Cavendish; co-owner of the Duchess Society
Cats: Nick Bottom, Buster
Tropes: Forbidden romance, bluestocking, working heroine, matchmaker, class difference
Best Historical Romance 2022 – Romantic_Pursuing_Feels

THE SCANDALOUS VIXEN

Roan Darlington/Duke of Leighton
Helena Astley/Self-Made Shipping Heiress, rookery girl
Cat: Rufus
Tropes: Class difference, enemies to lovers, fake courtship, working heroine, hero falls first

THE WICKED WALLFLOWER

Xander Macauley/Half-brother of Oliver Aspinwall, Earl of Stanford
Philippa "Pippa" Darlington/Little sister to the Duke of Leighton
Cat: Rufus
Tropes: Class difference, age gap, friend's little sister, heroine nurses hero back to health, slow burn/pining
Best Historical Romance 2022 – Thirteen Instagram reviewer's lists!

ONE WEDDING AND AN EARL

Oliver "Ollie" Aspinwall/Earl of Stanford, half-brother of Xander Macauley
Necessity Byrne/Infamous landscape designer, rookery girl
Cat: Delilah
Tropes: Grump/sunshine, forced proximity, scarred hero, class difference, enemies to lovers

TWO SCANDALS AND A SCOT

Dashiell Campbell/Author, cardsharp
Theodosia Astley/Sister to Pippa and the Duke of Leighton by
  marriage
Cat: Mr. Darcy
Dog: Wordsworth
Tropes: Friends to lovers, marriage of convenience, bookish hero-
  ine, reformed rake, class difference

THREE SINS AND A SCOUNDREL

Jasper Noble/Man with secrets
Tropes: Second chance, hidden past, reformed rake
Coming 2024!

THE GOVERNESS GAMBLE

Holiday Novella
Chance Allerton/Viscount Remington
Francine Shaw/American heiress
Tropes: Class difference, curvy heroine, reformed rake,
  wallflower
New England Reader's Choice Finalist – Best Novella

Also by Tracy Sumner

The Duchess Society Series

The Ice Duchess *(Prequel)*

The Brazen Bluestocking

The Scandalous Vixen

The Wicked Wallflower

One Wedding and an Earl

Two Scandals and a Scot

Three Sins and a Scoundrel (Coming 2024)

Christmas novella: The Governess Gamble

League of Lords Series

The Lady is Trouble

The Rake is Taken

The Duke is Wicked

The Hellion is Tamed

Garrett Brothers Series

Tides of Love

Tides of Passion

Tides of Desire: A Christmas Romance

Southern Heat Series

To Seduce a Rogue

To Desire a Scoundrel: A Christmas Seduction

Standalone Regency romances

Tempting the Scoundrel

Chasing the Duke

About Tracy Sumner

USA TODAY bestselling and award-winning author Tracy Sumner's storytelling career began when she picked up a historical romance on a college beach trip, and she fondly blames LaVyrle Spencer for her obsession with the genre. She's a recipient of the National Reader's Choice, and her novels have been translated into Dutch, German, Portuguese and Spanish. She lived in New York, Paris and Taipei before finding her way back to the Lowcountry of South Carolina.

When not writing sizzling love stories about feisty heroines and their temperamental-but-entirely-lovable heroes, Tracy enjoys reading, snowboarding, college football (Go Tigers!), yoga, and travel. She loves to hear from romance readers!

Connect with Tracy: www.tracy-sumner.com

facebook.com/Tracysumnerauthor
twitter.com/sumnertrac
instagram.com/tracysumnerromance
bookbub.com/profile/tracy-sumner
amazon.com/Tracy-Sumner/e/B000APFV3G

Acknowledgments

Thanks to my amazing Facebook reader's team, the Contrary Countesses, for always being there to discuss ideas about works-in-progress. And big thank you to the Ton & the Tartans Facebook group who helped me figure out a critical plot point in *Two Scandals and a Scot*! Also, I'm happy to have made their companion group, Upturned Petticoats and Undone Cravats, happy with my latest release (*One Wedding and an Earl*). The heat *was* fairly sizzling! I was moving to NYC during the writing and can only say that I must have been in a mood! 😏

And to Laura L, who wanted to see how much Dash was going to have to grovel to gain Theo's love. I hope it's enough! Scottish begging is so, so sexy. Nothing hotter than a Scot!

And, finally, to Melinda G, fellow Southern girl and cheerleader extraordinaire! I could not do it without your support!

Made in the USA
Columbia, SC
17 May 2023

16854740R00155